The moon splashed a powdery blue beam across the bed. Cathy's head was tucked under my chin, her arm flung across my waist and her leg straddling my calves. Her snore sounded like a cat's purr. I lifted her hand and kissed her wrist. She cuddled closer, mumbling contentedly. She had to be innocent, I repeated inside my head like a mantra.

Her skin looked as smooth as a starlit lake on a still night. My fingertips glided over her arm. She responded by kissing my shoulder. Her eyes opened, their brilliant blue dappled with flecks of moonlight. "I want you," she said. There was a question in her voice. I stilled her doubts and my own by turning toward her, outlining her lips with my tongue.

"Mmmmmm." She sucked and nibbled at my neck. A groan rose in me like a wave. "I want you," she whispered as she tenderly eased me onto my back. She lifted my nightshirt over my head, my body instantly beading with goosebumps. Gently, she circled my breast with the edge of her palm. I could feel the bruises where Carl had dug his fingers into me. I raised my hand to stop her, but then her breath fluttered over my nipple and my protest melted into a sigh.

I Left My Heart

A Robin Miller Mystery

BY JAYE MAIMAN

The Naiad Press, Inc.
1993

Printed in the United States of America on acid-free paper
First Edition
Second Printing January, 1993

Edited by Christine Cassidy
Cover design by Pat Tong and Bonnie Liss
   (Phoenix Graphics)
Typeset by Sandi Stancil

Library of Congress Cataloging-in-Publication Data

Maiman, Janice, 1957—
   I left my heart / by Janice Maiman.
      p.   cm.
   ISBN 0-941483-72-X   : $9.95
   I. Title.
PS3563.A3826612   1991
813'.54—dc20
                                                    90-22726
                                                       CIP

To Vivian Roll.
You are still the wind beneath my wings.
Wherever you are, I hope you're proud of me.

Acknowledgments

Someone once said that writing a book is like giving birth. And we all know that labor pains are no picnic. This book's creation would not have been possible without the hand-holding and administering of some very special people. My thanks go to Barbara Grier for bringing my book to light; to Christi Cassidy and Katherine Forrest for their careful edits; to Vanessa Ferro of the New York City Police Department for her insights and encouragement; to my many friends and occasional editors; to Dinah for reading each manuscript page ten times and still loving me when I asked her to read the same page "just one more time"; and to my parents, whose unconditional love and acceptance are the greatest gifts I have ever received.

About the Author

Jaye Maiman was born on October 31, 1957, and so learned early on that life is a series of tricks and treats. She grew up in Coney Island, Brooklyn, not far from the rumble of the Cyclone and the tantalizing aroma of Nathan's French fries. She now lives in Park Slope, Brooklyn, with her two cats Teaka and Livy. They can often be found sitting in their bay window, watching the action on Seventh Avenue and plotting future Robin Miller mysteries. The best ideas come from the cats.

Chapter 1

"Would you like a headset?"

I looked up at the flight attendant as if she were speaking Rumanian. "What . . . oh. A headset. Sure."

The flight attendant flashed me the standard why-do-I-get-all-the-jerks smile and handed me a plastic bag containing a coiled headset. Music. Just what I needed. I plugged the rubber cord into the armrest and began flipping the dial, searching for Broadway tunes. I clicked past the country station and froze. Tony Bennett's voice crackled into my ears. "I Left My Heart." My lips automatically mouthed the words. Suddenly, my eyes filled with tears; my ears burned like the hood of a race car.

Christ. She can't be dead. Not Mary.

"Robin? It's Patty. Patty Allen. Mary's friend."

"Mary?" I say dumbly, as if there were more than one Mary in my life, as if somehow the name were foreign, unknown.

"Mary Oswell."

"Yes. Of course." Mary. Cobalt blue eyes. An egg-shaped birthmark on the soft curve of her belly. Breasts that defy gravity. "How is she?" I mumble casually. "It's been nearly a year since we talked."

"Was it that long? I'm sorry."

Something in her tone, something about the pauses in the conversation, my own lack of curiosity about why this near stranger decided to call me at nine o'clock on a Friday night, hit me between the eyes like a bee sting. "Is something wrong?" I ask, my tongue thick in my mouth.

"Look, is anyone with you? Do you live with someone?"

"What happened?" Damn this woman. Damn this phone. My heart's shrinking, and she's making small talk.

"I'm sorry to be the one to tell you this, but Mary died last week. There was an accident . . . an allergic reaction to something she ate . . . she named you as her beneficiary. Do you think you can fly out here? Her lawyer . . .

Patty continues talking, but my rushing blood drowns her out, pounding against my skin and

2

organs like hard surf. No. *That one word repeats like a series of whitecaps smashing down on cracked shells.* No. *Not Mary.*

"We'd like to remind you that the captain has turned on the seat-belt sign. If you are walking around the cabin, please return to your seats."

Thankfully, the flight attendant's words cut into Tony Bennett's finale. I pulled off the headset, shoved it into the seat pocket, and dug out a roll of fruit-flavored Tums.

"I hate flying, don't you?" The high-pitched voice came from the elderly woman sitting next to me, her wiry hands knitting at breakneck speed. "Especially such long flights. Five hours. I would never leave New York at all, but my son lives in San Francisco, and he and his wife just had another child. A baby boy. It seems awfully unfair that I have to fly five hours just to see my grandchildren. Do you have any children?"

My mouth curled into a reluctant smile. I shook my head no, popped a pink Tums, and began rummaging through my Land's End briefcase. My luck, I thought. First Tony Bennett and now a nervous grandmother.

"Are you married? I didn't notice a ring."

"No."

"My son married when he was just eighteen. Broke my heart. I thought he'd go to law school. At least college, but no. He wanted to sing. Imagine . . ."

Maybe if I don't look up, she'll stop talking.

"Are you a lawyer? You look like a lawyer."

Lots of people have told me that. I don't know

why. When I think of lawyers, I envision double-breasted suits, wire-rimmed glasses, beady eyes, and pants pressed so precisely that they look as if they might crack. On the other hand, I was wearing a forest-green mesh polo, unironed gabardine pants, and white Nike sneakers with the laces tied on the side — personal quirk Mary had found endearing and friends just find odd.

"It's your eyes," my seatmate added, as if she were reading my mind. "They're so intense. And your build. The lawyer who handled my divorce years ago was built like you. Thin, small hips. She burnt off calories like a marathon runner, constantly dashing from the law library to the courthouse to her office. I got out of breath just looking at her."

She had me there. Mary used to dare me to sit still for five minutes. I wasn't even allowed to move my hands. It was sheer torture.

"Actually, I'm a writer," I mumbled. One look at the mad knitter told me I had made a bad mistake. She looked even more intrigued, her needles clacking so fast they started to blur. "As a matter of fact, I have a deadline to meet. Would it bother you if I do a little work?"

"Oh no. Not at all. What type of writing do you do?"

Here come the questions, I groaned to myself. I decided it was time to fight dirty. "Financial analyses."

"Oh." She fell silent.

I opened my notebook and started writing furiously. Mary was right. Nothing stops a conversation faster than telling someone you write

4

financial analyses. Happily, I don't do anything of the kind. That was Mary's specialty. Mine is travel literature. And, of course, my bread and butter: romance novels.

Amanda slid behind the bedroom door. Her flimsy nightgown grew wet with perspiration. She could hear Roger's soft moan as he embraced Emily. "I can't wait any longer," he growled harshly. "But Amanda may hear us," Emily protested. Roger laughed and ripped her blouse open. "Amanda's a fool," he said as his hungry lips pressed into her pulsing cleavage.

Four hours later, Amanda was running half-naked through the garden and I was about to land in San Francisco.

* * * * *

The lobby fireplace was blazing as I checked into the Hotel Vintage Court. On the couch opposite the fire sat a woman in a tight black dress with three-inch thick shoulder pads. She sipped a glass of red wine, her lips barely grazing the edge of the glass, her shapely legs crossed at the ankles. Her companion, a distinguished-looking man with a shock of white hair, whispered into her ear. A shiver went through me. How long had it been since I was that cozy with someone?

"Single or double?"

Startled, I turned back to the registration desk. The clerk had unnaturally black hair and a hooked

5

nose. He reminded me of a hotel manager in Atlanta who told me that women should never travel alone unless they wanted to get laid by strangers.

"I want a room on the sixth or seventh floor, facing Bush Street. With a window seat," I said a bit too brusquely.

"You've been here before?"

"And reviewed it twice. Can I have my key please."

"Of course." He looked at my signature. "Robin Miller. You wrote the piece that ran in *Travel & Leisure* about a year ago. We received a lot of calls after that."

"Glad to hear it," I murmured, lifting the key from his hand. Usually I don't mind chatting with hotel staff, but that night I just wanted to crawl into bed, slip on my Walkman, and have Rosemary Clooney invite me to her house.

The room was just as I remembered it. Laura Ashley bedspreads. A wide window seat with six pastel-blue throw pillows. The white curtains fluttering as a cool breeze spilled in from the open windows. Every piece of furniture was soft white, even the small desk near the door.

The last time I stayed here, in 1988, I was on assignment for *Travel and Leisure,* and Mary was hurt that I chose not to stay at her apartment. We had one of our usual arguments, with Mary calmly explaining that our history had nothing to do with our present. I came close to screaming. But Mary didn't lose her cool. She rarely did.

In the four years we had lived together, I heard

her raise her voice only twice. Once, when she discovered two teenagers torturing a cat in an alleyway. Then two years later, when I told her that her Grace Kelly sangfroid was killing me. That time, she actually threw a book at me. I think I may have applauded.

The phone rang, interrupting my reverie. I was about to ignore it when I realized that the caller was probably Patty.

"I just wanted to check that you arrived okay." It was Patty.

"Sure. Other than the knitting-needle menace that sat next to me, the flight was fine."

"Did you make arrangements to see Mary's lawyer?"

I closed my eyes, remembering how, dry-eyed and fiercely rational, I had dialed my travel agent and the lawyer's office first thing Saturday morning. "Yes. I'm seeing him tomorrow morning."

"Fine . . . look . . . Pete and I thought, well, given everything, that maybe you'd like to come to dinner tomorrow night. A few of Mary's friends are coming over. Since you missed her funeral . . ."

"I'd like that." Two nights ago, I didn't have the strength to discuss Mary's death. I took out my address book and leafed through the pages. "You still live near the Presidio, don't you?"

"I'm surprised you remember. Come over around seven o'clock, that way we'll have some time to talk."

"Thanks. See you tomorrow."

I stared at my address book. Patty's address was in Mary's handwriting.

"Here, let me write it down. Your handwriting is awful." Mary grabs the address book and begins scribbling. "I'm only going to stay at Patty's for a few days, till I find an apartment."

"Mary, I doubt we'll be talking that much."

"There you go. Robin, we can still be friends. I want us to. Four years is a long time to throw away."

I turn away and start sorting through the mail on the kitchen table. I will not cry again.

"What did I do now?" she asks, a plaintive tone sneaking into her voice.

"Nothing, Mary." I tear through the mail with a vengeance.

"You don't know how much I love you," she says softly.

My throat starts constricting. In a few minutes I will start gasping for air.

"I never meant to hurt you."

I look at her. A fatal error. The sobs come hard and fast. I could kick myself.

"Oh, Robin." Mary sighs as she wraps me in her arms. "I'm sorry. Please don't cry. You'll be okay. Geeja and Mallomar will take care of you." She moves away and starts looking for the cats. "C'mon girls, Mommy needs you."

I stare at her back, my fingers curled into hard fists. It's not the girls I need. It's you, Mary. You.

I dropped the address book on the night table, leaned back on the king-size pillows, and closed my eyes. In the distance, a cable car bell rang out.

When Mary moved to San Francisco three years

8

ago, she carried my world with her. Five months passed before we spoke. Five months of leaping at the phone each time it rang. Five months of waking up in the middle of the night, sweat-drenched and searching for her body. Five months of stumbling on her remnants: dirty sneakers hidden in the corner of the closet, a night shirt that made me heady with her scent, the travel toothbrush she had left in my carry-on. And after those five months, she called to ask me for my sister's new telephone number. "I'm writing a series on the new tax laws and Barbara's the best CPA I know," she had explained.

I shook my head. The city was getting to me. Only one way to escape. I turned on the television and spun the tuner. News. A car chase. Then I smiled. Lucy and Ethel were frantically shoving chocolates into their mouths as the conveyer belt sped up. I collapsed on the bed and kicked off my shoes.

* * * * *

A page out of *Better Homes & Gardens,* I thought as I sunk into an armchair that could have easily held two women and a Great Dane. The well-cushioned furniture and highly polished accessories, including several carved eagles and one discreet silver cross, were a little too traditional American for my taste, but the overall effect was somehow appealing.

"Miriam can't talk yet, but she loves Raffi's voice," Patty explained as she turned off the Raffi videotape that had been playing when I arrived. "As you can see, it puts her straight to sleep." She bent over the edge of the crib near the television set and kissed her daughter's forehead.

I had forgotten how pretty Patty was. Her shoulder-length hair was bleached golden by the sun. Her hazel eyes had a trace of gray in them, reflecting the color of her trim shirtwaist dress. For a moment she reminded me of Mary. I turned away. A walnut bookcase held an odd combination of military novels, Mormon treatises, wine guides, and Dr. Seuss books.

"Maybe I should try it sometime," I said absent-mindedly.

"Try what?" Patty looked startled, as if she had forgotten my presence.

"Raffi's music."

"Oh. You've had trouble sleeping?"

When haven't I had trouble sleeping? I'm an insomniac. At three o'clock in the morning you can usually find me cleaning the refrigerator or re-alphabetizing my compact disc collection. Understandably, sleep's a sore issue. I decided to deflect the question. "Why didn't you call me as soon as Mary died?"

"I did," Patty answered defensively. "But I got your answering machine, and that's not the type of message you leave on someone's tape. Then, in the craziness of the next few days, I just forgot." She tucked a blanket around Miriam and sat down opposite me. "When her lawyer told me that I was the executor of the estate and you the sole beneficiary, I felt awful. You did see Carl today, didn't you?"

10

Carl was Mary's lawyer. A tall, impeccably handsome man, his pinkie ring held the diamond the size of a small gumball. I had stared at it obsessively, the sparkle making it easier to separate myself from the legalese filling the room like noxious gas fumes.

"Yes. I was there the whole morning. He's one smooth character."

"To tell you the truth, Mary wanted to change lawyers. She and Carl had a falling out a while ago. But she could never find the time. You used to date a lawyer, didn't you?"

I looked up, surprised. "How do you know that?"

"Mary talked about you constantly. For instance, I bet you had lunch at Roxanne's today."

I nodded, dumbfounded.

"Mary once told me that whenever you have business in San Francisco, you go to Roxanne's for lunch." Patty dragged her upper teeth over her bottom lip, her eyes misting over. "I miss her more than I imagined possible." Suddenly, she looked very uncomfortable. "Pete should be home soon. You know he's a captain in the Army, don't you? He's been stationed at the Presidio four years now . . . which is pretty unusual. Most Army families move around more than gypsies." Twisting her wedding band, she stood up. "Would you like some wine?"

"Love some. Only white, though. Red gives me a headache."

Patty swept out of the room, nibbling at a fingernail like a squirrel.

What had come over her? Her mood had managed a 180-degree flip — from a blissful

Madonna to a harried housewife in less time than microwaved popcorn takes to pop. If the thought of Pete could make her that nervous . . .

The doorbell chimed.

"Robin, would you mind getting that? It's probably Cathy or Liz."

I opened the door and found myself staring at a man wearing a Beau Bridges smile and a slightly rumpled military uniform. "You're not Cathy or Liz, are you?" I asked with a crooked grin.

He chuckled. "Good guess. I'm Pete. Could you give me a hand with these?" He nodded toward the two overstuffed A&P bags that were balanced precariously on one raised knee.

"Sorry." I grabbed one bag and let him pass.

"Thanks," he shouted over his shoulder. "Hey Patty, I'm home!"

"Pete?" Patty scampered around the corner. "Why'd you ring the bell?"

"I couldn't get to my key," he said as he handed her one bag and turned to remove the other one from my arms. "I picked up some dessert and Pampers, plus some stuff for the barbecue at Ted's tomorrow." He paused to smile at me. "Excuse us while we unpack."

As soon as they had pushed through the swinging doors leading into the kitchen, Miriam woke up with a piercing howl. I started for the crib, but before I had taken two steps, Patty whisked in and lifted Miriam into her arms. "Sorry," she said almost shyly. She wrapped Miriam in a fuzzy, pink cocoon and shushed her as she climbed the stairs to what I presumed was the bedroom.

My thoughts returned to Pete. He was not at all

what I expected. Laugh lines radiated from the corners of his eyes, which were a gentle brown. His tousled mess of sandy hair peaked in a Dennis-the-Menace cowlick. All in all, he looked more like a Disney character than a captain in the Army. Patty's earlier agitation couldn't possibly have stemmed from anticipating his arrival.

"Sorry for this craziness," Pete apologized as he strode back into the room. "I bet you want to retreat to the safe quiet of your hotel room."

He was incredibly charming. And dead right. "No, this is very pleasant," I lied.

Pete flopped into a well-worn easy chair covered in cadet-blue corduroy. "Right." He nodded conspiratorially. "Patty tells me you write all those Laurel Carter romance novels."

Oh God, I thought. That's why he's being so nice. He must think I'm straight. Straight and horny. I started to squirm in my seat.

"My mom reads them all the time. She says nobody writes steamy love stories the way you do."

How do I tell him the truth?

"I didn't have the heart to tell her you're gay. It would destroy her fantasies. She imagines you as a fifty-five-year-old enchantress with silver hair and a mink coat draped over your shoulders. Probably nothing underneath."

I settled back against the armchair. Pete was a bundle of surprises. "I could send her an autographed copy of my new book, if you like," I offered, suddenly feeling more comfortable than I had all day long.

"Perfect," Pete hooted. "She'll be beside herself. I can see her now. Parading around the beauty parlor with a new perm, waving the book, and bragging that she and Laurel are *that* close." He lifted his hand and twisted two fingers together. Then, without hesitating, he leaned over to yank off his heavy, scuffed shoes.

"Hope this isn't too rude." He began rubbing his feet. "My dogs are killing me."

"Believe me, I understand." Watching Pete, I became conscious of the tightness in my own muscles. Maybe I should drive up to Calistoga for a body massage.

"How'd you get into that stuff anyway? The romances, I mean. Being gay and all that, I wouldn't think that it's your cup of tea."

"Actually, it's a funny story . . ."

"What is?" Patty interjected as she strolled in. She now looked uncharacteristically calm, her thin lips lifted in a private smile.

"Robin was just about to tell me how she became a romance writer."

"Oh. I'd like to hear this." She picked up a glass of red wine she had left on top of the television and took a quick sip. Pete cocked his head at her and she laughed. "Just one sip, silly." She sat down on the arm of the easy chair and leaned against Pete, whose face immediately relaxed into a broad smile.

Inexplicably unnerved by the picture of domestic bliss before me, I launched into my story with a verve. "About six years ago, my friend Tom was desperately searching for a job. Finally, he found one with Harbor Romances. Tom's a great editor with a superb sense of what's marketable and what's not. But back then, he didn't have much experience —

and he had few author contacts. Of course, he never mentioned that in his interviews.

"So, he gets the job and his first assignment is to find an author for a new series of romances. Tom panicked. He called me up and pleaded with me to submit an outline for a romance novel, plus a few chapters. I thought he was nuts. A straight romance? At the time, I was writing a review of an American history textbook. 'No,' he said, 'An S&M thriller set in the back room of the Anvil. Of course I want a straight romance. We're talking commercial publishing honey.' Then he tells me that if they accept my work, I could get a five- to ten-thousand-dollar advance, plus a generous royalty contract. This was before Mary got her inheritance. At the time, we were living on Bumble Bee tuna. I wrote three chapters that weekend, and an outline for two other stories that same week. Needless to say, I got the contract. Plus."

Patty laughed. "Mary said she could always tell when you were writing a Laurel Carter novel because you'd be sitting at the word processor giggling like a crazy woman."

I smiled at the memory of Mary peeking around the corner to watch me write, unaware that I could see her in the reflection of the screen. "That's a pretty accurate description."

The room suddenly became unbearably quiet.

"Okay, enough chatting," Pete announced as he rose from the chair. "Time to get serious about dinner. Do you like garlic?"

"Like is too weak a word," I said, relieved to be discussing the one uncomplicated passion in my life.

"My concept of heaven is a trip to the Gilroy Garlic Festival."

Pete grinned. "Well, I better go throw in a few more cloves or we'll be fighting for garlic at the dinner table." The swinging doors closed behind him.

"He's something else," I said, turning to Patty.

Her eyes were still fixed on the kitchen doors. "He's one of a kind," she sighed. "You may not understand this, but he's been my saving grace."

I smiled stiffly.

"I'd be lost without him," she added with a pale grimace. "You know, I'm happier now than I've ever been."

She had a funny way of showing it, I reflected.

* * * * *

Cathy and Liz arrived a few minutes later. I heard the two women talking even before the doorbell rang.

"Hope we're not too late," cooed a chunky, dark-haired woman with deep dimples and a St. Tropez tan. "If we are, it's all my fault. Cat was right on time. But I split my jeans and had to sew them." She sailed over to me and embraced me like a long, lost friend. "Hi. I'm Liz. This," she said, looking back to the woman still standing in the doorway, "is Cathy."

I stretched out my hand. Cathy shook it. Reluctantly.

"Why don't the three of you sit down in the living room while Pete and I get everything ready." Patty gestured toward the L-shaped sofa. Obediently, we shuffled into the living room and took our places.

"I hate meeting new people," Liz confessed. "You never know what to say, especially under these circumstances. Just last month, a second cousin of mine died. The funeral was awful. And the wake . . ."

While Liz rambled on about her cousin's funeral, I snuck a closer look at Cathy. A small flutter in my stomach told me that trouble was around the corner. Cathy was the type of woman who could make you breathless within seconds. Her eyes were deep turquoise, the color of the Caribbean on an overcast day. Long, golden eyelashes cast a pale shadow on her cheeks. Skin the color of toast, legs that begged for exploration. I sighed heavily. She reminded me of Mary, of how much I still longed for her, ached to make love to her. I shifted in my seat uncomfortably.

"Geez Louise. I'm sorry Robin. This must be upsetting you," Liz murmured, misinterpreting my gesture.

"No, it's all right," I said, snapping back to the moment. "Actually, the main reason I'm here is to talk about Mary. When Patty called me, she didn't say much about her death. Just that it was some kind of allergic reaction to something she ate. Mary's lawyer told me the same thing. It's pretty surprising since she was so careful."

Liz leaned forward. "The police think —"

"The police? What do the police have to do with this?"

"Initially, there was some question as to whether Mary's death was an accident or not," Cathy explained more diplomatically than I liked.

"What are you talking about?"

"No one told you?" interrupted Liz. "They found a note in her typewriter."

My body went numb.

Cathy stood up and started to pace. "Do we have to go into all this?"

Liz glared at me with uncertainty. I nodded.

"Adam — that's my brother-in-law — works with the detective who investigated Mary's death." She wiped her palms on her pants nervously. "He said the letter sounded like the start of a suicide note. Something like 'I can't go on like this any more. It's time that I tell you . . .'"

Cathy spun around, clearly annoyed. "Look, the point is they ruled out suicide. Didn't they, Liz?"

"Yes," she said, wincing at Cathy's tone. "For a couple of reasons. Mary and I were planning a weekend in L.A. We confirmed our reservations the week before she died. And she had just mailed her tax return that Saturday. She owed six or seven hundred dollars to the IRS. I remembered her bitching about it. Adam said people don't usually pay their taxes and *then* kill themselves . . . that's when the police started thinking that maybe it was murder."

I felt the room tilt.

"For God's sake, Liz . . ." Cathy hissed.

"It looked like she might have tried running for help." Liz took a deep breath. "She was in the house down by Big Sur. Apparently, she got as far as the front door. A neighbor found her there the next day. A real pain in the ass. The neighbor, I mean. Cathy, you must know her . . ."

"Martha Spinks," Cathy responded coldly.

All at once, I imagined Mary in a carefully

ironed sweatsuit, stretched out in her doorway, one arm reaching for help. I covered my eyes to dispel the image burning in front of me.

"In the end, the coroner decided it was just an unfortunate accident. You know how allergic Mary was. The autopsy showed that she ate clam dip a few hours earlier. They don't know for sure, but they think that's what made her go into shock."

"Clams?" I jerked my head up. "Mary ate clams all the time. It couldn't have been clams." When we lived together, I used to tease Mary that her insatiable sex drive derived solely from her daily dose of clam dip.

"They say it happens like that sometimes." Liz hesitated. "You can eat clams twelve days in a row, and on the thirteenth, you just —"

"Was there anything else in her system?"

"I'm not sure. You'd have to ask the police. A Detective Ryan was in charge of the case. Maybe my brother-in-law can arrange a meeting for you."

Cathy sat down between us. Her sea-green eyes were moist. "That's enough for now," she said wearily.

Yes. It was more than enough. Something was wrong. Dangerously wrong.

Chapter 2

Dinner reminded me of a Twilight Zone episode in which time stops. Pete and Liz chatted effortlessly, but the rest of us fumbled along like flies in molasses. Patty started and ended every sentence mid-stream, as if she were talking to herself and wasn't very interested in what she was saying. Cathy chewed every scrap of food twenty-five times. I know, because I counted each movement of her jaw. The rest of the time I spent counting every garlic clove and grain of rice on my plate. Anything but talk. Or think.

The next morning, Liz called me. Apparently Detective Thomas Ryan owed her brother-in-law a favor. And an interview with me was the payback. I thanked her and then sat at the edge of the bed, staring at the phone number. Five minutes passed before I dialed the police station, shivering non-stop.

* * * * *

"Thank you for seeing me," I said as I sat down on a wooden chair that looked as if it had been attacked by rabid dogs.

"No problem." Detective Ryan was about forty-five years old. His hair was prematurely gray, and his face was gnarled and puffy from lack of sleep. His annoyance at my visit was almost palpable. To some degree, I couldn't blame him.

"I'd like to know everything you have on Mary Oswell's death."

"You told me that on the phone. I'll answer your questions, but that's it. So what do you want to know?"

"How did she die?"

He sneered at me. "Anaphy . . . wait a sec." He pawed through a file on the desk. "Yeah. Anaphylactic shock. Bit word for a stupid death. In simpler terms, something she ate didn't agree with her."

I winced at his cavalier tone. "What exactly did the autopsy show?"

"You deaf? Anaphylactic shock."

"I mean . . . what was in her system?"

"Let me look. Clams . . . Yeah, the doctor thought that was what did it. Can't trust goddamn seafood today. Don't eat the crap myself. Good for

21

you, my daughter says. Sure. And the next thing you know, you're keeling over from mercury poisoning or —"

"Is that it? Clams? Nothing else?" I was one step away from committing homicide. How do you get information from a Neanderthal?

"Nah. Crackers. A trace of lemon. Yogurt. Some salad stuff, lettuce, carrots. Penicillin . . ."

"Penicillin?" Bingo.

"Yeah. Apparently, she had a cold or infection." Ryan squinted at me. "Why the face?"

"Mary was allergic to penicillin."

"That's not what she told her doctor. And none of her friends told me any different." He picked up a pen and started clicking the cap on and off.

"Mary and I used to be roommates. I'm telling you, she wouldn't take penicillin. Not when she had strep throat, and not when she had an ear infection."

He narrowed his eyes and made a sucking sound with his lips, like he was nursing a bottle. "She did this time. Who knows, maybe she just got careless."

"Mary wasn't the careless type."

Raised in a strict Mormon household, with a mother who belonged on page one of the Guiness Book of Health Fanatics, Mary was hyper-conscious of her diet. She had exactly six allergies, and she compulsively checked the list of ingredients on every product she ate, drank, washed in, or cleaned her toilet bowl with.

Ryan spun the pen on his desk. "Look, I'm just telling you what I know. Maybe you got things twisted. Maybe she was allergic to some other type of antibiotic —"

"For God's sake, she wore an allergy identification tag that listed penicillin. Didn't anyone bother to read it?"

His eyes snapped to my face. "What allergy tag?"

My heart skipped. "The one she wore on a gold rope. Around her neck."

He placed his palms flat on the desk, his face clouding with uncertainty for the first time. "There was no tag. No one mentioned any tag." He paused. "When was the last time you saw each other?"

I answered reluctantly, knowing I was about to give him a way out. "Years."

"Years." He scratched his chin. "Years. So maybe years ago she wore this tag. But not last month. Right?"

"It's worth exploring, isn't it? I mean, there are a lot of things about Mary's death that say it wasn't accidental. Maybe if you spoke to the doctor —"

"Look, I checked this all out. Met the damn doctor who prescribed the penicillin. A nice-looking guy. Young, but smart. He works at a clinic near your friend's office. She ran in one afternoon during her lunch break, said she was on deadline and needed some medicine. So he gave her a prescription. No big mystery there."

"Except that she failed to mention she was allergic to penicillin. Maybe it wasn't even her. Did he describe her?"

"He didn't remember her. He has fifty people in and out of there every day." He rubbed his temple with his index finger. The message was clear. I was giving him one royal headache. "I see you're concerned, but I gotta tell you, you're barking up a tree that's got no fruit. Maybe the doctor lied to cover his ass. Maybe she couldn't read his handwriting. In any case, what we got here is an accident. Pure and simple."

"The label was typed on the bottle. She would have read the label."

"Maybe she forgot."

"Not Mary."

"Look, I don't know what else I can tell you. You want me to say it's suicide? I don't know. If what you're telling me is true, there's a good chance you may be right. But nothing's conclusive. As for murder, we had no solid leads of any kind."

He leaned back, his eyes glazing over. "Hell . . . I don't mean to be a hardass. I understand your position more than you realize. My wife was killed five years ago. It took me two years to stop obsessing over the case. You see what I'm saying?"

I knew I should feel sympathy, but my fists were still clenched and my teeth were grinding against one another. "I don't want you to do the impossible," I said with frustration bordering on rage. "I just want you to investigate. You *do* do that occasionally, don't you?" As soon as the words were out of my mouth, I knew I had crossed the line.

Ryan's eyes darkened. He pushed back his chair abruptly and stood up. "I think this interview is over." He swept the file to one corner just as a young patrolman rushed in out of breath.

"Murphy's got a lead on Peters . . . we gotta move now!"

"Awright!" Ryan slapped the desk and glared at me. "You. Outta here. Now." He pointed to the door, his nostrils flaring. I took my time gathering my jacket and then stood up suddenly, spilling the contents of my briefcase on the floor. I shrugged coyly and knelt down to retrieve my possessions.

"Aw . . . dammit," he groaned, kicking his seat back at the same time. He glanced down at me, spat into a garbage can and stalked out of the office. "John, get someone to escort her outta here," he shouted over his shoulder. The young cop ran after him, shooting questions.

I looked at the desk with an arched eyebrow, wondering how many years I'd get for borrowing police property. If the judge was a Laurel Carter fan, I might get lucky. I decided to take the chance. I swept the file into my briefcase and shot out of the office.

* * * * *

In my thirty years on this planet, I have probably read hundreds of mysteries. But they don't prepare you for the real thing. The sheer numbing weight of suspicion. The panic that makes every inch of your body burn. I tried hard to evoke Sherlock Holmes, James Bond. Cool, detached reason. Action without anxiety.

Instead, I sat at the head of my hotel bed, mindlessly shoving crisp Bremner wafers into my mouth, the crumbs spraying the police records scattered around me. Medical records, interview notes, the two-line letter Mary had written exactly as Liz had remembered it. A sealed envelope with the word *Photographs* printed on it in cold, square letters. A life reduced to scraps of paper with frayed edges and coffee stains.

I sorted through the pile and picked up a list of

articles found on the "victim's" body. Mary's body. My mouth went dry as I ticked off the items. Seiko watch. The one her Uncle Thomas gave her when she turned thirty. Opal pinkie ring. I glanced down at the matching ring I still wore. The air grew oppressively still.

The peal of the phone broke the silence.

"So your plane didn't crash. That's good to know."

It was my housemate, Dinah. For the last three years, we've shared a brownstone in Park Slope, Brooklyn.

"I forgot to call. Sorry." I took a deep breath and filled her in on the details.

"Rob, you're out of your league. Let the police deal with this. Come home."

"I can't. Not now. I need to know what happened. If it was suicide or —"

"You know what this is about, don't you?"

I rolled my eyes. "Don't do this to me now." Dinah's a psychologist, which can be mighty inconvenient at times.

"You have to stop feeling like you're responsible every time someone you love dies. This is not your fault . . . and you can't make things better by putting yourself into danger."

My defenses locked into place. They usually did whenever Dinah referred, however obliquely, to the accidental death of my younger sister. "Look. I know you're trying to help. But this is the wrong time. Okay?"

"Whether it was suicide or murder, you aren't the reason Mary's dead."

I felt an all-too-familiar knot in the side of my neck. If Dinah didn't lay off soon, my back muscles would go into a two-day spasm. "Enough." The word felt like a brick.

Dinah knew the tone well enough. "Okay. But think about what I'm saying. And stay in touch. I'm going to worry like a Jewish grandmother till I hear from you."

I smiled in spite of myself. "Oy. I'll call in a few days. Love you."

I hung up. My hands were sweaty. I wiped them on the pillow case and then picked up the envelope marked *Photographs*. Gingerly, I slid my finger under the flap and lifted one corner. The first picture showed the outside of the house in Big Sur. Nothing seemed unusual. Then I noticed Mary's body sprawled in the doorway. Bile sprung into my throat.

"Robin, you have to come out to the house. I can hear the ocean from my deck. Listen."

A familiar whoosh *filled my ear.*

"Can you hear it? That's the Pacific Ocean right at my doorstep. Seagulls too. I keep thinking about that poet you love. What's his name?"

"Robinson Jeffers."

"Of course. Well, now I know why he wrote all those wonderful poems about hawks and churning water. It's exquisite out here. When are you coming out west again?"

"I'm not sure, Mary."

"Find reason to get out here. I want to share this with you."

I never went. She sent me photographs. Pictures of a typewriter basking in the sun on her driftwood-gray deck. Pictures of her posing with friends I didn't know, one woman leaning on her arm. Now this. A black and white photograph of her twisted body, spanning the doorway of the home I had been terrified to visit.

I'm sorry, Mary. I should have gone.

I leaned back against the headboard and closed my eyes hard. I must have fallen asleep because the next thing I knew, someone was pounding on my door with what sounded like a baseball bat.

I stumbled toward the door. "Who is it?" My mouth tasted mildewed cardboard. I glanced over to the alarm clock. It was 1:10 in the morning.

"Detective Ryan."

Just what I need, I groaned to myself. The Return of Godzilla. "Can you hold on a minute while I put something on?"

"Sure." I imagined him leering on the other side of the door.

The bed was littered with the police records, interspersed with my own notes, and thoroughly coated with cracker crumbs. I crawled into the center of the bed and started to sort through the papers in a silent frenzy.

"You decent yet?" Ryan called.

Ignoring him, I slipped the police records back into the manila envelope, put the file in the desk drawer on top of my own notes, and stalked to the door.

"C'mon! You can put on a damn robe. I won't bite," he bellowed.

I opened the door. Ryan appeared even more disgruntled than he had yesterday. His eyes were bloodshot and his steel-gray hair looked as if he had been tugging on it all night long. Standing with legs akimbo, he surveyed every corner of the room like a hawk.

"Would you like a drink, Detective?"

His eyes snapped back to me. "Honey, I could haul your ass in right now. Where's the goddamn file?"

Crossing my arms, I tried to keep my eyes from shifting to the desk. He snickered. "Jesus, you're an easy one to read." He spun toward the desk, yanked open the drawer, and grabbed the file. "Piece of cake," he muttered to himself. He spilled the contents onto the desk, studying each individual item with a meticulousness that surprised me.

"Looks like everything's here. Plus some cracker crumbs." He slid close to me, so close his stale breath swept over my face. "Did you find what you want?"

"No. But I will." I derived great satisfaction from knowing my breath smelled no better than his.

"You're stubborn as a mule, Miller." He methodically slapped the file against his left hand. "You know, I could make your life pretty damn unpleasant . . . a few days down at Central . . ." He bit the inside of his cheek, his eyes narrowing. "I shoulda never left you in my office like I did."

"Should I say thank you?"

Unexpectedly, he smiled. His bulldog jowls lifted in a grimace that looked almost amiable. "You're a sassy bitch, aren't you? You remind me of my own daughter. 'Cept I wanted her to be a cop and she decided to be a goddamn social worker. Stubborn like her mother," he snorted on his way out the door.

"How did your wife die?" I blurted.

He stopped dead in his tracks. After a few

seconds, he turned and looked at me. "I used to drink too much," he said quietly, his voice tight with sarcasm. But his eyes told the truth. He was still hurting. I suddenly felt embarrassed.

"She got tired of the fighting, so one day she moved out to some sleazebag hotel . . . and the next week she was robbed, sodomized, and clubbed to death." He steadied himself against the doorjamb and glared at me over his shoulder. "Any more questions?"

I felt my lips quiver. He just stared at me and nodded. "Tell you one thing that's not in these files . . ." He was taunting me now. "This pavement princess I know —"

"Pavement princess?"

He snorted. "A hooker. She tells me she saw your friend a couple of days before she died. She was hanging around a joint down in the Tenderloin district, right about Mission and Eighth."

He paused to watch my reaction. "A good place to buy cheap sex or score some crack. Now, maybe your friend was just passing by, and maybe she wasn't."

"What are you trying to say?"

"You wanna play detective, honey? Detect." The door slammed shut.

Ryan was right. If I was ever going to find out what happened to Mary, I was going to have to do a lot more than spar with a burnt-out cop who seemed to have more than his share of ghosts. I sat down at the desk and pulled out my copious but barely legible notes.

Fact: Mary's body was found on Sunday, April 16, by a neighbor with the melodious name of

Martha Sparks. The autopsy showed she had died from anaphylactic shock. Time of death was estimated at 7:30 the previous evening.

Fact: A vial of penicillin was found in her medicine chest. The drug was prescribed on April 6 by Dr. Timothy Harrison and filled by Jack Day's pharmacy.

Fact: A note was left in her typewriter that seemed to indicate she had been fed up with something — or someone — in her life.

Fact: The telephone was found off the hook. The police assume that she tried to call someone for help before staggering toward the front door.

And then there was the missing allergy ID. Without that, the police and forensic team had been forced to work in the dark.

It was almost eight o'clock when I threw my notebook down. I dialed Patty's number, tossing my legs onto the desk and tilting my seat back till it threatened to fall. When Patty answered the phone, I practically bit her head off. "Look Patty, I want you to write down every damn thing you remember about Mary, her friends, her enemies, her habits, the number of times she peed each day. Everything. I'll be by this afternoon to pick up whatever you've written."

"We have a barbecue tonight. I'm making the cole slaw," Patty stammered. I pictured her perplexed expression and my Dick Tracy act started to fall apart.

"Can't you make some notes while you're cooking?"

"It's kind of hard, Robin. I mean, I have Miriam to worry about and —"

31

"How about tomorrow? Can you be back to me by tomorrow?"

"Sure." She hesitated. "What's this about?"

"Did you know the cops found penicillin in Mary's system?"

"No." She sounded surprised.

"You were her best friend . . . you have to know she wouldn't take penicillin by accident." The wires buzzed with silence. "And she wasn't wearing her allergy ID tag."

"She said she lost it swimming at the gym. That was in March." I could hear Patty breathing shallowly. "Look, I didn't know about the penicillin, but if that's true —"

"I'm asking the same thing. Did she kill herself?"

"If she did . . . Robin, you're not going to like what I have to say."

"I don't like any of this . . ."

"She was depressed for a while. I'd never seen her like that. She was always the one to pick me up. We'd be having lunch and all of a sudden she'd start to cry." She waited for me to react. I knew Mary didn't cry easily. Obviously, Patty wanted me to acknowledge that fact. I kept silent.

"Mary didn't cry easily," Patty added, a sliver of irritation sneaking into her tone. "I'm sure you know that. She loved you a lot more than you realize."

I looked at myself in the mirror hanging over the desk. My eyes were bloodshot. My skin looked flaky. I need a good facial, I thought.

"Are you listening?"

"Yeah." I stood up, anchoring the phone between my chin and shoulder. God, my muscles were tight. I pressed my palms against the wall and stretched my calf muscles.

"She missed you. She said she kept reaching out to you and you kept pulling back." Patty was revved now. "She never really got over the breakup, you know. There were a lot of casual dates, but no one ever came close."

I straightened up and rested my forehead on the wall. Patty was right. I didn't want to hear this.

"All I heard was Robin this and Robin that. She drove a lot of people away. I thought time would help, but this past year was really bad. She bought the house down in Big Sur with the money her parents left her years ago, thinking you'd come out and fall in love with it . . . and her."

My mouth tasted like sour milk. I sat down at the desk and started tapping the pencil against the notepad. "What are you trying to say? That Mary killed herself because of me?" I practically spat into the phone.

"No. I don't know." She sputtered like a balloon stuck with a pin. "I'm sorry if it sounded that way. It's just that she was depressed."

"Did you tell this to the cops?"

"No. Why would I? It wouldn't bring Mary back, would it? And if the police had ruled her death a suicide, her whole life would have been torn apart in the papers. I couldn't do that to her."

I hung up from Patty, irritated by her provincial attitude and disturbed by her insinuation.

Was she right? Had I let Mary down? All of a sudden, I remembered a message Mary had left on my answering machine. In November, two weeks after my birthday. Before hanging up, she had said something about needing to talk to me. I got the message when I came home from a trip to Puerto Rico. I didn't call back, pissed that she had missed my birthday for the first time since our breakup.

Was the note in Mary's typewriter for me? "I can't go on like this anymore. It's time that I tell you . . ." Tell me what?

I had to think this through calmly, keep my feelings separate. I retreated to the bathroom and popped two extra-strength aspirin. The normally gentle clang of the cable car sounded like cymbals crashing during the finale of the *1812 Overture*. A back-firing car supplied the cannon shots.

Did Mary really kill herself? Certainly, suicide would answer a lot of questions. Mary had asked the doctor to prescribe penicillin for her precisely because she knew the effects. She drove down to the house in Big Sur and took the phone off the hook so that no one could interrupt her. At some point, she removed her allergy tag and took the penicillin. Afterwards, panic struck. Realizing her mistake, she started to run for help, but collapsed before she could find it.

The scenario had an undeniable logic. But it felt wrong. Too pat, like the ending of a gruesome fairy tale. And it still left too many unanswered questions. If she had started a suicide note, why had she stopped mid-sentence? And why had she bothered to mail her taxes the morning before?

I stood at the window and scratched at an ancient drip of paint. What if the person at the doctor's was not Mary, but someone masquerading as her . . . someone who knew her well enough to know that a single dosage of penicillin could kill her as effectively as a gunshot?

But why would anyone want to kill Mary? I started pacing like a caged leopard. Distanced from the details of her daily existence, I could barely speculate on who hated or feared her enough to poison her.

Patty was quirky and uptight, but she was hardly a candidate for murder. She and Mary had been friends since meeting as defiant Mormon teenagers in Salt Lake City. Mary used to say that if it wasn't for Patty, she'd be a martyred Mormon wife, sneaking sherry in the basement of the church while her husband bragged about her recipe for shortbread cookies. Pete was a possibility. Few men feel kindly to their wives' lesbian friends. But then, Pete didn't strike me as a homicidal homophobe. Of course, there were Liz and Cathy. And Carl Lawrence, Mary's attorney. I also had to consider Martha Sparks, the pain-in-the-ass neighbor in Big Sur. But I didn't know any of them well enough to even venture a guess at what they could gain from Mary's death. And why the hell had Mary been strolling around the Tenderloin?

My insistent pacing was starting to wear down the carpet — and my nerves. I grabbed a can of juice from the miniature refrigerator near the bathroom door and stormed out of the room.

Chapter 3

I didn't know where I was headed, but fifteen minutes and a cable car later I found myself standing outside the offices of the *San Francisco Tribune*, the place where Mary used to work.

On the fifth floor, a female security guard with short, frosted hair and a body like a linebacker asked me for ID. I leaned over her desk and whispered confidentially, "I'm a private investigator working for Sandra and Joseph Oswell, Mary's parents. I need to see her files, speak to her coworkers."

Surprisingly, I was finding that lying was a lot easier than writing romance novels. I just hoped that she didn't know that Mary's parents had both died years ago.

The guard's gaze wandered over my chest. "I'd like to help you, but . . ."

Taking that hint, I moved my mouth closer to her ear. "The family will be very grateful." I paused, letting my warm breath tease the tips of her earlobes. "So will I."

Goosebumps rose on her muscular arms.

Soon after, I was being escorted into Mary's old office. The guard winked at me as she unlocked the door. "If you need anything else, let me know." She squeezed my hand as if it were an orange and she fully intended to make juice. Only by sheer will did I prevent myself from wincing in pain.

"By the way, the name's Sam. I'll make sure no one disturbs you."

With my right hand held limply, like a dog favoring an injured paw, I searched Mary's drawers, my heart thumping loudly. The top desk drawer held nothing but paper clips and three sugar packets with pictures of Amelia Earhart on the front. I moved down to the file drawer.

"Private Investigator Miller, I presume." I jumped back from the desk and hit my head on the edge of a picture frame.

"Sorry, I didn't mean to startle you," Cathy purred with a smile that would have made my cats proud. She was leaning against the doorway, the edge of her milk-white rayon dress draped appealingly around her never-ending legs. I started to sweat. At that moment, her resemblance to Mary was overwhelming.

She slinked over to me. "Are you okay? You look a little wobbly."

God. She smelled like ripe peaches. I closed my eyes, struggling to still my sudden desperate need to make love, to lose myself in someone's arms. "No, I'm fine." I sat down on the edge of the desk and tried to recover my dignity. "What are you doing here?"

"I work here. Catherine Chapman, entertainment critic. You can read my review of *Dangerous Scoundrels* tomorrow. It stunk, by the way."

"I didn't realize you were a writer."

"You weren't paying attention at dinner, then." She was teasing me. "Liz must have mentioned it four or five times."

"Is Liz . . . are you and Liz . . ."

"Lovers? No. Just friends. She manages a gay bookstore on Castro. That's where we met."

She leaned against the wall and tucked a strand of coppery hair behind one ear. "Now it's my turn. Why are you here?"

"Why'd you call me 'private investigator?' "

"Not good at answering questions, are you? Sam told me. She knew Mary and I were very good friends. She wanted to make sure you were legit." One corner of her mouth turned up. "You made quite an impression on her."

"For some reason, that scares me."

Cathy laughed. "I can understand that. Now, do you want to answer my question?"

"I'm looking into Mary's death. I thought maybe I'd find something in her desk, but it seems as if someone got here before me."

"I have most of her files. She was incredibly private, and the prospect of burly policemen digging through her papers made me crazy, so I took what I could and snuck the files home."

I realized I was scowling.

Cathy looked amused. "Why don't you come over tonight and we'll go over the papers together?"

A queer mixture of lust and fear swept through me. "I'd like that. Where do you live?"

"On West Clay, near the Presidio." She tore a piece of paper from the notepad on the desk and wrote down her address. "Come by around six-thirty. I'll cook dinner."

"You don't have to . . ."

"No, I don't." She opened the office door. "By the way, if I were you, I'd leave by the back exit. Sam can be pretty persistent."

I watched her sashay down the hall, my palms moist and my heart beating a mile a minute. Then I shook my head. Back to business, Miller.

I finished searching the desk, then rummaged through the file cabinets on the back wall. In the last drawer, I found a phone directory for the newspaper staff. I flipped to the listing for the finance division, then slipped the book into my briefcase and headed out the door.

As I turned the corner, I noticed an in-box on top of a small oak cabinet overflowing with interoffice envelopes. I pulled out a handful of correspondence addressed to Mary. Apparently, the mail room hadn't deleted her name yet.

After a few seconds, I found an envelope marked "Personal." I peeled the flap open. Apparently the mail room wasn't the only department that had failed to update its records. Inside the envelope was a check stapled to a copy of an expense report. I glanced through the items casually and was about to toss it aside when a date caught my eye. April 6.

I checked my notebook. Sure enough, that was the date Mary had supposedly run to the doctor during her lunch break. But according to the expense report, Mary had submitted a receipt for a luncheon at Aunt Hatties, an upscale restaurant in Berkeley. I tucked the report into my pocket. Mary's death was starting to look a lot like murder.

* * * * *

According to the staff directory, Mary's editor was Helene McNeil, located in room 507. I tapped down the hall like I owned the place and found myself standing outside a corner office with a six-foot wide glass partition veiled by vertical blinds. I knocked on the door.

"Yeah!"

I flinched involuntarily, instantly switching on my bitch alert. Straightening my shoulders and pulling myself to my full five-nine, I swung into the room. "Ms. McNeil?"

A hard-edged blonde in a gray pinstripe suit sat at the desk, her ice-blue eyes squinting at me

40

through thick cigarette smoke, her nails bitten to the quick.

"Who the hell are you?" she growled.

I crossed over and placed my palms on the desk, leaning into the smoke like a firebrand. "I'm a private investigator, Ms. McNeil. Now, I'm going to ask you a few questions, and I expect some answers." My voice was scratchy from the smoke, but I thought it enhanced my menace. I was wrong.

Helene leaned back, pulled a pink-tipped cigarette out of her mouth, then licked her bottom lip and smiled. "You're not a cop, right?"

"Right," I said, a sense of unease stealing over me.

"Then get the hell out of here."

Obviously, I had used the wrong tactic. I sat down in a hard-backed visitor's chair and stared at her. Her shoulder-length hair was thick and wavy, the color of egg yolk. I figured it was courtesy of Clairol. She reminded me of an aging playboy bunny, with small Betty Boop lips coated with pasty lipstick. Cotton-candy pink. Make-up caked in the wrinkles surrounding her eyes and mouth. She was probably in her mid-forties, but she looked a lot closer to fifty-five.

She seemed perfectly content with our staring match, so I decided to try another approach. "Would you be surprised if I used the word murder?"

"Why should I?" She talked around her cigarette, her lipstick so thick that her lips seemed stuck together. "Mary was a bitch. A good reporter, but a bitch." Her eyes held a challenge.

"Do you mind elaborating?"

She scratched the side of her nose and laughed. It sounded like chalk screeching over a blackboard. "Why the hell not?" She stabbed the cigarette into a tin ashtray shaped like the state of California, the laugh turning into a deep, rattling cough.

"Mary was an ambitious dyke who would stop at nothing to get what she wanted. You look shocked. Sorry sister, but you want facts . . . I'll give you facts." She stood up and leaned over me, a mischievous gleam in her eye. "I used to be the news editor. I was the best around . . . I *am* the best around," she rumbled into my face, her breath an acrid mixture of cigarette smoke, cherry Lifesavers and Scotch. "Then I got sent down here," she said, gesturing with disgust at her office door. "Finance. This is not my beat, and everyone knows it."

She fell back into her seat, a self-satisfied grin distorting her face. "Politics." She spat the word out like it was the answer to all my questions. We stared at each other again for a beat or two, and then she rummaged in her suit pocket for another cigarette. I watched her in silence.

"The new publisher took a disliking to me. Thought he'd send me down here and let me drown. But I've been hanging on . . ." She paused to light her cigarette. "Mary was looking to bump me out. Kept stories from me. Contradicted my orders. Crashed meetings I told her to stay out of. It might've worked too, if someone hadn't gotten to her."

"Why do you think she was killed?" I asked quietly.

"You deaf? I told you . . . she was a bitch. Her

42

career was everything. She wanted to destroy people. Me included." She inhaled cigarette smoke like it was oxygen and she was gasping for her last breath. "I always say, what goes around, comes around. She was on some hot story. Wouldn't let me in on it. The way I see it, someone got to her before she got to them." She started to rock her chair back and forth.

"You tell the police any of this?"

"No. From what I hear, the jerks never got past square one. No motive, no means." She smiled at me. "I didn't say anything because sometimes murder can be justified . . ." She reached over the desk and pointed her cigarette at me. For a horrifying moment, I thought she might poke its hot tip into my cheek. "How long have you been in this business?"

"A few years."

She nodded like she had anticipated my answer. "I was in news for eighteen years. I've seen some awful stuff go on in this city. Suicides, decapitation, rape." She dropped the cigarette into the ashtray and watched it burn. "After twelve years, I found myself starting to sympathize with some of the criminals . . . life can be hell sometimes. Live long enough and you'll know what I mean." She grew unnaturally still, her eyes glazed over.

I wasn't going to get anything more out of her right then, so I jotted down my hotel number and stabbed the note onto her memo spindle. I left her staring at the ashtray.

I had one more person to see before I could head back to the hotel. Richard Klein, the paper's food columnist. I had worked with Richard in the past, long before Mary joined the paper. We had attended conventions together and had even spent a week in Hawaii working on a series of travel articles. But when Mary moved to San Francisco, the two of them quickly developed a solid friendship that had locked me out.

"Knock, knock," I said, poking my head into his office.

Rich looked like a young Richard Chamberlain. He glanced up and flashed me a dazzling smile. "Well, well." He lifted his long, lanky body and walked over to hug me. "Hello stranger," he muttered into my ear. "Come on," he said, leading me by the hand. "Have a seat."

I sat down and waited till he had settled into his chair.

"That's an ominous look you have," he said, only half-joking.

"This isn't really a social visit." My voice was strained. I wanted to hug him, but if I allowed even a small crack in my defenses, I knew I'd fall apart. "I need to ask you some questions."

"Fine. But lighten up. It's me, remember?"

I took out a notepad and pen, struggling to stay indifferent. "I think someone may have killed Mary." I filled him in on what I had learned so far. "Can you think of any reason why someone would want to kill her?"

"Hell no. Mary was an angel. You know that."

There was an edge to his words. My eyes locked on his.

"She was crazy about you, Robin."

"Dammit Rich, she moved out here by choice."

"Right. I'm sure Allen thought the same thing."

44

Allen was Rich's ex. They had been together for six years. Two years ago, Rich had moved out. I didn't know why. By that time, Rich and I had stopped talking. When I asked Mary what had happened between them, she had begged off, muttering something about not wanting to violate confidences.

"I was sorry to hear about the two of you. Why'd you leave?"

"Ancient history," he said, his lips verging on a pout. Then his eyes softened. "How can I help you?"

"Did Mary have any enemies?"

He raised his eyebrows and tilted his head at me.

I noted the sarcasm and stepped around it. "I just spoke to Helene McNeil. She wasn't real fond of Mary."

"No surprise there. She hates half the staff. But Mary was on the top of her list. She had some cockamamie idea that Mary was after her job. Between you and me, she had reason to worry. Not that Mary was trying to edge her out. She was just that good. And Helene, well, let me put it this way . . . she's her own worst enemy. She'll be out of a job by the end of this year."

"Because of her drinking?"

"That's just part of it. She's a mean-assed woman. I once saw her make a fifty-year-old news reporter weep like a baby . . . a man who hadn't even cried when his mother died. That's when the publisher demoted her. I think he was hoping she'd leave in a huff. Instead, she's hanging onto this job by her ragged fingernails." Rich punctuated his remarks with a grimace, stretching his fingers out

45

like a cat's claw. He was always given to dramatics, a fact that had endeared him to me from the start.

I smiled and some of the tension in the room dissipated.

"By the way," he said, his green eyes sparking. "It's good to see you again."

This time, we both laughed.

"Okay, okay. Enough mush," I said.

"Aw, you're such a softie."

"Do you think Helene's capable of murder?"

He looked off to the side for a second and then swung his attention back. "Yes."

"Anybody else who might have reason to hurt Mary?"

He sighed heavily and dropped his head back, his eyes fixing on the ceiling. "That's a hard —" Suddenly, he lifted his head and stared at me. "Sam's girlfriend. You know Sam, the security guard? She was crazy about Mary. Every morning, she'd bring her coffee . . . and every afternoon she'd be in there with flowers, or candy, or a new paperback."

He leaned forward. "Well, her girlfriend is this pretty, petite thing that scares the life out of me. One day, Mary and I were having lunch in a coffee shop around the corner and Sharon Goodman . . . that's her name . . . Sharon barrels in steaming. First of all — you'll love this — she's wearing a leather jacket with studs all over it. And lime green socks with pink stripes. She runs over to us and starts yelling her head off at Mary. The two of us practically sunk under the table."

Without warning, Rich stood up, put one hand on his hip and wagged the other under my nose. "Sam's mine! Mine! Do you hear me? I know what you're up to, Miss High Class, and I won't let you get away with it'" he squealed in a falsetto voice. "I tell you, she was a bat out of hell. Try to imagine Madonna with flames spitting from her mouth and you've got the picture." He leaned back on the edge of the desk. "Funny thing is, she's got a soft spot for animals. Once a week, she comes in here with some stray she's found, pleading with people to adopt some greasy cat or three-legged dog." He shook his head. "Maybe she reserves all her tenderness for animals."

* * * * *

I took a cab back to the hotel, left a message for Detective Ryan, and spent the next two hours showering, plucking and moisturizing. Then I made the mistake of lying down. An hour later I awoke, my hair sticking out at right angles to my scalp. I scampered into the bathroom and stuck my head under the faucet. Then I towel-dried my short, choppy locks — which thankfully fell back into a semblance of chic disarray — and darted into the hallway.

"Whoops. You almost knocked me over."

Carl Lawrence, Mary's attorney, cupped his massive hands around my shoulders. His mouth was fixed in a studied, toothy, and determinedly masculine grin. His jet black hair revealed each careful stroke of a narrow-toothed comb.

"I brought some papers for you to sign." A burgundy faux-marble folder was tucked elegantly into his armpit.

"You should have called first."

"I did. When you didn't call back, I thought I'd stop by."

"I never got the message." In fact, I had never even checked with the front desk.

"No problem." He dropped his arms and crossed them over his crotch. "The papers are self-explanatory, but nevertheless I expect you may have some questions. I took the liberty of making reservations for us at Masa's. It's just downstairs and the food's fabulous." His eyes surveyed my khaki pants and sneakers. "Why don't you slip on a dress while I wait in the lobby."

"Excuse me, Lancelot, but I have an appointment already."

The sarcasm slid off him like eggs from a teflon pan. "My loss. And yours, too. Masa's is in a class all its own."

I gently tugged the folder out from under his arm and slipped it under the door. "Papers delivered."

"How about dinner tomorrow night?"

"Why don't I just stop by your office."

He chuckled, half-heartedly. "You misread me, my dear. I'm a very respectable attorney who hopes to one day be a very respectable mayor. What's more, I have a very respectable girlfriend who would, no doubt, kill me in a very respectable fashion if she even suspected that I was cheating on her. You have nothing to fear from me, unless you are inexplicably terrified by men who have a healthy appreciation for well-toned women with lovely olive skin, intriguing green eyes, and incredible intelligence."

Oh, for a large sack of manure, I thought, recalling a line from a Woody Allen film.

48

"Carl, it's been an unparalleled pleasure. Live long and prosper." I flashed him the Vulcan hand salutation in lieu of the gesture I really wanted to make, and trotted down the steps.

* * * * *

Cathy's house was the color of ripe honeydew, with a peaked roof and a small balcony lined with geraniums and irises. I was admiring the Victorian detailing when I suddenly noticed feet dangling over the roof edge.

"Hello!" I yelled skyward, feeling more than slightly foolish.

First a forehead, then those devastating eyes appeared at the roof edge. "Sorry, I'll be right down."

Okay, I commented to myself. We all have our quirks.

The door opened. Cathy stood there, breathless. Her cheeks were bright red and her carefully sculptured hair was delightfully windblown. She wore a pair of faded Levis and a man-tailored dungaree shirt which revealed a tan "V" at the base of her neck. The "V" led to a paler rise of flesh. For a split second, I forgot how to breathe.

"God, I *am* sorry. The time just got away from me. After you left the office, I had this awful fight with my editor." She took me by the arm and led me into the hallway. "He wants me to start reviewing television movies — which he knows I despise. Have a seat in the living room. I'll be right back." She disappeared around a corner.

The living room was almost completely black and white, with an occasional splash of red. An alabaster couch was smothered with black and white pillows of various shapes, sizes, and patterns. Two club chairs, covered in matching fabric, faced the couch. In the center of the sitting area was a rya rug bearing a crisp black-and-white geometric pattern. A stone fireplace stood on the opposite side of the room. On the mantle were two red candles and a photograph in a red glass frame.

"Don't be afraid to sit down."

I turned to find Cathy standing just inches behind me, with two wine glasses in her hands. "I remembered that you only drink white. Hope you like this. It's a Beringer special reserved Chardonnay. I love it."

I took the wine from her, once again amazed by the sheer physicality of her presence. She rearranged the throw pillows on the couch and patted the space next to her. "Come on. Sit down."

I obeyed, my breathing turning somewhat irregular.

"You know, we didn't have much time to talk the other night. I hardly know anything about you."

"There's not much to know." I struggled to sound casual. What was it about her that made me act so damn juvenile? Sure, it had been months — in fact, almost a year — since I had been intimate with anyone. But still, I couldn't remember feeling this fluttery. Except with Mary. The first time I met Mary.

Cathy tittered. "Don't tell me you're modest. How unusual." Just then, an overweight tabby waddled into the room. The relief was overwhelming.

"You have a cat!" I announced as if I were relaying some great new discovery.

50

"Meet Mr. Tubbs. Tubbs, I'd like you to meet Robin Miller."

Tubbs sniffed my shoelaces, then paused with his mouth held open. His gaze drifted up to my face. After sizing me up a few more seconds, he granted me acceptance. With surprising agility, Tubbs leapt onto my lap and began kneading my thighs. I slipped my fingers behind his left ear and started rubbing that hard-to-reach crease.

"I take it you're a cat lover."

"You bet. I have two back home. A friend's watching them for me."

"A live-in friend, I presume." Cathy's curiosity was encouraging.

"Not quite. We share a brownstone in Brooklyn. I live on top, and she has the bottom floors."

"An interesting arrangement." She made the words sound intensely sexual. I focused all my attention on Tubbs, rubbing his narrow chin with the back of my thumb.

"I think Tubbs has fallen for you," Cathy said, leaning toward me.

"The feeling's mutual." I shifted Tubbs' dead weight and crossed my legs tightly. My breathing was becoming unbearably shallow.

Unexpectedly, she stood up. "I better get dinner started. Do you like chicken Kiev?"

I looked up and met her eyes for the first time since my arrival. Her gaze was charged, but whether with attraction or warning, I couldn't tell. "Fine. That's fine." When she left the room, I took a huge swallow of air. Please God, I whispered to myself, don't let her be involved in Mary's death.

"Why don't you come in here while I cook?"

51

Cathy hollered from the kitchen. I walked in, hoping my trembling knees wouldn't betray me.

Cathy was standing over a bowl of rolled chicken pieces, brushing them with melted butter. A five-inch Magnavox television was playing on the countertop.

"Hope you don't mind. I always watch the news while I cook. It relaxes me." She tossed me an open smile. "So does sitting on the roof. I actually had someone build me some steps and a small ledge up there. Whenever I get upset, I just crawl out on the roof and stare at the clouds."

I started to say something in response when the news caught my attention.

"Lucille Ball died today in a hospital in Los Angeles. Her doctors say . . ."

As the newscaster droned on, the room started to fade. All the stress and tension of the past few days swept over me. I found myself sitting on the kitchen floor, my arms wrapped around my knees, the sobs coming hard and fast.

"Shhh." Cathy was sitting next to me, sweeping my hair away from my face. She gently pulled my head to her shoulder. I sniveled into her collar. "Go ahead," she murmured. "Let it out."

At her words, a sound bellowed from me, a sound that a wounded animal might make.

We must have sat there for twenty minutes before Tubbs walked in and decided to take advantage of the situation by jumping onto the counter and swiping a piece of chicken.

"Drop it, Tubbs!" Cathy screamed. Tubbs dropped his catch and darted out of the room. I started to half-laugh, wiping the back of my hand over my nose, which had started to run. Cathy handed me a

52

box of Kleenex and I unceremoniously blew my nose while she stood there, gazing down at me with undisguised concern. "Look, why don't we forget about dinner for now and just go inside and talk." She extended her hand to me.

"Good idea," I answered with a sigh, the tears temporarily tucked behind a fragile barrier. I followed her into the living room and dropped heavily into a club chair.

"Want to tell me what happened in there?" Cathy probed gently.

"Who knows? The straw that broke the camel's back, I guess. Lucy's always been a tonic for me. Like your sitting on the roof. I turn on one of those early episodes and all the craziness of my life recedes. I don't know. Maybe it's just safer to cry about her." And maybe it's safer to feel attracted to you than to admit how much I want Mary back, I thought suddenly.

I balled the tissue up in my fist, realizing all at once that this was the first time I had allowed myself to cry over Mary. "It's too scary to think about Mary's death. When I think that she's gone . . ." My voice cracked. I fell silent, knowing that the tears were threatening to break through again.

"Why did the two of you ever break up? It couldn't have been lack of love."

"No. Far from it." I closed my eyes, remembering the way Mary looked when we first met. She was sitting in my sister's accounting office, biting the eraser of a pencil. I had walked in unannounced.

"Sorry." I start to close the door.
"Come in, Robin." Barbara waves me in. "I'd like

you to meet Mary Oswell, one of my most valued clients. She's a writer for the Wall Street Journal."

Mary rises to greet me, her eyes catching mine with a start. Oh yes, I whisper to myself. Oh yes.

"It's a pleasure to meet you." Mary squeezes my hand a little too long, with a pressure that tells me the feeling's mutual.

"There was pure electricity between us. We were in bed two hours after we met." I laughed. "Neither one of us had ever done anything like that before."

"So what happened?"

"Time, I guess. The passion stayed with us, but the easy forgiveness of new lovers faded fast. Mary was always so controlled, so even-tempered. I know she loved me, but the only time she really showed it was when we were in bed. Other times, she acted like a distant relation. The final blow came when my father died. He and I hadn't been close for years. More than years, actually. Something had happened when I was a kid . . ."

"Your sister's death?"

My head started to pound. "Mary told you about that?" I asked, surprised.

"She said you still blamed yourself. She wanted to make everything okay but couldn't. It made her feel impotent."

I tried to imagine Mary talking like that. The words didn't match my memory. Whenever Carol's death had come up, Mary changed the subject. "It was an accident, silly. You have to put it behind you," she used to say. Right. Forget I shot my own sister to death. No problem, Mary.

"What happened exactly?"

I stared blindly at Cathy, suddenly transported back to the dark, musty closet in my parent's bedroom. The sound of Carol's muffled giggles.

"We were playing in a closet. Carol — that was her name — was just five years old. I was three. My father had a twenty-two caliber pistol hidden in a shoe box. I found it and started fooling around with it. The gun went off." I started to feel sick, the pit of my stomach soft and sour, like a rotten peach.

"I'm sorry. It was stupid of me to bring it up."

"No, it's all right. To tell you the truth, it's never too far from mind. Anyway, my father never forgave himself — or me. Whenever he looked at me, I could see the pain and anger. So we just stopped talking. He and my mother moved to Florida when I was eighteen. I visited them once a year, at most. But for some reason, his death tore me apart. Mary tried to console me in her own way, I suppose. But it wasn't enough. I needed her emotion, I needed her to *feel* my pain, but she just stood outside, like she always did, telling me time would take care of everything." The old anger rose. "Things fell apart after that. The love was there, but so was a bridge that neither of us knew how to cross."

I rubbed my eyes and shifted into a more comfortable position. "When Patty called to tell Mary about the job opening at the newspaper . . . now that I think about it, you must have been the one that told Patty about the job." Cathy nodded silently. "Anyway, when she heard about it, she leaped at the chance. I think it provided the escape hatch we both needed."

I sagged back in the chair, feeling more exhausted than I had ever felt. "I never really got over her. The past three years I've been with three other women. None of them lasted more than a month or so." I took a slow sip of wine.

Cathy walked over to me, then knelt by my side. "You've been through a lot." She covered my hand with hers. At her touch, I sunk deeper into the chair. She gazed up at me, her eyes reflecting my fatigue.

I leaned my head back and closed my eyes, concentrating on the warmth of her fingers as they drew small circles on the back of my hand. With my eyes closed, I could pretend it was Mary, letting me know everything was all right. I smiled to myself and let the world disappear.

* * * * *

When I woke up, I was still in the club chair, my feet on a hassock that hadn't been there previously. A cotton-mesh blanket was draped over me. I looked at my watch. It was 6:10 in the morning. For an insomniac, I was doing an unusual amount of sleeping lately.

"Good morning!" Cathy scampered past the hallway in a T-shirt and jogging pants. She hopped back with one sneaker on and the other one in her hand. "I must say that I've had women fall asleep on me before . . . but never quite in that fashion." She bent over to tie her laces. "How are you feeling?"

"Ridiculous," I replied, standing up and straightening my clothes. "That was incredibly rude of me."

"Not at all. Although, I *was* surprised. Mary

made a big thing out of your insomnia. In fact, I took it as a compliment." She tucked in her T-shirt and grinned. "It's nice knowing you felt safe enough to fall asleep like that."

"I think you may be pushing it."

She shot me an endearingly crooked smile. "Maybe. Look, I'm going for a short run. Why don't you pour yourself some juice? Take a shower too, if you like. The bathroom's upstairs. I'll be back in about twenty minutes."

The door slammed behind her, leaving me puzzled and unnerved. What was I supposed to do? Wander through a stranger's home? I started to head for the kitchen, the only room I felt comfortable exploring, then stopped suddenly. I took a closer look at the picture on the fireplace mantle.

Cathy was standing with her arms around Patty, their cheeks pressed together as they grinned into the camera. Behind them was a lit Christmas tree. At the right side of the picture, other couples stood with hands entwined.

Mary was grasping the hand of a petite woman with dark eyes. She looked incredibly young. Next to them was a slightly slimmer Liz wrapped around a tall, androgynous blonde with an aquiline nose.

I took the picture off the mantle and stared at it. Mary was wearing the forest green fisherman's sweater I had given her as a birthday present two weeks after we met. That was in December 1982. I remembered how disappointed I was when she told me that she had agreed to spend Christmas with friends in San Francisco.

Patty had been gay back then. And Cathy had been her lover.

Chapter 4

"Why didn't you mention that you and Patty had
been lovers?" I hurled the words at Cathy before she
had even stepped through the front door. Her smile
flattened instantly.

"Why should I? That was years ago. In case you
haven't noticed, she's straight now. Straight and very
happily married." She kicked her sneakers across the
hallway with more force than was necessary. They
bounced off the wall and landed at my feet.
"Besides, I thought you knew. Patty and I didn't
break up till 'eighty-four. You and Mary were still

honeymooners back then. Don't tell me she never confided to you about Patty's troubles — the seven-year relationship that sunk faster than the Titanic."

Cathy stomped over to the fireplace, picked up the picture, and waved it at me. "Is this why you're asking me about Patty? Damn." She slapped it face down on the mantle. "What's the point, Robin?"

Suddenly, I wasn't sure. Deflated, I waved my hands feebly. "Forget it. You're right. It just seemed important somehow." I reached for the knob of the front door.

"Fine, Robin. Just walk out. Christ, you're just like the rest of them." Cathy was standing in the middle of her living room, her hands resting on her hips, her face flushed with anger, her T-shirt damp with sweat.

"What do you suggest I do?"

Cathy didn't answer. She just glared at me, the dare in her eyes unmistakable. I strode back into the room, stopping less than a foot away from her. I could feel her breath on my face. It smelled of mint. For a moment, anger and suspicion receded and something deeper, more compelling surged through me like a lightning stroke cracking the night open.

Cathy blinked. When she opened her eyes, the change was perceptible. "Maybe you better leave." Her voice was low, the muted rumble of retreating thunder. Neither of us moved. She dropped her eyes, her voice becoming as small as a splash of rain from a single leaf. "Please."

* * * * *

I walked aimlessly for close to an hour, cursing myself for forgetting Mary's files at Cathy's house. Finally, I sat down on a bench facing the Golden Gate Bridge. The morning fog hung on the far end of the bridge like a cotton ball, the top edge brushed with sunlight.

A stray dog, his once-golden fur matted with a dark liquid, nosed a garbage can next to me. With fierce determination, he began pawing at a McDonald's bag buried behind the grating under a full load of other people's junk. The dog looked up at me, his moist walnut eyes torn between suspicion and hope. I started to dig through the garbage. Finally, I found the McDonald's bag, tore it open, shooing away flies the entire time. Sure enough, half a Quarter Pounder lurked beneath a pile of crumpled napkins. I tossed the meat to the dog, who devoured it in two bites. His tail was in full swing by then.

"Good luck, kid." I smiled at the dog and pulled a tissue from my back pocket. Wiping my hands, I started to walk away. The dog followed. I spun around and stared down at him. He seemed to understand. Dropping his head, he changed directions. My eyes burned as I watched him fade down the slope.

* * * * *

I collapsed on a small patch of grass and focused on the growing circle of people waiting for the cable car to turn around for the steep climb up Nob Hill. How had I ended up here?

I blew my nose and tried to clear my head. Why had I freaked out when I remembered Cathy had been with Patty? Was I jealous? Or was I just pissed at myself for forgetting?

Mary had always referred to Patty and Cathy as a model couple. She was devastated when they broke up. We had planned a trip to Denmark that year, but instead Mary flew out to San Francisco to comfort Patty. They spent one week sobbing on each other's shoulders about lousy lesbian relationships, and another week driving out to Utah where Patty's parents lived. After two days in their Mormon homeland, enduring virulent lectures on the sins of booze, drugs and lesbianism, Mary decided enough was enough. We met in Denver and spent three exquisite days in a hotel room with a view of snow-capped mountains we never managed to visit.

Six months later, Patty called to tell us that she had met and married a soldier. "I'm back in the fold," she had informed Mary, only half-joking. For years before, it had been part of their shtick, keeping track of the number of ex-communicated Mormons they knew.

Mary had hung up the phone slightly dazed. Then, typically, she had looked up at me and quipped, "Another good ex-Mormon lost . . . I think we're down to fifteen."

I ran my hands through my hair, the memory making me queasy. How the hell was I going to find out who killed Mary if I couldn't even keep track of the past.

Annoyed with myself, I stood up, marched over to the nearest pay phone, and dialed information. I wrote the number on the back of my hand. The phone rang six times. I was about to hang up when the phone clicked. "Cathy?"

The pause seemed interminable. "What do you want?"

I pressed the phone to my ear to dull the traffic sounds. "Mary's papers."

"I'll leave a key under the doormat," she said, as if instructing a licensed exterminator. "The papers are in my office upstairs. On the desk." She hung up. The phone buzzed into my ear like an irritated wasp. The sting was poisonous.

* * * * *

Cathy's office was so impeccably arranged I thought I'd find a rope barring access to the room and a small historical marker tacked near the door.

Pale oak bookcases lined three walls of the room. The books were organized by subject, author, and title. I half expected to see small typewritten catalog numbers glued to the binders. Nearest the door were classics: a row of Shakespeare, several volumes of Dickens, a few novels of Hardy, and a two-inch thick, leather-bound edition of seventeenth-century poetry. The next case contained volumes on the entertainment industry, including Molly Haskell's book on women in film and several oversized picture books on old movies. I pulled one out at random and found myself chortling out loud. Who would have thought Cathy would have a fondness for Godzilla movies and horror flicks?

A postcard flickered to the ground. I picked it up.

On the front was a black and white photograph of the Bride of Frankenstein. I turned the card over.

"Darling, I know I've been awful. Sometimes you must feel like you've married the Bride of Frankenstein. I'm sorry. These have been hard times for me, for us, but I'm going to change. I promise. From now on, the only 'turning on' I'm going to do is with you. Love your wild woman, Patty."

Embarrassed, I slid the postcard back into the book and returned it to the shelf. It was hard to reconcile the Patty I had seen a few nights ago with the woman who had written that card. I tried to remember why she and Cathy broke up. Then it hit me. Patty had had a drinking problem.

In her letters to Mary, Patty had always minimized her alcoholism, joking that it ran in the family. But that last year with Cathy was different. Patty knew she was sinking fast but didn't know how to pull herself out. Her letters had been desperate, confused. In her version of the breakup, Cathy had abandoned her just when she needed her most. I wondered how much of that story was true.

From the immense, highly polished oak desk near the window, I caught the distinct vestige of lemon-based Pledge. The surface was bare except for a slim MacIntosh computer, a plastic case of carefully labeled computer disks, and a black metal file containing Mary's records. I sat down guardedly, as if I were in a mausoleum and might disturb the dead.

Mary's handwriting was decisive, each individual character perfectly formed. The first folder contained notes on the Technical Corrections Act of 1988. I shoved that one back into the file so fast I ended up with a mean paper cut. Sucking the index finger on my right hand, I opened the next folder. This one was more promising.

Exxon Valdez. Impact on industry. Investigate Paul T. Buttons for local angle. Pollution in Bay area?

The next few pages were filled with the same type of cryptic notes. This was Mary's "thinking" folder. She used to keep a similar one by our bedside. One time she had even interrupted our lovemaking to jot down a revelation she had had while burrowing between my knees.

C.L. Buying chicken in meat market. Check out video. Connection with S.R.?

Then, two pages later:

C.L. source of funds? 8pm, Selma. Time to take off white gloves. Nail this one!

Adrenaline coursed through me. For the first time, I felt as if I had a real lead. Mary was investigating someone, and she had been prepared to play rough. Maybe too rough.

I scoured the rest of her files looking for a similar reference. All I could find was "C.L. Transfer records to floor safe in Big Sur. Dead on arrival."

The door slammed downstairs. I heard the jangle of keys being tossed onto a table, then measured steps on the stairs.

"You're still here?" Cathy had on a silk, teal blue dress tied loosely at the waist. The fabric hugged each luscious curve. She unclipped her pearl earrings with one deft hand.

"I'm just about finished." I began slipping the folders back into the metal file. The initials in Mary's notes popped into mind. I turned toward Cathy. "What's your middle name?"

Her eyebrows gathered in puzzlement. "Linda. Why?"

"Just curious."

"That's a new one. Sure you don't want to know my sign?" She sat on the edge of the desk, the silk pulling tight around her trim thighs. "Listen, maybe we should start over." She looked expectant — her mouth parted, her lips moist.

"Not tonight. I need to think some things through." Like who's C.L. and why the hell do your first two initials match? I thought.

"Fine," she said with a tense smile. She squeezed my hand, sending fire up the base of my spine. As I left the room, I glanced over my shoulder. Cathy's honey-toned arms were reaching backwards to undo her zipper. I swallowed hard and bumbled down the steps.

* * * * *

Back in the hotel, I called the police station again. Ryan was out of town till tomorrow. I told his assistant to make sure he called me as soon as possible, then I huddled over the small hotel desk with a cup of lukewarm coffee from the corner restaurant.

I picked up my notes. Mary's first reference to C.L. sounded almost like an errand list: buy chicken, check out video. But Mary had added that question about a connection to someone or something abbreviated S.R. I quickly reviewed the people in Mary's life I had met or heard about. No one's initials came close.

The second note was no less confusing. Source of funds for what? Selma, Alabama? Or was Selma a person?

All of a sudden, my head started to buzz and my fingers tingled. The feeling was vaguely familiar. Then it hit me. This is how I feel when I'm drafting a new book, juggling plot lines and characters till my head spins. Okay, I thought. Take it from there.

On a hotel notepad, I jotted down a list of suspects and possible motives. Cathy Chapman, subject of investigation? Helene McNeil, professional jealousy. Sam and her girlfriend Sharon, sexual tensions. Then I jotted down Martha Sparks' name. Did she have anything to gain from Mary's death? I'd have to drive to Big Sur to interview her. I bit the end of the pencil absentmindedly. Consider all possibilities, I reminded myself.

It was just after seven. I dialed Patty's number. Pete's good-humored voice boomed into my ear. "She's putting Miriam to bed. Hold on and I'll get her." Pete put the phone down and shuffled into another room. I heard him holler up to Patty.

"Hi. Let me just close the door." Somehow, Patty

managed to sound both timid and wired, like a
teenage girl sneaking a phone call to her boyfriend
behind her parents' backs. While I waited for her to
get back on the phone, I added Patty's and Pete's
names to the suspect list. In the background, there
was the thud of a closing door.

"I'm sorry I never got back to you. How are
you?"

"I need to ask you some questions."

"Well, Pete and I were just about to sit down
and have some dessert." She hesitated. "All right."

"Did Mary know anyone with the initials C.L. or
S.R.?"

A second or so passed. "They don't ring a bell."

"What about Selma?"

"Selma? No way. I'd remember that name. Why
are you asking?"

"I went through Mary's work notes. I think she
may have been investigating someone."

There was a sharp intake of air.

"Carl. Carl Lawrence. Mary was furious with
him. She said he had turned out to be another
hypocritical pig."

C.L. I came close to breaking into a chorus of
"Hallelujah." Cathy wasn't C.L. And I had made the
unforgivable mistake of leaving before that zipper
was slid down into the sweet hollow of her back.

"Is there anything else? I really want to get back
to Pete."

"Do you know why she was so upset with Carl?"

"No. She didn't really want to talk about it. All
she said is 'I'm gonna nail this one to the wall.'"

I kissed the phone.

Chapter 5

I felt strangely exhilarated. For the first time in nearly three years, I slipped on a pair of sweat pants and went out for a jog. I lasted about six blocks.

In the heart of Chinatown, lungs burning and stomach growling, I stumbled into the nearest restaurant and ordered sweet and sour soup, General Tso's chicken with extra hot peppers, and garlicky string beans.

Sawing my chopsticks against each other to remove any splinters, I surveyed the room. It was not one of San Francisco's more elegant restaurants. The kitchen was open to public view. Carbon-black woks larger than my bathroom sink rocked on top of a greasy, overcrowded stove. The cook was a thin, wiry man with unusually large hands. He alternated between flinging utensils into a vat of brown-tinged soap suds and frantically stirring the woks till food slopped over the edge and sizzled on the stove. Two heavy-set women stood off to the side, chopping vegetables so fast I got dizzy watching them. Ginger, garlic, and high-pitched Chinese voices spiced the air. I poured myself a cup of pale green tea and grinned. The place reminded me of New York, and for a short while, it was nice to be back amid the oily hubbub.

Afterwards, I strolled back to the hotel, a mint toothpick in my mouth and a fortune cookie in my hand. I cracked the cookie open and unrolled the slip of paper: "To seek truth is noble, to uncover lies is brave."

* * * * *

I changed into a pair of cotton pajamas and settled down with my notes. So far, I had more potential suspects to consider than I would have thought possible. I reviewed the list. Based on Mary's notes, I decided to start with the hotshot lawyer.

"Carl, it's Robin. Sorry for calling so late."

The television set was playing without sound. I switched channels, fascinated by the pantomime. When I hit the Discovery channel, I leaned back. A whale was spinning in sun-dappled water. As I watched, a musty cloud of blood exploded from near her tail. All at once, a small, charcoal-gray body dropped from her rear.

"Did you hear what I just said?"

Oops. "Sorry Carl, I was just pulling on some pj's," I said, trying to sound flirtatious.

"No problem." His voice was cloyingly cheerful. "I said I was disappointed that you didn't come by the office today."

I bet he was. "I was tied up." Just make believe you're writing one of your Harbor Romances, I thought.

Carl chortled. "Not literally, I hope."

God, this was too easy. It was like playing one of those high-tech organs you see in shopping malls. Hit one lousy key and out comes "That's Amore."

I tittered. "Of course not. Though it might be worth considering under the right circumstances." I looked in the mirror and bit my bottom lip to keep from laughing out loud. My hair was spiked up from my brief shot at jogging. My T-shirt had a bright cranberry stain right over my breast, where I had dripped sweet and sour soup, and my gymnasium-gray sweatpants were sagging. No doubt about it — I was a veritable sex kitten.

"And what might those be?" Carl asked coyly.

"Who knows?" I had to cut this short or I'd start gagging. "I've had second thoughts about dinner. Do you think we could get together tomorrow night?"

"Tomorrow's Friday."

"Is that a problem?"

"Is this a date?" he said, doing his best to sound witty and provocative.

"Let's just say an appointment."

He let out a whistle that made me flinch. "You're on. How's Gaylords? It has a great view of the bay."

"Gaylords is perfect. See you around seven. And Carl . . . don't be late." I let my voice get husky, aiming for a Brenda Vaccaro timbre. It came out a little too throaty, as if I were suffering from tonsilitis. Luckily, Carl was too impressed by his own powers of persuasion to notice.

"My timing is *always* perfect."

I clunked the phone down. Not always Carl. Not always.

* * * * *

The conversation with Carl nudged my creative powers into action. For the next six or seven hours, I cradled myself in a cocoon of pillows and worked on my novel. Now that Amanda realized that Roger was a cad, all I had to do was reconcile her with Matthew and resolve the mystery of her parentage. By the time I stood up and arched my back in my best cat-like stretch, I was a mere chapter away from finishing *Love's Lost Flame.*

The digital clock informed me it was a quarter to five in the morning with a little plastic click. Well, I thought, insomnia does have its advantages. I sauntered into the bathroom, splashed shampoo into the tub, and turned the faucet on full power.

Nothing like a hot bath, I thought as I eased into the steaming, avocado-scented water. My body was beaded with sweat as the water rose steadily higher. I tried to see myself as a stranger might. Not too bad, I commented.

I'm blessed with one of those bodies that can

somehow digest Twinkies and Ring Dings and still look as if it's just emerged from a hard day at the gym. My breasts are a little too full for my taste — though apparently not for my lovers'. Personally, I've always envied women who can go braless without risking mammillary whiplash.

Without warning, I had a vivid image of Cathy lounging seductively in a double bathtub, her small, firm breasts floating on crystal clear water. A shiver of excitement raised goosebumps along my exposed flesh. I closed my eyes and surrendered to the fantasy, but as it started to froth, our bodies slipping among fruity soap suds, I realized that Cathy's face had transformed into Mary's. Instantly, my sexual excitement dissolved. I sobbed, my chest heaving in the now lukewarm bath water.

I drained the tub and turned the shower on. This was no time for fantasies, I thought. I had to make peace with Mary.

My skin was as red as an unripe cherry. I scrubbed hard, my teeth clenched. If Carl was the one who had killed Mary, I was going to squash him like a water bug under the wheels of a Mack truck.

After a quick, unsatisfying breakfast at Roxanne's, I walked to Ryan's precinct station. He was sitting in his office, his feet crossed on his desk, a cup of curdled coffee in one hand and a folded newspaper in the other. He was clean-shaven, which made me hopeful. In my limited experience with men, I've always found that a recent shave makes them a bit more civilized. Ryan upheld my theory.

"Well, if it isn't Detective Miller herself." He swung his feet down and gave me a cheeky grin. "Sit down." He gestured to my favorite wood chair.

"You look as if you've had some sleep."

His grin widened, revealing a set of teeth that could have belonged to the Tin Man. "On target, lady. Nailed this son of a bitch I've been tailing for nearly a year. Mean bastard, too. Took a shot at me and my partner, but I got him good." He squinted at me. "No comment?"

"Did you kill him?"

"He's hanging on. Scum always do. Want to know what he's in for?" Ryan leaned over his desk, adopting the manner of someone about to tell you the plot of the last *Friday the 13th* release. I braced myself for the worst. "Murder. Grizzly stuff. We found bodies stacked in his basement like slices of Wonder Bread, limbs scattered all over." He leaned back, his hands clasped behind his head.

I felt my face turn green. "I need your help," I said, grimacing as acid shot into my mouth.

A shadow crossed his face. His eyes flicked to a silver picture frame standing at the corner of his desk. The picture hadn't been there on my previous visit. I didn't have to look at it to know that it was a photograph of his wife.

"I shouldn't have done that," he said more to himself than to me. "What do you want?"

I passed him the expense report and pointed out the luncheon date.

"Damn! Where'd you get this?"

I told him about my visit to Mary's office.

His shoulders slumped. "How the hell did we miss this?"

"The report was issued after you completed your investigation. I found it in the interoffice mail."

Biting a cuticle on his thumb, he read the rest of

73

the report, then muttered under his breath, "That's why we couldn't find the damn date book." He rubbed his eyes wearily. "We'll follow up on this right away . . . is there anything else?"

"Do you have anything on Carl Lawrence?"

"Lawrence? He's a big-time lawyer, isn't he? I've seen him on the tube a lot. Supposed to be pretty popular with women."

"That's him."

"I've heard people say that he's getting into politics. May even run for mayor. The Robert Redford candidate."

I nodded.

"He's too pretty. Don't trust pretty men. I don't mean swishes either. I mean the kind that slick back their hair and smile like they're another goddamn Elvis. What about him?"

"I think he may have had something to do with Mary's death. I went through some notes of hers . . . she was conducting an investigation on him for a newspaper story."

Ryan suddenly looked more awake. "Wasn't he her lawyer?"

"Yes. But someone told me they had argued recently. I think it's a good lead."

Ryan assented silently. He stood up and crossed the room to a file cabinet that looked as if it had been kicked at least sixty or seventy times. He opened a drawer and pulled out a dog-eared folder. I recognized it as Mary's, though it looked a lot more worn. With a start, I realized that Ryan must have been reviewing the file again.

"Nothing here. My partner interviewed him. He may be hell with the ladies, but he looks clean on paper. In fact, he's done a lot of work with the department. Helped out on some big cases." He sat down opposite me. "Any ideas on what she was looking for?"

I pulled out my own notes and slid them across the desk. "I found those in Mary's papers, but I couldn't make heads nor tails of them."

Ryan quickly scanned the page. "If you're gonna get into this business, you better start thinking differently," he mumbled, absorbed in thought. He pointed a spade-shaped finger with a ragged nail at the first note. "This here is crystal clear. 'Buying chicken in a meat market.' Mary must have found out C.L. was buying himself some young prostitutes to screw around with. The video part I don't get. Maybe he's into porn, or blackmail."

He tapped the note. "S.R. I've got buddies in Vice. I'll see if that rings a bell with anyone." His face turned grim. He looked up at me, his eyes intense and surprisingly intelligent. "You know, you may have found something here. Maybe you should back off this."

"I can't." Suddenly, I trusted this man more than anyone else in San Francisco. "She was my lover for four years. I have to do this."

Ryan's eyes drifted over me in a quick assessment. "I thought that might be the case. Okay. But you stay out of the way."

"No problem."

"I doubt that." He slid my notes back across the table. "Selma's the pavement princess I told you about. The one who saw Mary down in the Tenderloin."

I felt like a kid who had just grabbed the brass

ring on a carousel ride. I dropped my notes into my bag. For good measure, I told Ryan about Helene McNeil and Sam's jealous lover.

He chuckled. "Doesn't sound like much to me. You'd probably be able to come up with suspects like that for almost any guy in the street. Lawrence is a different story."

"What about Martha Sparks . . . the one that found Mary's body?"

"She's something else. An uptight WASP who's into everybody's business . . ." He grimaced at the ceiling for a brief moment, then shook his head. "I don't think so. Not that women like that don't kill. I've seen plenty upper-class ladies who could slice you up with a bread knife and then go shopping in Neiman Marcus without a second thought. But my gut instinct is she's clean."

He asked me a few more questions and then let me leave after promising him that I wouldn't make any foolish moves. I wasn't sure how he would view my date with Carl, so I conveniently forgot to bring it up.

I spent the latter part of the afternoon writing up my notes and sketching a plan of action. Then I took a one-hour nap, showered, and primed myself for a night of living fiction.

Chapter 6

Gaylords is one of my favorite San Francisco restaurants. I'm a spice and carbohydrate junkie and Gaylords provides the ideal fix: doughy poori dotted with onion, saffron-colored curry flowing over tender chunks of lamb. My mouth began to water.

Just outside the entrance, I hesitated. For a moment, I was unwilling to spoil my appetite by dining with Carl.

"You have legs!" Carl announced with exaggerated amazement. He was standing behind me in a *GQ* pose. He had removed his tie and opened several buttons of a custom-made silk shirt. I could tell by the way the expensive fabric clung to him that his hairy chest was well-defined. With a mild shock, I realized that many women must actually find him sexy. I looked at his face and noticed that he seemed to be waiting for a response. Unfortunately, my sexual repartee had not yet shifted into gear.

"Nice legs, too," he added, as if he were pumping gas to a stalled car.

I lowered my eyes, hoping that gesture would suffice for the moment.

"I think you just blushed," he noted with delight. He lifted my chin with his hand. I fought the impulse to bite his thumb. "Don't you know what that does to a man?"

No, I thought. And I'd rather not find out. "Let's go inside," I said as meekly as I could manage.

Carl steered me into the restaurant by the elbow. It made me feel like a little red wagon.

The maitre d' — a handsome, gray-haired man with skin the color of milk-rich coffee — strode over to greet us. "What a pleasure," he said with genuine enthusiasm. Carl beamed from ear to ear. So did I, knowing what was coming.

"Robin, it's been too long." Sahid rolled me into his arms. I clung to him gratefully.

"How have you been?" he said, holding me at arm's length.

I glanced at Carl, who had moved off to the side. His smile was plastered onto his face like wallpaper. "Good. How's Harry? Has he moved in yet?"

"Better than that. We've bought a house in Pacific Heights. You'd love it. Big bay windows. A fireplace at the foot of the bed. A kitchen that makes Harry weep."

"Talking about kitchens, make sure you tell him that I'm still waiting for his recipe for red-pepper sauce."

Sahid winked. "I'll tell him, but I can make no promises. Harry guards his secrets like a sneaky politician."

With that comment, Carl's patience had run out. "Can we sit down now?" he snapped.

Sahid nodded and led us to a table overlooking the bay. "By the way," Carl said, tapping Sahid's shoulder like a boxer priming for a knock-out. "I'm a lawyer — and a politician — and I don't appreciate wisecracks about my profession."

Sahid looked at me with a question in his eyes. I answered with an almost imperceptible shrug.

"My apologies, sir. It was a thoughtless joke. Most unnecessary." He backed off with a small bow. Carl seemed mollified by what I knew to be Sahid's carefully practiced impersonation of a humble Indian servant. It was his way of saying "Up yours."

Carl gazed after him with a look of unearned triumph and then turned on me. "I didn't know you had a fan club here," he said accusingly.

"Sahid and I go back years. His mother runs a restaurant on East Sixth Street in Manhattan. She makes the best chicken kurma on the planet."

Carl didn't bother to listen. He sat down and opened his menu petulantly. I decided it was time to improve his mood. "Do you work out a lot?"

Carl's head sprung upright, his eyes brightening with well-fed egotism. "As a matter of fact, I work out a couple of hours every day . . . but you can't

79

really appreciate the results with clothes on." He smirked. "You must work out too. I bet you don't have an ounce of fat on you, except where it counts."

At that moment, the waiter appeared. Since I was starving, I ordered the Maharaja's feast. Carl raised an eyebrow with surprise. He ordered a variety of vegetarian dishes and a bottle of Sauvignon Blanc.

"You must be hungry," he quipped.

"I'm always hungry."

Carl leaned back and licked his lips. I knew I was supposed to get a charge out of that, but all I could think of was an animated snake from some otherwise forgotten Disney film. "You know you're not the typical lesbian."

I practically choked on a piece of poori. "Excuse me," I croaked.

Carl seemed amused at my reaction. "Of course, neither was Mary. I often wondered if she swung both ways. I assume you two were lovers once."

My face flushed with anger. Calm down, I warned myself. Don't blow it. "Once. A long time ago."

"Do you still *indulge*?" He stressed the word as if we were discussing banana split sundaes with extra hot fudge and wet walnuts.

"I'm not sure indulge is the right word." I tried to make the statement coy. What I wanted to do was spear him with my fork.

"That good, is it?" His smile darkened and his eyes clouded over. "Have you ever done it with a couple?" His voice had an edge to it now, like a teenager whispering about hard-ons.

I tore off a piece of poori and dunked it into a dish of mango chutney, then slowly sucked the hot liquid off in what I hoped was a seductive manner. What response was he looking for? "Only once. In college." Good answer, I thought. He was nearly salivating.

"Two girls and a guy?"

Whatever you say, asshole. "Yes." I felt my lips curling with disdain. I grabbed the glass of wine the waiter had poured and gulped half the contents.

Carl was leaning over the table like a wolf waiting for his prey's last gasp. "You're not going to leave me hanging, are you?" His eyebrows arched, reminding me of Jack Nicholson in one of his sleazier roles.

"You know, you haven't told me anything about yourself. That's not very polite," I countered.

With dismay, I watched the features of his face rearrange themselves in slow motion. It was like one of those horror flicks you catch at four in the morning, when the werewolf metamorphoses into a man frame by frame.

"I'm afraid my own life is quite boring. Despite what you may occasionally hear on the nightly news. I get my vicarious thrills through . . . people like you." He was lying through his teeth.

"I find that hard to believe."

"A lot of people do, but honestly, I'm so squeaky clean the press falls asleep when they interview me."

"You have to play around sometimes . . . even if only on a rare occasion or two," I said teasingly.

"Not when you're in politics." His posture had altered. He was sitting upright, one arm braced on the back of his chair, his neck stiff, his chin lifted to emphasize the square line of his jaw. He was going to be a harder nut to crack than I had expected.

"So it's all just word play, then?" I licked the edge of the wine glass, praying that Sahid wouldn't see me and burst into hysterics.

"Something like that," Carl muttered to himself, his eyes glittering expectantly. "You're not what I expected," he added with a note of surprise.

"What did you expect?"

"I'm not sure. The other night you were so frosty, I thought you might have a serious problem with men . . . or me," he confessed.

"I don't like to be rushed."

"Rushed into what?" Carl's question had a provocative sting to it.

"Into anything. Even into playful, totally meaningless repartee."

Carl spread his hands out on the table and nodded appreciatively. If this was a test, I had just aced the exam.

The waiter interrupted our brief staring match. Carl's plate held a careful arrangement of matir paneer, mixed vegetables in a kurma sauce, and curried spinach. I watched him eat with impeccable etiquette, chewing each forkful ten times.

"I thought you were starved," he said, pointing at my untouched plate.

"I was. But my appetite has shifted focus."

Carl tittered. "Eat up, my lady. Energy is of the essence."

I soon found out that Carl couldn't eat and flirt at the same time. During the meal, he reviewed my legal status as Mary's beneficiary with unnerving professionalism. He dabbed the edges of his mouth with a maroon napkin, then pulled a sheaf of papers out of his portfolio.

While he squeezed a slice of lemon into his water glass, I read through the documents. With a quick signature, I became the owner of a house in Big Sur, a co-op apartment in the city, and the recipient of some $236,000 in stock holdings, insurance, and pension funds. Carl tossed me a set of keys.

"Congratulations," he said offhandedly.

I blinked my eyes twice, reminding myself that I had plenty of time to mourn and rage. Right then, I had a job to do.

I took a deep breath. "Have you been down to Big Sur?"

"You mean the house? No. Not that I didn't try to wrangle an invitation out of Mary. She was one cold cookie." He folded his napkin into a neat square and tucked it under the edge of his dinner plate. The plate was so clean I would have sworn my cats had taken their tongues to it. "Let's get back to you. Do you think you may move out here now that you own a house on the coast?"

"Well, I haven't even seen the place. Besides, I don't think California's right for me."

"California's got a lot to offer." He rubbed the side of his face, distorting his features like a cartoon impression on stretched-out Silly Putty.

The conversation hit a wall. We both sipped wine, waiting for the tension to break. I decided to take out the battering ram. "How close were you to Mary?"

"Not very. I was her lawyer."

"I heard the two of you fought recently."

Carl's eyes narrowed. "Heard where?"

"I don't remember. Is it true?"

He adjusted his shirt collar, which hadn't needed fixing, and stared at me for a beat or two. "I guess so," he said at last. "She was headstrong. You must know that. Anyway, we had a legal disagreement. I gave her advice she didn't like. No big deal."

"I'm surprised she never wrote about you."

The table started to vibrate. I didn't have to look under the table to know that Carl had begun unconsciously bobbing one leg up and down — a telltale sign of frayed nerves. Back off, Miller, I told myself, or he's going to sprint for the door.

I rearranged the features of my face with an effort. "After all, you *are* one of the city's most prominent lawyers. And an eligible bachelor."

His smile was forced. "I won't be eligible for long. I'm engaged."

"Funny you didn't mention that the other day."

"We haven't made an official announcement yet. After all," he said with a smirk, "a lot of women are going to be heartbroken."

"And still you agreed to dine with a single woman. Pretty naughty."

His face muscles relaxed. "You're a queer, remember. When I told Jackie that, any incipient jealousy went out the window. She thinks I'm dining with a three-hundred-pound softball player with no tits and a crewcut. God, if she saw you, she'd go nuts."

And if I had a bat, mister, you'd be in deep shit. "So what's the fascination with lesbians?" I asked, my smile cranking into place.

"Don't play with me," he snapped. I jumped back

against my seat, startled by his sudden temper. "Sorry," he muttered, first checking to see if anyone had noticed his outburst and then glancing down at his solid gold Seiko. "It's getting late . . . why don't we go for a stroll. I know this nice, quiet path that leads to the bridge — it's incredibly beautiful at night."

What do you say when a murder suspect invites you for a late night stroll on deserted streets? I shrugged. "Sounds wonderful."

Carl was right. The Golden Gate Bridge spanned the night like a string of pearls displayed on cobalt glass.

With the evening breeze wafting around us and the city noise muted, the time was perfect for relaxed conversation. I got the ball rolling by asking Carl about his background. The ball never came back. He launched into a twenty-minute monologue on how his parents were working-class: a high school teacher and a car mechanic. He financed law school by working in his father's garage. I had the distinct impression that his words were scripted, probably lifted straight from his press kit.

All of a sudden, he spun around and propelled me toward the railing overlooking the Bay. "I love this city," he said with unusual intensity. "And I'm going to run it one day. I can feel it right here." He punched himself in the gut.

"It must be wonderful to have a dream like that," I said, trying to keep my teeth from chattering. For a split second, I thought he was going to throw me over the railing.

He turned abruptly and grabbed me by the shoulders. "It's no dream. That's what makes it so great. I can't go into the details, but I've got so much party backing, I'm going to slide into office like a nail through cardboard."

"But it takes more than party backing, doesn't it? A campaign's expensive. There's advertising, polling, direct mail . . ."

"Yes, yes . . ." His excitement was contagious. My heart was jumping around like a school kid on the first day of summer. "And I've got it all. The money, the expertise, the public relations staff. It's just a matter of time. A matter of time."

He wandered off ahead of me, then turned to me, his eyes catching the reflection of a nearby streetlight. "When was the last time you slept with a man?"

Oh lord, I thought, here it comes. "It's been a while." About twelve years, to be exact.

He walked over to me and wrapped his hands around my waist. Panic welled up inside me. Maybe I had played my part too well.

"Carl, I'm not ready. Not tonight."

His lips brushed the top of my head, his palms flat against my back, pressing me to him. "Don't play games," he whispered. "You've been asking for it all night." He punctuated his words with a small swivel of his hips.

"Carl," I mumbled into his chest, sweat breaking out on my forehead. "I'm really beat. I was up all last night working on a project."

"So tonight, you'll work on me."

How was I going to get out of this? Then it hit me. "Can I be honest?"

"Mmmm."

"I'm waiting for the results of a . . . medical test.

I should hear in a day or two." It wasn't an elegant lie, but it was effective.

He held me at arm's length. "You serious?" I could see the dismay sparkling in his eyes.

"I'm sure it'll be negative, but till I know for sure . . ."

"Yeah, yeah," he said nervously. "No point in taking unnecessary chances. We can wait." He backed off. "Do you need a lift?"

"No. I'll just catch a cab." I squeezed his shoulder and spun around. There was a taxi stand back at Ghiradhelli Square, which was close to a mile away. I made it there in under twelve minutes.

* * * * *

When I got back to the hotel, I found a note under my door: "I took the chance you'd be in. Sorry I missed you. Maybe we can get together tomorrow. Call me. Cat."

I undressed, cursing to myself and tossing clothes into various corners of the room. The night had been a complete waste. I had spent an entire evening playing juvenile seductress, only to find out facts I probably could have discovered in Carl's press file. I imagined how different the evening might have been if I had stayed home.

Limp with disappointment, I fell backwards onto the bed. I blinked twice and focused on an odd pattern of hairline cracks scattered across the ceiling. They reminded me of a street map. I traced them with my eyes. If that were Coit Tower, I mused, that crack would be Market and the real thin line over there would be Mission.

All of a sudden, a light bulb went off in my head.

I sat upright and checked my watch. It was 11:10. I dressed hastily, pulling on a pair of old sweats, my heart thumping with adrenaline.

* * * * *

The taxi dropped me off at Mission and Fourth, in front of an all-night liquor store. I bought a bottle of cheap bourbon, the type I used to drink at University of Virginia football games, then stepped outside and took a long swig. I could feel the alcohol burn a path down into my stomach. I spilled some on my hands to make sure I smelled like the real thing, then I staggered toward Eighth. I spent the next three hours curled up against the refrigerator-cold grating of a check-cashing joint, nursing the bottle like a three-month old.

My butt was numb and my head was starting to do loops, but then my luck kicked in. A 1985 midnight blue Camaro rolled up to the corner, its muffler coughing out a curl of steel-gray smoke. I rolled my head to the side for a better view. A tall, red-haired woman stepped out, her legs as thin as bedposts. When she straightened up, my interest piqued.

She had on the type of outfit I thought only Cher could get away with: a skin-tight, tiger-striped dress with strategically placed cut-outs, and red high heels that looked as if they could double as can openers. Before she had even closed the door, the car screeched away. "You were great, Selma," the driver bellowed out the car window. My head snapped upright. Pay dirt. Ryan had been right.

Selma straightened her skirt, scanning the street from the corners of her eyes. Something in her posture made me realize that she had already noted my presence. I stood up. "Hey," I yelled in my New York best. Selma turned to face me. She was a study in contrasts. I was surprised to find that her eyes reminded me of my grandmother's — they had that same penetrating look of concern. Her bushy shoulder-length hair was dyed copper red, just a shade or two darker than the blush on her cheeks. She looked at least fifty, but her legs could have belonged to a twenty-year-old dancer.

"What can I do for you, honey?"

My mouth opened and closed like a ventriloquist's puppet without a voice.

"You looking for action?" she asked doubtfully.

I shook my head and felt the street spin. Shit . . . that bourbon was strong. "Just talk," I said, almost inaudibly.

She raised an eyebrow. "What kind of talk, baby?" she asked seductively.

"Do you know Detective Thomas Ryan?" I asked in my most authoritative voice.

"Tom? Yeah, sure." She took a step back and crossed her arms across her chest. "Is there a problem?"

"Did you tell him that you saw a woman hanging around the Tenderloin a couple days before she died?"

Selma's face contorted into a disgusted grin. "Honey, people die out here every day. Some of them

89

I happen to see. Some I don't. You got someone particular in mind?"

My Adam's apple suddenly felt as big as a golf ball. "A woman died in Big Sur about two weeks ago. Attractive. Blonde hair, blue eyes. About my height . . ." I looked down at myself. "Shapelier, though."

"Marilyn Monroe," Selma said matter-of-factly.

"Excuse me?"

"Marilyn Monroe." Her eyes shifted. A window slammed in the distance. She waited a few seconds before continuing, her body taut, braced for impact. When she spoke again, her tone had dropped to a whisper. "When I saw her cruising down Eddy Street, I said to myself, 'This one's built like Marilyn.' Great tits, tight buns. She coulda made a fortune in my business."

"Then you did see her."

"Sure I did, honey. Ryan tells you something, you know it's right on." She paused to scratch a mole on her chin. Her fingernails were sharper than a cat's.

I took a step back. "When did you see her?"

"A few days before she died. There was a piece in the paper. She was a reporter, right? Damn shame. I mentioned it to Ryan just the other day 'cause it's been sitting on my mind."

"What do you mean?"

"She was digging around hard. Fact is, she scared half the girls off the street. She was asking questions you just don't ask around here."

"Like what?"

The grandmother look returned. "Why don't you

90

leave this be, honey. It don't matter much now, you know."

I stared back, making my eyes as hard as cement. We stood there like that a full minute. Selma finally blinked.

"She was asking about Spider."

"Spider?"

Selma tilted her head back and laughed so hard she started to cough. "You're a real chicken, ain't ya? Okay baby, I'll tell you this much. Spider Rose is a street king. He's got a stable of girls bigger than most high schools. You get one free the first time, like a lollipop at the dentist. It's a treat. Next time, you pay. Get the picture?"

She adjusted her bra strap and looked over her shoulder almost too casually. I followed her gaze. All I could see was a shadowed doorway and a rumpled Macy's shopping bag. "Spider's who you go to if you got peculiar tastes," Selma added in a tighter voice. "You wanna make it with a goat, you call him and he'll bring you a damn catalog of farm animals."

"So he's involved with porn."

"Honey, he *is* porn. Cheap shit. He videotapes everything. You shit in one of his bathrooms and it's on tape. Must sell pretty well, though. He's got two silver Mercedes and a big house near Twin Peaks. Now, I haven't told you nothing you can't find out from his police records. That's where I stop. You want more, you better get yourself some big men with bigger guns."

"Does Ryan know all this?"

"He knows your friend was walking where she

91

wasn't supposed to. That's it . . . and that's more than enough. You bring Spider's name up to the cops and you better be real fond of the taste of acid." As if she suddenly heard herself, she turned on her heel and loped away.

Chapter 7

The next morning I woke up in a foul mood. My head was pounding and my mouth tasted like the thick paste kids use in kindergarten crafts. I downed a V-8, which made my mouth taste like paste spread on tin, then brushed my teeth for a good ten minutes. Afterwards, I shimmied into my sweat clothes. Maybe a run would clean me out.

It was Saturday morning and the sun had just started to rise. The streets had an expectant silence. I jogged down to the Embarcardero and back at a slow pace, pausing only at streetlights. My lungs burned, but the pain was nowhere as intense as it had been the other night. I wiped the sweat off my brow with the back of my forearm. A sense of power spread through me.

The elevator doors opened and I sauntered into the hallway with John Wayne-sized strides. I halted suddenly. Cathy was sitting outside my door, her head tilted to one side. She was snoring and a small pool of saliva clung to the corner of her mouth. Drool had never looked so adorable.

She was wearing an oversized, powder-blue T-shirt with a scoop neck and a pair of lavender biking pants, the kind that fit like a second layer of skin. They shimmered in the dim light. My heart was still flip-flopping from the run, but at the sight of her it leapt into gymnastic feats worthy of the Olympics. Waves of hot and cold flashed over me as if I were stuck in a revolving door halfway between heaven and hell.

Cathy stirred, jerking backwards at my presence. "You're awake!" She stood up awkwardly, her face turning a shade of magenta.

I glanced down at my black-on-black Swatch. It was just after eight. "It's a little early for visits, isn't it?"

Her smile was shy. "I didn't sleep well last night. I woke up so early I decided that I might as well go for a run. I ended up here." She hesitated. "I didn't want to wake you, so . . ." A nervous laugh punctuated her remark. This was a side of Cathy I hadn't seen yet. I liked it. "So I sat down and took a nap."

"Why don't you come in?" I opened the door, taking in the room's disarray. My bra was hooked onto the back of the desk chair. The dress I had worn last night was draped over the television set. I looked for my panties and failed to find them. I almost slammed the door in Cathy's face. "I'm usually pretty neat," I said as I darted around the room, picking up clothes and tucking them into dresser drawers.

Cathy cleared a spot on the bed and sat down. "I didn't know you were a runner."

"I'm not." Where the hell were the panties?

"You're in good shape."

I was about to return the compliment with bedroom eyes when I noticed that Cathy was sitting on my panties. Real life is never as romantic as fiction. "Excuse me," I said, tugging the underwear out from under her buttocks. Her laugh was hearty. It reminded me of the way Mary would laugh whenever I massaged her feet. As soon as I touched her arch, she'd burst into hysterics.

"Do you have plans for today?" Cathy asked.

"No, not really," I said, mentally reviewing the list of tasks I had originally planned for this afternoon.

Cathy must have seen a hint of doubt cross my face. She stood up. "God, this was pretty rude. Showing up here at eight o'clock, hoping you'd drop everything." She backed off toward the door. "Why don't I call later."

Just as she was opening the door to leave, I caught her arm by the wrist. She let go of the door and it closed with a distinct click. We stood facing each other, our eyes locked. Her lips parted expectantly.

"Stay," I said with more breath than sound.

That one word had extraordinary power. Cathy touched my cheek then kissed me hard on the mouth. She tasted of toothpaste. I can't swear to it, but I think my toes curled.

I enfolded her in my arms, feeling her chest rise and fall against mine. Steam seemed to rise from where our bodies touched. Our kisses grew deeper, more urgent. One of her hands pressed the small of my back. A small, involuntary moan slipped out of me.

Cathy broke off the kiss, resting her forehead in the curve of my neck. My hands were trembling. "Whew . . . I didn't expect that," she whispered breathlessly.

I didn't want words then. My arms still encircling her, I started to edge toward the bed.

"No." Her voice was barely audible. "Not yet." She lifted her face from my shoulder. Her eyes were moist and her cheeks fever-red. "I'm not real good at this." I closed my eyes as she placed a raindrop-sized kiss on my mouth.

My body was running in eight different directions. What was she doing to me? I dropped my arms and crossed the room to the window seat. The bed separated us. "What just happened?" I asked, crossing my legs tightly to still the painful throb. "Did I do something wrong?" A defensive note had crept into my voice.

Cathy sat down on the bed, her back half-turned to me. "It's not you." She brushed her hair back from her face. "I wish I could explain it to you, but I can't. Not now." She glanced at me over her shoulder, her eyes as demanding as those of a lost child.

I shifted my gaze to the windows, starting only slightly when I heard the door click.

Ten minutes later the phone rang. I continued staring out the window, watching tourists chase after a cable car. The ringing stopped momentarily, then began again. I closed my eyes, trying to shut out the sound. Finally, I gave in.

"Christ, I'm sorry," a winded Cathy sputtered into the phone. "I feel like an awkward adolescent. Can we start over? I'm down at Sears coffee shop . . . you know the place?"

"Yeah," I said, one hand curling the phone wire into a tight ball.

"How about it? A nice hot breakfast?"

Food's my downfall. I nodded to myself and muttered agreement.

* * * * *

Cathy looked mildly annoyed as she took a deep sip of her second or third cup of coffee. The cup had a paper-thin crack along one side. "You haven't heard a thing I've said," she said.

I was having a hard time keeping up with her mood swings. I pretended not to hear her and continued to focus on the menu.

Sears is a small, old-fashioned coffee shop that makes ordering breakfast as much fun as choosing a pint of Ben & Jerry's ice cream. I asked the waitress for scrambled eggs with artichokes and a side order of extra crisp bacon. A metallic clang from across the table made my eyes jerk back toward Cathy. She had purposely dropped her silverware on the table.

"Good morning," she said sarcastically.

97

"Sorry. My brain's going a mile a minute," I lied. The fact was my mind was a grimy blank, like a subway tunnel. I felt tired, tense, and out of control. And Cathy's push-pull wasn't helping a bit.

She said, "Why don't you let me in on what's happening?"

"I'm not sure myself."

"Do you have any leads?"

I shrugged, all of a sudden realizing how much I needed to discuss my suspicions out loud. I found myself telling Cathy about Mary's notes, the expense report, my conversations with McNeil, Rich, and Selma, and dinner with Carl.

At the end, she leaned back and pursed her lips. "You thought I was C.L., didn't you?"

Before my mouth could answer, my eyes must have.

"I thought so." She narrowed her eyes and nodded. I almost expected her to toss her coffee at me. Instead, she reached across the table and touched my hand so lightly I had to look down to make sure it had really happened. "Do you trust me now?" she asked in a gravelly voice.

I said yes with as much conviction as I could, but a nagging doubt still lingered. I tried to push it away.

"Good." She removed her hand and sat upright. "Then give." Her tone had changed abruptly.

"Give what? I've told you what I know."

"Then tell me what you don't know."

I was starting to get a little peeved at her persistence when the waitress returned with our orders. I kept quiet until she had placed the toasted bran muffin in front of Cathy. I looked at her plate and then back at mine. Dime-sized chunks of artichoke poked out of the eggs and the finger-length bacon strips were just slightly burned on the edges. "Is that all you're going to eat?" I pointed to the bran muffin with disbelief.

"Don't change the subject. I want to know what you make of all this."

I snapped a piece of bacon off with my fingers. I decided it was easier to answer her questions than to continue this game of dodge ball. "All right. Here's what I think. I think McNeil, Sharon, and Martha Sparks are long shots. Right now, I'm focusing on Carl. I think Mary found out about some kind of connection between him and Spider Rose. That kind of information would destroy his career. From her notes, it seems like she was focusing her investigation on Carl, but that doesn't mean that Spider didn't find out and decide to stop Mary himself." I paused to sprinkle salt and pepper on my eggs.

"Spider doesn't strike me like the type who would kill someone with a lethal dose of penicillin," Cathy said.

"My thoughts exactly. So that leads me back to Carl. If Mary was threatening to expose the fact that he's connected to a big-time pimp — he'd have an awful lot to lose."

"So where do we go from here?"

"We?" I asked.

Cathy's cheeks dimpled. "Even the Lone Ranger had his Tonto."

"I don't think it's a good idea."

She continued as if she hadn't heard me. "Superman had Lois, Holmes had Watson . . ."

"This could get dangerous."

"Cagney had Lacey."

At the mention of my favorite police team, I broke into laughter. "Okay, okay. You win."

She reached across the table and shook my hand. For a split second, I imagined Cagney and Lacey making it in a shower. Then I sobered up. This wasn't a goddamn television show, and if Cathy wanted to be my partner she was going to have to do a lot more than make cute jokes.

* * * * *

After breakfast, I dragged Cathy into a nearby stationery store and bought a jumbo packet of 5" x 7" index cards, a box of red markers, and a small metal file. It felt like the first day of a new school year. Cathy had to stop me from buying a pencil case with a picture of Wonder Woman on the cover.

We paid for our P.I. supplies, as Cathy called them, went back to the hotel, showered — separately, of course — and then taxied to Cathy's house. With the index cards laid on her kitchen table, we spent the next three hours writing down every pertinent fact about Mary's death, plus a list of everyone we needed to question:

Interview Carl again. Try to pin down connection with Spider. Find out about his fiancée. Could she be the woman in doctor's office? Find out more about McNeil and Sharon. Question doctor and pharmacist. Check out Mary's apartment. Go down to Big Sur and talk to Mary's neighbors, especially

100

*Martha Sparks. Call Ryan and ask him about
Spider and the follow-up on the business
lunch. Ask Patty and Liz about other people
in Mary's life.*

Around three o'clock, Cathy stood up and
stretched. "We need a break," she said. Since my
neck muscles felt like they were about to snap, I
readily agreed. "Why don't I make us some
sandwiches?" She started rummaging through the
refrigerator, not waiting for an answer.

"Do you mind if I make a quick phone call?"

"Not at all. Why don't you use the one upstairs?"

Cathy's office was exactly the way I had left it a
few days ago. The phone was tucked into a corner of
one of the bookcases. As I picked it up, I noticed
that the cord disappeared into a hole drilled into the
backboard. Mary must have loved her neatness, I
thought.

I dialed Patty's number from memory. After five
rings she finally picked up. I could hear Raffi
singing in the background. "Hi Patty. Sorry to bother
you again, but I have some more questions." Miriam
was making baby noises near the phone.

"This is getting annoying, Robin. Can't you let it
go? All you're going to do is hurt people."

"The only person I want to hurt is the one who
killed Mary." I sat down in the desk chair and
propped my feet up on the edge of the bookcase.
"Patty, I need your help. You knew Mary better
than anyone else. Including me."

"What do you need to know?"

"Anything you know about Carl Lawrence. His
girlfriend's name. Why Mary called him a hypocrite.
The names of Mary's neighbors in Big Sur."

"Can you wait a minute? Miriam's tape just ended and I have to put something else on." There was a distinct clunk as Patty dropped the phone. While she was gone, I rummaged through Cathy's drawers and found a legal pad and a magic marker.

"Okay, I'm going to make this short," Patty said, just slightly out of breath. "I hate talking on the phone while Miriam's awake. Carl's girlfriend is a nurse at the university hospital. I can't remember her name . . ."

"Jackie. Her first name's Jackie."

"Right. Jackie Collins . . . no, that's not it. She has a very common Irish surname. Starts with a *C* like Cummings, Connors . . ."

I felt like I was on a game show. Name ten Irish surnames starting with the letter *C*.

"Dolan! That's it. Jackie Dolan."

So much for the letter *C*. I was about to suggest that Patty pay better attention to her Sesame Street lessons when she spat out the names of several friends who Mary may have talked to shortly before she died. "You should really talk to Liz. She and Mary were pretty close near the end. The neighbor in Big Sur will probably be a waste of time. She's a nasty gossip . . . wait a second, I forgot someone. Helene McNeil."

"Her editor?"

"Yes. She has a house in Carmel, maybe forty minutes from Mary's place. A real shrew, that one. Once she barged into the house on a Saturday night, drunk as all get-out, demanding Mary's resignation. She passed out right on the deck. We had to scoop her up and drive her home. Next day, she called

Mary to complain about how we had parked the car. We laughed over that one for weeks."

I put an asterisk next to McNeil's name. "Did you visit her often?"

"Huh? Mary, you mean? Yes . . . well, maybe not that often. The last time I was there was just after Christmas, I think. She had a small party. Several of us went down there. I even brought Pete and Miriam."

"Anything else on Helene or Carl?"

"No. You might ask Cathy though. She knows both of them pretty well. In fact, Carl's her lawyer too. In fact, I think he does work for most of the newspaper staff. That's how Mary met him."

"What about a woman named Sharon Goodman? I understand she's involved with the security guard at the newspaper."

"Sharon's a weirdo. Into punk rock, skull earrings, all that stuff. She works for a florist on Van Ness . . . American Country Gardens. You should definitely talk to her. She used to call Mary up and leave ugly messages on her machine."

"Thanks Patty, you've been a lot of help."

"You're not going to give up, are you?"

"You can count on that. I'll let you know as soon as I have some solid evidence. Send Pete my regards."

I wiped my heel prints from the bookcase shelf, and scanned my notes. Why didn't Cathy tell me that McNeil lived near Mary . . . or that Carl was her lawyer? Maybe I had crossed her off the suspect list a little too soon.

When I got back downstairs, Cathy was sliding

103

two peanut butter and jelly sandwiches and some golden apples into a Glad bag. She wiggled it in front of me like bait.

"How about a picnic? I think we can both use some air."

Looking at her open smile and her bright eyes, it was hard to imagine that she was anything but what she seemed. And at the moment, she seemed incredibly enticing. "A picnic would be wonderful."

Cathy's white Volvo was parked in the driveway. She unlocked the doors and jumped in. The interior smelled like new leather. The windows were crystal clear. She probably owns cases of Glass Plus, I speculated.

While she drove, my eyes fixed on the speedometer. Somehow, she managed to drive at precisely 45 miles an hour, no more and no less. Her hands clutched the wheel in the ten o'clock and two o'clock positions recommended by my high school driving teacher. She'd be mincemeat in New York traffic. We cruised into the Golden State Park and pulled up outside of Stowe Lake.

Cathy walked around the car, took me by the hand and led me up to the boat house. "Do you like pedal boats or rowboats?"

"I love anything that has anything to do with water."

We ended up renting a rowboat. Cathy slipped the paper bag carrying our lunch under one bench and sat down on the opposite one. As I climbed in, I noticed that she was watching me intently. I immediately picked up the oars. I like to be in control, even in a rowboat.

The air was still and unusually warm for early

May. As I propelled us to the center of the lake, a trickle of sweat tickled the small of my back. "This was a great idea," I said, sinking into the rhythm of the oars.

Cathy smiled. "I can see why Mary fell for you."

I closed my eyes. I didn't want to think about Mary right then. I didn't want to think about anything. My muscles were warming up and my mind was quieting. Suddenly, the boat dipped.

I opened my eyes to find Cathy crawling towards me. She sat down between my legs and draped her arms over my thighs. Rowing suddenly seemed uncomfortably sexual. I dropped the oars and reached for one of the sandwiches. Cathy caught my arm and kissed my wrist.

"I like the way you taste," she said as she turned my hand over and licked the center of my palm.

Great timing, I thought.

She tilted her head back, waiting for a kiss. I kissed her forehead.

"Is there a problem?" she asked.

"Nothing that four walls and a king-sized bed couldn't fix."

She twisted around and circled my waist with her arms. I clutched the sides of the boat, fully expecting us to capsize.

"Don't tell me that you're embarrassed about being affectionate in public?" she asked teasingly.

"Not at all."

Her hands dropped to the curve of my buttocks. I wanted to scream. The ache between my legs was unbearable and we were about ten feet away from another boat filled with cackling teenagers. Around the perimeter of the lake, mothers rocked babies in their arms, elderly couples tossed bread crumbs to pigeons, and tourists snapped pictures.

"Why don't we head back to your house?" I said anxiously.

Cathy reached up to kiss the base of my neck.

"C'mon," I whined.

She chuckled, sending small puffs of breath over my flesh.

I took another look at the rowboat filled with teenagers. They were pointing at us. One adolescent male with a straggly beard and crew cut was poking a finger in and out of a circle he had made with his other hand. "Cathy, people are watching us."

"Let them," she whispered.

I grabbed the oars and started rowing like mad to a more secluded spot right beyond a small bridge. Cathy steadied herself by clinging tightly to me. Never before and never since have I rowed that fast.

If you've ever fooled around in a rowboat, you know how tricky it can be. We ended up twisted between the two benches, panting and sopping wet. Our clothes looked as if they had been pulled out sometime during the final cycle of a malfunctioning washing machine. I peered over the edge of the boat, thankful we hadn't attracted a crowd.

Cathy slipped her hand under my polo shirt and began to edge her fingers upward.

"Whoa . . . enough's enough. We could be arrested."

"I want to feel you."

"You've felt enough for now." I sat up and pulled my shirt down. My pants were plastered to me and I was starting to feel chilled. Cathy, on the other hand, looked incredibly content. Her smile reminded me of the Cheshire Cat.

"Why now and not this morning?" I asked suddenly.

Her eyes were closed. For a moment, I thought she was sleeping.

"I have my reasons," she said unexpectedly. "Besides, this is one of my little quirks . . ." She rubbed the inside of my thigh, sending a tremble through me. "Public places turn me on. Don't you find it exciting?"

How could I say no? "Maybe we should head back."

"Mmmm," she cooed.

I took the oars and started rowing us back to the dock, wondering all the time what I had got myself into.

By the time we arrived at Cathy's house, the sun was setting. Our clothes had dried, but we smelled of lake water and algae. I closed the door behind me and stalked up to Cathy. "Why don't we take a slow shower?" I asked, pulling her into my arms. I kissed her neck and imagined rubbing soapy hands over her breasts, down her belly.

"Why don't you go first? I want to put on some coffee." She extracted herself from my arms and disappeared around a corner.

The rest of the night Cathy remained distant. We went over the notes we had written earlier and ate dinner silently. Our only physical contact came when I called a cab and got ready to leave. She kissed me passionately, patted me on the behind, and instructed me to call her first thing in the morning.

I walked out of her house as bewildered as an American wandering through a Chinese marketplace.

When I got back to the hotel, I took a long, steamy bath and tried to make sense of the afternoon. The thought crossed my mind that Cathy might be playing with me. Then I remembered the way she melted under my hands and I shook my head. The passion was real, that much I was sure of. Could she be shy? The question made me smile. No one bold enough to attack me in public could rightly be called shy. Maybe she had a real sexual dysfunction. I made a mental note to call Dinah, my therapist-friend-for-all-seasons.

I lifted my leg out of the water and ran the razor over my calf, nicking myself suddenly as Patty's words came back to me. Carl was Cathy's lawyer too, but for some reason she had conveniently failed to mention that while we were writing up our notes. Could Cathy be trying to distract me from Mary's death? If so, she was doing one hell of a job.

I dunked my head under the water, suspicion sweeping over me. Cathy had seemed unusually eager to help me investigate Carl. Maybe the two of them were more than just lawyer and client. I tried to imagine the two of them in bed and found that it was a lot easier to do than I liked.

I got out of the tub and patted myself dry. The metal file and index cards were waiting for me on the desk. I sat down buck-naked and started reading through them again. I made a note to ask Cathy about Carl and Helene. I also resolved to keep my legs closed until I got some satisfactory answers.

* * * * *

The next morning, I left a message for Cathy at the hotel desk and headed to the library. The temperature had dropped overnight and goose bumps popped up all along my arms. I bought a San Francisco sweatshirt from a street vendor and jogged the rest of the way.

The microfilm room was silent except for the shushing made by a reel of tape sliding between glass plates. I requested several back issues of local newspapers and sat down at one of the viewers that could make photocopies.

I hit the jackpot on the sixth reel. Under the headline "Lawrence Hosts AIDS Fund-raiser" was a picture of Carl and his girlfriend Jackie Dolan. The caption read, "Carl Lawrence and steady companion Jacqueline Dolan hosted one of the city's most successful fund-raisers on behalf of AIDS research at the elegant Chez Pierre." The irony was overwhelming.

The accompanying story noted that during a recent press conference Lawrence, "who has dedicated his career to battling San Francisco's drug and prostitution rings," hinted that his campaign to fight the city's problems might compel him to run in the next mayoral race.

I took a closer look at Jackie and tried to determine whether she could have successfully impersonated Mary. The ink smears and dot matrix of the newspaper print made it difficult to make an accurate assessment. She looked about the right height and weight, but her hair was long, dark, and wavy. I tried to picture her in a wig. After squinting at the screen until my eyes began to tear, I realized that I'd have to meet Jackie face to face.

I slipped a quarter in the coin slot, stabbed a red button, and made a copy of the page. Then I continued my search. Three reels later, I found several articles with Mary's byline. The first was an innocuous article on IRAs that Mary could have written in her sleep. The second column was far more interesting: the economics of political campaigns.

As always, her writing was razor-sharp. She covered the basic regulatory restrictions on political contributions, then moved on to the methods candidates commonly use to circumvent those restrictions. Near the end of the article was an uncharacteristic editorial comment on the need for an objective system of monitoring campaign funding.

Increasingly, politicians are turning to graft, bribery, kickbacks and backdoor funding to build their campaign coffers. Without an enhanced system of control operated by an independent review board of government officials, certified public accountants, and concerned citizens, we may soon find our cities, states and country governed by people who — if the truth be told — we would more quickly send to jail than to office.

The article appeared on March 31, just two weeks before Mary died. I slipped another quarter in and waited for the slick photocopy to drop on the table.

By the time I left the library, it was early afternoon and my hands stunk of ink and photographic chemicals. I stopped at a McDonald's for a Quarter-Pounder with cheese and a large order of fries, then I called the hotel for messages. There were two. Cathy had called exactly at ten o'clock and Ryan at 11:05. I dialed Ryan's number and got an elderly woman with a heavy Irish brogue.

"Tommy, it's a lady for you," she hollered into my ear.

Five seconds later, Ryan grunted into the phone. "Miller?"

"Yeah," I responded gruffly. This was getting to be a game. Who could out-tough whom?

"Got some news for you. About S.R."

"Spider Rose. Known for being able to supply goats on demand."

There was a moment's silence as Ryan digested my comment. "Who'd you talk to?"

"Selma."

"You're a jackass, Miller. You keep this up and in a few days I'm gonna be peeling your ass out of some dark alley. I don't need the extra work."

"No one saw us."

"Right. Where'd you meet her?"

It was my turn to hesitate. "I was discreet."

"Were you alone?"

"Of course." I could feel my face reddening.

"Well, there's no use in my running down Vice's records with you over the phone. There's nothing much in here anyway. The guy's pure Teflon. We can't get anything to stick. By the way, I've also asked some people about Lawrence. Nothing there either." He paused. "We confirmed her business luncheon on the day she was supposed to be at the doctor's . . . you were right. She was at Aunt Hattie's."

I filled him in on what I found out during dinner with Carl and read him excerpts from the newspaper articles.

"Not bad. Tell you what, tomorrow I'll start digging into Lawrence myself. Find out about his sources of funding. You better take a good look at his girlfriend."

"I plan to."

"But Miller, you go near this Spider Rose and I'm gonna find a way of hauling your ass into jail."

"Your concern is touching."

"Concern, bullshit! There's enough blood on the streets without yours." He hung up.

It was nice to have Ryan on my side.

Chapter 8

Later that afternoon, I rented a silver Subaru GL from a downtown agency. Not only was I tired of taxis, but I was in desperate need of a long, fast drive. Back home, when I get real antsy after a string of sleepless nights, I'll pick up around midnight and drive all the way out to the Poconos where a few of my good friends live. I'll leave a box of candy or a dirty book with a note on their doorstep and turn around. By the time I get back to Brooklyn, it's close to five in the morning. Most times, I sleep like a baby for the next few nights.

I bought myself an ice-cold bottle of Yoo-Hoo and slid into the car with a grin of satisfaction. Within minutes, I had crossed the Golden Gate Bridge and was speeding out to Muir Woods, taking the turns with a derring-do that Mary would have applauded. Unfortunately, when I got up to the woods the parking lot was jam-packed. For a moment, I felt like I had stumbled through the twilight zone and landed in one of those infuriating mall parking lots that are never, never empty. I edged into a narrow spot at the far end of the lot and scrunched down in my seat.

For the next few minutes, I watched the tourists watch the redwoods. It was cold and foggy and you could see only a third of the trees' lengths, but the tourists kept snapping pictures anyway.

Another car drove up near me and two elderly women emerged. They were both wearing chinos and cream-white fisherman sweaters. One was a little overweight with short, stark-white hair and a deep tan. She strapped on a charcoal backpack with incredibly grace. Her friend had gray, wavy hair that just swept the top of her shoulders. Even from a distance, I could see that her eyes were the cool blue of a frozen alpine lake.

The blue-eyed wonder opened the car trunk and pulled out a green army blanket. She turned to say something to her companion with a smirk I was determined to memorize. The other woman laughed and strolled over to her. They kissed discreetly, with eyes open. All at once, the white-haired woman nodded in the direction of a pick-up truck that was cruising toward our end of the parking lot. They parted abruptly.

It wasn't until they had disappeared into the woods that I realized that I was crying and smiling all at the same time. I figured it was time to head back to San Francisco.

After I crossed the bridge, I found myself driving toward Cathy's house. As soon as I realized what I was doing, I veered in a different direction, ended up on Castro Street, and parked next to a meter on which someone had painted a rainbow. I chuckled. Someone had painted the fire hydrant as well.

I started up the street, sidestepping a group of men in black leather and studs who were arguing about the attractiveness of a character in *Dynasty*, then I squeezed between two men who reminded me of Archie and Reggie. I emerged about three steps away from the entrance to A Different Light, the west coast version of a terrific gay bookstore in New York City.

The air was faintly musty, as it should be in all good bookstores. The store was long and narrow, with counters and running shelves stretching so far back I had to squint to see the rear wall.

I stationed myself near the first counter and surveyed the room — the first thing that any smart lesbian does when entering a new gay environment. Right in front of me, skimming through a book titled *Womon Sex and Goddess Forgiveness* was an anorectic woman with a faint mustache. Her opossum-brown hair looked as if it had last been washed during the rainstorm at Woodstock. Her ears were studded with four sets of silver double axes. Around her neck hung a somewhat tarnished silver necklace with an amethyst pendant. I gazed down to her Birkenstock sandals and the telltale curl of hair peeking out from under the cuff of her faded jeans. As she flipped through the pages, I noticed she had "Dyke" tattooed on her forearm in blue ink. The tattoo was redundant.

Next to her, scanning the shelf of mysteries, was a Kate Jackson look-alike wearing an Anne Klein cashmere cardigan in fashion-forward teal. Her scoop-necked blouse was tucked neatly into crisply ironed pants the color of fresh lox. I positioned myself between the two of them, feeling like one of the three bears awaiting the judgement of Goldilocks.

"Robin! What are you doing here?" I turned to find Liz barreling down on me with frightening enthusiasm. "Why didn't you come over and say hi?"

She pushed aside the Kate Jackson look-alike with a firm bump of her hips. Indignantly, the woman slid over to the next section, tutting under her breath like an old woman. Shortly afterward, I noticed that she rather surreptitiously picked up a book of lesbian erotica.

"I just got here a few minutes ago," I said distractedly. "I wasn't even sure you'd be working today."

"Actually, I'm not. But I spend a lot of my spare time here . . . for obvious reasons," she said, glancing over her shoulder at an athletic-looking woman with curly blonde hair and Dolly Parton breasts. "It's a great place to meet people." She poked me in the ribs with one finger. The bracelets on her wrists jangled whenever she gestured. She jangled a lot.

"I'd love to see your black book sometime," I quipped.

Liz giggled, making me feel a lot wittier than I

am. Up close, she was really quite attractive. She smiled with her whole face. Her dimples were so deep, I wanted to measure them for the *Guiness Book of World Records*. Her hair was a thick, walnut brown and exuded a trace of vanilla. All at once I realized that she probably did own a black book — and a thick one, at that.

"C'mon to the back. There's some chairs and a lot more quiet." She grabbed me by the hand, surprising me with the delicious softness of her palm. In the back, she pointed at one chair and eased into another. "So talk to me," she said with an exaggerated Jewish accent.

Normally, people like Liz make me feel as if I had just binged on candy apples and Hershey bars. But Liz was different. She was genuinely good-hearted. If she caught a fly in her house, I'd bet she would cup it in her hands and escort it to the door like a cherished quest. She made me feel safe.

"I need to ask you some questions about Mary."

She nodded. "Patty told me you might be passing by. She said you were worrying yourself to death."

"That's Patty's interpretation. I'm investigating Mary's death . . . I'm convinced she was murdered."

She tapped my knee like a doctor testing for a reflex. "Do you think Mary's death was an accident?" I asked testily.

"No. Not any more." Liz paused, apparently distracted by a customer who had stopped nearby. I turned to check her out. Liz had good taste. "Patty told me about the penicillin. You're right about that. Mary was a fanatic about avoiding stuff she was allergic to. Whenever I cooked dinner for her — and

117

I did that a lot — she'd call me up the night before and remind me to not use any tomato or ginger. Like I had forgotten."

"Did Patty tell you she thinks it might have been suicide?"

"She mentioned it. It took me by surprise, that's for sure. Mary had been through some hard times, but she was doing fine the last few months or so."

"But she had been depressed?" I asked, my guilt resurfacing like the Loch Ness monster.

Liz shrugged reluctantly. She started plucking at the binding of a book that had fallen on its side. "The breakup was hard on her too. Ever since she moved out here, I've been trying to perk her up." Her smile was embarrassed. "To be honest, I had one mean crush on her. But she wasn't interested. Kept to herself a lot. Then she went through a period of sleeping around like she was a damn mattress-tester . . ."

I felt the color drain from my face.

"Is this okay? My telling you all this?" Liz asked.

I was grinding my teeth so hard that bolts of pain were shooting up my jawline. "No problem. Go ahead."

"Okay. Well after a while, she quieted down again. Like when a really heavy storm finally passes. She seemed calmer. So I thought I'd give it another shot. Sometimes friends make the best lovers, you know." She squeezed my knee playfully. I surprised myself by blushing. God, my hormones were working overtime these days. "But it was still, 'Liz, I love you . . . but not like that.' Then a few months ago, she met someone."

"Excuse me?"

She squinted at me like my mother used to when she suspected I was catching a cold. "You're having a hard time, aren't you?" She leaned back and shook her head. "You two were real stupid. Never saw two people who were still so hung up on each other after so many years."

My temples throbbed. I leaned back in my chair and smiled with effort. "She started seeing someone, you were saying," I said as casually as I could under the circumstances.

"Yeah," Liz said doubtfully. "But she was real secretive. No names. No description. Nothing. I figured she didn't want to risk the evil eye. My sister was like that. Didn't tell me she was pregnant until she looked as if she had swallowed a whole cantaloupe. Then she wouldn't tell me the baby's name till it was born. David Thomas McCarthy. Pretty impressive, huh?"

Liz was starting to wear me out, but I had a lot more questions that needed answering. "Are you sure she was seeing someone?"

"Of course I am. We had lunch one day and she had that afterglow. You can't miss it. I said to her, 'Mary Oswell, you've been fooling around, haven't you?' and she got as shy as a schoolgirl. I asked questions and she shushed me up. Said she wasn't going to spoil it with words. Said she wanted to savor it by herself for a while."

I was shrinking in my seat. Had she really fallen in love again? "How come Patty didn't know about this?"

"Got me. Maybe Mary didn't tell anyone but me. She wasn't much for confidences, you know."

"Did she ever mention someone named Sam?"

"The security guard?" she asked with a note of surprise. I nodded. "Yeah. You mean . . . Sam and Mary. God, I never thought of the two of them together. But it's possible." She shook her head, a wry smile puckering her lips. "Boy, wouldn't that be a slap in the face."

I knew exactly how she felt.

"To tell the truth, she used to talk about Sam a fair amount. She once told me that under Sam's macho facade was a lost puppy. And you know how she felt about strays. I'll tell you one thing . . . if she *was* involved with Sam, I sure as shit hope Sharon Goodman didn't know about it."

"Why?"

"Have you met her yet? She's a real tiger." Liz's face lit up. "She's about five-three, at the most. Short-cropped, punky hair. Milky skin. Tight, teenager tits. Full buttocks . . ."

"I get the picture."

"No, you don't. She's great-looking, no question about that. But she's absolutely wild. For example, she went topless at last year's gay march. But even that wasn't enough for her. She had painted her body with neon paint. She stayed that way the whole day." She smiled coyly. "I would have paid big bucks for one of those black lights."

"Do you think she's capable of murder?"

"Honey, she's capable of anything. And she hated Mary. Called her a tight-assed WASP."

"What about Helene McNeil?"

Her eyes sparkled with amusement. "You're on a roll, aren't you? McNeil's another basket case. Though I don't think she could stay sober enough to plan a murder. Besides, personal jealousy's a much better motive than professional jealousy, don't you think?"

I was starting to think that Liz would probably make a great talk-show host. She'd give Oprah a run for her money. "What do you know about Martha Sparks?"

"The nosy goose? That was Mary's name for her. Not much, really. She was always dropping by. Made a point of putting down gays every chance she could. But you should have seen the way she looked Mary over. Like she was planning to feast on her body. You know what I mean?"

An image flashed before me of Mary generously lathering her breasts with fresh whipped cream. A birthday present to me four years ago. "Yes," I said with a small voice.

"Would she have any reason to kill Mary?"

"Who knows? Maybe she got tired of having temptation just a stone's throw away from her own backyard."

"How about Carl Lawrence? Did Mary mention him?"

"Yeah. She talked about him a couple of times. He was constantly on the make. She told me he reminded her of a dog in heat . . . you know how they latch onto your leg and hump away like mad."

"Do you know what they argued about?"

"Everything. At least near the end. You know, she used him as a reviewer for her more technical columns. They had a couple of rip-roaring fights a few months go. Mary didn't go into specifics. She rarely did."

"Did you get the sense that she may have been investigating him?"

Liz smiled at me. "You're good at this. You could do this for a living. Be a private eye, I mean."

"Hmmm," I said, noncommittal. "Right now I need to figure this out."

"You think Lawrence had something to do with Mary's death."

"It's a possibility. He's Cathy's lawyer too, isn't he?"

"Gee, I'm not sure about that one. She never mentioned him to me, so I couldn't be certain."

"Is there any possibility that Cathy's bisexual?"

Liz laughed so hard she started snorting. "Cathy? Good God, no way! She had an absolute fit when Patty had her conversion. No. She's gay through and through."

"Are the two of you good friends?"

"Well . . . sometimes yes, sometimes no. She's another one who went through major changes when her relationship broke up. Patty really put her through the ringer. Patty had a real bad drinking problem. But it was on and off for years. Cathy would give her an ultimatum and she'd dry out for a few months. Then it would start up again." Liz pulled at her left earlobe like Carol Burnett. "They were together seven years, did you know that?"

I nodded. "Why'd they finally break up?"

"It was a lot of things I guess. I've always figured that Patty was one of those homophobic dykes. Couldn't stand the fact that the Mormons excommunicated her. You know their religion says something about not getting into heaven if you're not married?"

I nodded, remembering long conversations with Mary. I don't know if the "marriage is a key to

122

heaven" bit was actually part of their religion or their parents' scare tactics. In any case, the belief left quite a few scars on Mary's psyche, so I wasn't all that surprised to hear about Patty.

"But the drinking was the real problem," Liz added, catching my attention by tapping my knee. "Patty's drinking was real bad. And she started doing some drugs, too. Nothing too heavy, but enough to tilt the balance. You know she used to manage this store?"

The question stirred a faded memory. "I think so."

"Anyway, there was a woman working here back then. Judy . . . Joyce . . . something like that. I didn't think she was much to look at, but Patty was ga-ga over her. They started hanging out together. She was the one that got Patty using drugs. At first, she only used them occasionally — when Cat wasn't around. But things just got worse. Now, let me get this straight . . ."

Liz was a gold mine of information. With a surge of gratitude I let her rummage through her mental library.

"Maybe it was in 'eighty-four. I was seeing Doris back then. In any case, Cat was fighting with her like crazy. Then she had her mastectomy and . . ."

"Whoa . . . mastectomy?"

"You didn't know?"

"No. Patty never said anything to Mary. God, that must have been awful. Don't tell me Cathy left her after that."

"Cathy? No, no. Cathy's the one with the mastectomy," Liz said with surprise.

I felt my pulse quicken.

"Patty freaked out," Liz continued. "I think she thought Cat was going to die and leave her alone or something. So she started fooling around with this other woman. That was the final straw. Cat packed up and moved in with me for a few weeks. Patty had a real breakdown after that. Moved back to Utah. Lived with her parents for a while. Next thing we know, she's back in town all sobered up, wearing a wedding ring and a cross. Cathy went through the roof."

"You've been a lot of help," I said, my head spinning like a runaway carousel. I kissed Liz on the cheek, said yes to some invitation I barely heard, and retreated to my rented car.

Chapter 9

Mister Ed was nudging Wilbur with his muzzle when the phone rang. I sat on my bed and counted the rings. They stopped at five.

I'd been back at the hotel for a few hours, digesting everything that Liz had told me. I didn't feel any closer to solving Mary's murder, but I suddenly understood why Cathy had cut things off in the hotel room only to attack me in the park. My first reaction was relief. Thank God she wasn't a kinky, game-playing bisexual who conspired with a sex-crazed maniac to kill my ex-lover. Then I thought about the mastectomy.

Our lake encounter had been frenzied and awkward. Obviously, we hadn't undressed. All at once, I remembered how Cathy had clung to me, pinning me to the bottom of the boat with the right side of her body. I couldn't have touched her right breast without forcibly wedging my hand between us. Still, it had been wonderful. As I recalled how I felt when Cathy's hot breath circled my ear, the mastectomy suddenly seemed insignificant. It doesn't matter, I thought with a shock of pleasure. For a moment, I felt so sure of myself that I reached for the phone, but just as I started to dial my confidence shriveled like a sun-dried tomato. What if it did matter? What if the scar was really awful? What if I said or did the wrong thing? My mother had had a hysterectomy six years ago, but even today I can remember how I recoiled at the sight of the surgical staples that held her slabs of flesh together.

In the absence of a plan of action, I settled for rummaging through the hotel refrigerator, stuffing Ghiradhelli chocolate into my mouth with lightning speed. Within little more than an hour, I had consumed two chocolate bars, a bag of potato chips, half a triangle of Brie, and two Diet Cokes. The subsequent heartburn was unbearable.

I brushed my teeth, slithered into my sweats, and pulled on my sneakers. It was about eight and the night air was so crisp that I sprung into my jog with great expectations. That lasted for about seven minutes before my nightmare dinner threatened to reappear. I plopped down on a street corner, gasping for air like a beached whale.

When I got back to the hotel, Cathy was sitting in the lobby, sipping a glass of red wine and staring at the fireplace with a somber intensity that embarrassed me.

"Hi," I said in a small voice.

She looked at me in absolute, excruciating silence.

"When did you get here?" I asked.

Her eyes slid back to the fireplace.

I sat down on the camel couch, our thighs touching. "Sorry about not returning your calls."

"I started to worry about you," she said without emotion, her eyes still fixed on the flickering blue heart of the flame. I never considered that. That she might think something had happened to me.

"Sorry," I repeated with an awful sense of inadequacy.

She turned to face me, her eyes boring into mine like a hypnotist's. "I called everyone I could think of. Finally I reached Liz. She said you had stopped by the store." There was a fierce question in her eyes.

I looked around the room. Customers from Masa's were drifting in and out of the double glass doors like models for Giorgio Armani and Perry Ellis. "Why don't we go upstairs to talk?"

Her eyes snapped back to the fireplace. "What did you and Liz talk about?" She was rubbing her fingers along the sides of the wine glass with so much pleasure that I could hear a faint squeak.

"Mary, mostly."

"Mary . . . mostly," she repeated with an edge.

"Yes." I squirmed in my seat. Rarely have I felt that uncomfortable. My nausea was swelling, my armpits were damp, my clothes needed to be burned, and I was being bombarded by the tinkle of wine glasses and cocktail hour chatter. "Please come upstairs. We really need to talk, and this is not the right place."

She nodded almost imperceptibly.

We rode up in the elevator in a tense silence, relieved only by the piped-in chords of a Mozart piano concerto. I unlocked the door and stepped aside for Cathy. She faltered on the threshold. I gently nudged her with the palm of my hand. "Please."

She ambled to the window seat, pushed the curtain to one side, and stared down at the street.

"Sit down, Cat. Please."

She whirled around at the nickname and shot me a look that burned a hole through my head. I could almost smell the smoke. Then she turned around and knelt on the window seat, her back toward me.

"I had breast cancer a few years ago," she said in a thin monotone. She opened the window wider and stuck her head out as if she half expected a bird to come and perch. "The doctor said it wouldn't matter, that I was an attractive woman. Of course, she still had both breasts so what did she know?" She was almost whispering now, the anger being supplanted by a fatigue that was almost palpable. "Patty couldn't handle it. Neither could a lot of other women. Even your precious Mary."

I let her words sink in with a shudder, then I crossed the room and stood behind her, wanting desperately to hold her yet terrified to move my hands a single inch closer.

"You learn to adapt, you know?" Her voice was becoming scratchy, like a radio station fading under static. "I went with this one woman, Paula, who loved to make it in movie theaters. We'd go up to the balcony during off hours and fool around like teenagers. It was fun . . . at first." She sighed heavily.

I could see her shoulders rising and falling as she struggled to breathe evenly. "But after a while, I started to feel ridiculous. So one night I made us a special dinner — Australian lobster tails, long, tapered candles, red cloth napkins, a Liszt concerto playing softly on the stereo, a bottle of the best Pinot Noir I could find."

With each word, her voice grew huskier. "I even bought myself a silk teddy. After dinner, we slow-danced in the living room. Everything was perfect until we started to kiss. She touched me . . ." Her hand drifted to her right breast and her body began to sway lightly. I knew she was on the edge and I tensed my muscles, waiting to catch her. "She goddamn gagged. Gagged, for chrissakes. I could see her trying to mask it, but it was plain as day. She never even called me after that. And she was just one of many. So after a while, I just stopped trying. I took what I could and gave what little I had left."

She leaned her forehead on the window frame. "Now, I'm on empty." All at once, her body shook. Tight sobs jerked past her defenses. I wrapped myself around her, her body stuttering in my arms.

"God, don't, don't . . ." She pushed against me with all the strength of a wounded deer.

I kissed her eyes, her salt-lined cheeks, the elegant line of her jaw, the hollow of her neck where her blood pulsed wildly. I held her head next to mine and listened to her heartbeat echo through her. And when she finally quieted, I laid her down on the bed and curled around her.

Sometime in the night we awoke, our bodies moving against each other in a dream-like rhythm. My hand rested on her belly. She covered it with one of hers and pressed it tighter to her body. I brushed her hair to one side with my mouth and kissed the back of her neck, drawing my lips over her flesh. The sheets rustled as I raised myself on one elbow. The room was bathed in a pale, blue light, and the air smelled faintly like apricot.

We both had removed our jeans at some point in the night and now Cathy's legs were draped over mine. I bent over and licked the crease behind her ear. Her skin responded with a wave of goosebumps. I swept my hand over her left side, past the edge of her breast and down her waist, hips, thigh. Her body began undulating against me like a lake under a summer wind. She turned to face me, her eyes searching mine for a trace of doubt. I answered her by kissing her deeply, my arms pulling her to me.

She stopped me abruptly, raising my face with both her hands and staring at me with uncertainty. I moved so that I was kneeling above her. My hands skimmed her body like a butterfly. She closed her eyes with a soft moan. I started to unbutton her shirt. Her body shivered.

"Robin . . ." She reached for my hand.

"Shhhh." I kissed her eyes, then lower, to the curve of her neck. Carefully, I parted her shirt and unhooked her bra. Cathy's body had grown still beneath me. My fingers flowed over the thin ridge of scar tissue. There was a brief moment of disorientation and then the passion returned with an urgency.

My tongue grazed her nipple. Cathy put her hand on the back of my head and lowered me to her. I sucked at her nipple till it blossomed in my mouth. Cathy's body strained toward me, her belly arching against mine, one long, tight thigh raised between my legs. I began rubbing myself against her slowly, my body aching with need. She lifted her hips and pumped against me until I felt like I would explode. I gasped for breath. Not yet. Not yet.

I slid my mouth down her belly, nibbling at the tender curve of her waist, the rise of her hip bone, one hand still on her nipple, kneading it softly, like the touch of a feather. Cathy shuddered beneath me. "Yes," she said in a tight whisper. I stopped suddenly, my skin damp with sweat.

For a split instant, Cathy's voice had mingled with my memory of Mary, the raspy moans she made whenever my lips touched her breasts. I closed my eyes tighter. Mary's gone, I thought. She's gone, but you're still here. I felt my pulse quicken.

"Robin, please . . ." Cathy was staring at me with urgency and doubt. Don't blow this, I warned myself. This is what counts. This moment.

I drew my hands down the sides of her body and lowered myself to the foot of the bed. Her legs

131

opened for me. Touching her first with just my hot breath, I held onto her hips and pressed my tongue to the inside of her thigh.

"Please . . . please," she growled at me.

Trembling, I opened her with my mouth, her body reaching for me as I drew her in, sucking first gently, then with abandon.

"Yes . . . God . . . yes."

Each time she rocked against me, my own body throbbed more fiercely. Suddenly, her thighs tightened, her hips lifted abruptly, her hands slapped the bed. Beneath my lips, I could feel her pulse beating fast, the wings of a hummingbird. I nuzzled against her, pausing for just a moment before I touched her again with my tongue.

All night long, our moans filled the night like song.

* * * * *

Around ten o'clock, the phone woke us up with a tinny ring. I stretched my arms past Cathy's warm body and lifted the receiver. "Yeah," I yawned.

"Is Cathy there?" A shrill voice yelled into my ear.

"Who is this?"

"Patty. Is she there?"

"Yes."

"Do either of you have any idea what time it is?"

I squinted at the alarm clock. "A little after ten."

"Well, why don't you ask Cathy where she's supposed to be right now."

132

At the moment, she was running her tongue along the sensitive inside of my elbow.

"What are you getting at, Patty?" I said impatiently.

"She has a job, remember?"

"Shit!" I sat upright, suddenly a lot more awake.

"A friend of hers at the paper called me to say her editor's going wild. They had a staff meeting scheduled for nine. I can't tell you how scared I was when I called her house and no one answered."

"Okay, okay. Thanks for calling." I hung up before she could continue her harangue.

Cathy started down my body with intent.

"Whoa," I said, reluctantly extracting myself from under her. "That was Patty. You had a staff meeting this morning."

She rolled her eyes. "Damn. Brian will be crazed."

"According to Patty, he already is."

Cathy screwed her face into a grimace that made me laugh. "Why did she call here?"

"Who knows? Maybe she felt the vibrations at dinner the night we met."

She smiled. "You stared at me all night long. I came that close to dragging you home with me."

"You brute."

"And what I want right now, little lady, is some more of your sweet loving," she said in a hokey Southern accent.

Unbeknownst to her, Southern accents made me hornier than hell. I stumbled onto her and began nibbling at her shoulder. About two hours later, we finally managed to get showered and dressed. We spent another ten minutes kissing our way to the door.

"This time, when I call, you better answer," she said with mock toughness.

"Any time, anywhere."

"Now," she said huskily, moving in for another round.

"But not now," I countered, propelling her out the door with a wifely kiss. "We both have jobs to do."

As soon as Cathy was out the door, I slipped on my one decent pair of heels and took a good look at myself in the mirror. I was wearing a royal blue, thigh-length jacket over a sleeveless dress belted at the waist. For effect, I added a strand of pearls I'd bought for a dollar on a street corner in New York. Not bad, I thought. I looked like the consummate professional — that is, if you could ignore the private grin and telltale flush lingering from the night before.

I picked up my car from a lot near the hotel and headed for University Hospital. The traffic was awful, the radio stations kept drifting, and a thick pasty fog covered the city like soap scum at the bottom of a dirty tub. But I was undaunted.

I drove with one arm out the window, drumming the top of the car and humming show tunes as I passed quaint Victorian-style homes stacked along the boulevard like a string of fruit-flavored lifesavers: melon, strawberry, pale lime, grape. By the time I pulled into a spot near the hospital, I was belting out "Some Enchanted Evening," breaking off mid-chorus when I suddenly noticed a male medical student with acne scars peering into the car as though he were watching a particularly bad segment of *The Gong Show*. I gave him a small Queen Elizabeth-style wave and locked the door.

My mood plummeted as soon as I pushed through the hospital's double glass doors. The acrid smell hit me like a bug smashing into a windshield at sixty miles per. I had a sudden flashback to the day I dissected a frog in high school. All around me kids pecked at the coin-sized hearts and flung organs at each other, while I stood at my desk, overwhelmed by a sense of guilt. I remembered grimacing as my knife cut through the lifeless muscles and veins, formaldehyde squirting over my fingers. Mrs. Patterson, a sixty-year-old woman with blue-black hair tied in a bun and an upper torso like Joe Namath, had chided me from across the room. The other kids responded by tossing assorted frog parts at me. A sliver of rubbery liver had dropped into my shirt and clung to the inside of my bra.

I walked up to a small glass partition, shivering slightly from the memory. The information clerk was a woman of about fifty-five with hair the color and texture of late-summer hay. Blush was streaked over her cheeks like war paint. She had light brown eyes and the type of pug nose you can only buy from a doctor's catalog. Her blouse matched her blush. Dangling from her neck was a string of beads that reminded me of rock candy. Her name tag, pinned above her generous bosom, said "Betty Davis." I took a closer look at her face and suppressed a grin. She looked a little like Baby Jane.

"Can I help ya?" As she spoke, I caught a flash of neon pink gum tucked into the dark recesses of her mouth.

"You're a New Yorker, aren't you?" I asked with sudden insight.

"Yeah. How'd ya know?" She clacked her gum with one side of her mouth.

"I'm from Brooklyn."

"No shit." She leaned back in her seat. I noticed that her blouse was about two sizes too small. Her freckled midriff poked out between the buttonholes. "Queens," she said, answering a question I hadn't asked. "So what can I do for you, Brooklyn?"

"I'd like to see Jackie Dolan."

"Dolan, huh?" She stopped to examine a magenta-painted fingernail that had started to peel. "I hate this cheap stuff. Ya gotta do touch-ups every day." She started picking the nail polish off her thumb with the tip of another nail.

"Is she working today?"

"Who? Oh. Dolan? Yeah. What d'ya want with her?"

"I'm writing a book on nursing and a friend suggested that Jackie would be a great contact."

She squinted up at me like a hard-core New Yorker. "Wanna try another one on me, honey?"

"Excuse me?" I fumbled.

She concentrated on her nail again. By now, her blouse was littered with small magenta flecks that were starting to look like alligator scales. "You're here 'cause she's involved with that lawyer guy, the one that looks like a soap actor."

I shifted my weight uncomfortably. "You mean Carl Lawrence."

"Yeah. That's the one."

A door opened at the back of the office. Betty spun around and waved at the young woman who

136

had entered the room. "That's my relief. I'm on break now." She stood up abruptly and made a half-hearted attempt to smooth the wrinkles that arched across her blue polyester skirt. "Look, you want Dolan, she's in six-eleven." She tossed me a visitor's pass. "I don't give a shit why you want to see her. She's a bitch. Just do me a favor . . . make sure you piss her off but good."

I pinned the pass to my jacket and scurried over to the elevator.

The sixth floor hallway was painted that unique shade of hospital green, the color of mint chip ice cream melting on a dirty sidewalk. A faded sign instructed me that room 611 was somewhere off to the right. I turned the corner, my heels clacking at the tiles like a hammer. I should have worn sneakers, I thought.

I stopped at room 609 and pulled out my notepad. Under the flickering fluorescent lights, my hands took on a yellowish sheen, the color of an unhealthy urine sample. I wondered if just being in a hospital could make a person ill.

The door to 611 was open and I could hear a woman's voice. I held my breath and edged closer to the door. Jackie was sitting in a swivel chair in front of a large walnut desk, the phone tucked under her chin and her legs stretched out in front of her. She was flexing her feet the way they tell you to in those "How To Stay in Shape with Office Exercise" videotapes.

Almost instantly, I realized she was talking to Carl. Her voice had a wispy, lilting quality designed specifically for sexual banter. As she talked, she spun a long chestnut curl around her index finger.

I stepped to the side and scanned her office. The room was about ten by twelve feet, with a double casement window above the desk. One wall was taken up by beige two-drawer metal filing cabinets and a tabletop photocopier, while the other held a veritable photo gallery.

Most of the pictures were of Jackie, Carl, and various political dignitaries. In a few photos, the Ken and Barbie couple were flanked by well-known entertainers. On her desk was another 8" x 10" glossy of Carl that reminded me of the photographs actors bring to casting calls.

"Bye, bye bubbles," Jackie cooed into the phone, hanging up with a practiced sigh. It was only then that I realized that she had been fully aware of my presence. I strode in with more confidence than I felt. She swiveled around in her chair, emitting a small "oh" when she saw me. I bet she rehearsed that one in front of a mirror.

"Hi. My name's Robin Miller. I'm a free-lance journalist based in New York."

Jackie flashed me a generous smile. She stood up to her full height, towering over me by a good two inches. "Pleased to meet you," she said, shaking my hand with the perfect amount of pressure. "Please, have a seat." She rolled a chair over to me, then placed her butt on the edge of the desk, crossing her arms under her breasts so that her cleavage made a sudden, undeniable appearance.

Lord, she must drive men wild with that gesture. I have to admit I had a bit of difficulty raising my eyes to her face. "I met with Carl a few days ago. He may have mentioned my name."

She bit her lip pensively and shook her head.

"In any case, I was very impressed by him and decided to write an article on rising politicians. A sort of who's who for the nineties. Carl is undoubtedly one of the most promising candidates I've encountered. I realize I don't have an appointment, but I was hoping that you'd be able to help me with some background material on what makes the man tick."

Each word fanned the fire in her eyes. By the time I stopped talking, her eyes had that odd glow I normally associate with drug addicts. "What paper is this for?"

"To tell the truth, I don't have a firm commitment from any particular paper yet. But I do have solid contacts at *The New York Times* and the *Chicago Tribune*."

I dug into my jacket pocket and extracted my press card. "You can call the papers for verification, if you like."

She examined the card. "That won't be necessary."

"Do you mind if I ask you a few questions about yourself first?"

She shook her head, lifting her chin at the same time so that her hair rearranged itself on her neck in a perfect mass of curls.

"First off, I thought you were a nurse."

"I am," she giggled. "But I was promoted recently. I'm the administrative head of nursing now. I've just redecorated the office." She gestured over my head. "Do you like it?"

"It's pretty impressive."

"Not at all," she said, implying just the opposite. "Did you notice the photographs?" She glided over to the wall and started admiring them herself.

"You make a great-looking couple," I responded, barely turning around in my seat. She glanced at me over her shoulder and shrugged coyly.

"If you say so," she said, returning to the edge of the desk. She crossed her legs so that her tight linen skirt hiked up above her knee. "So what do you want to know?"

"When did you first meet Carl?"

Her eyebrows burrowed as she placed a finger over her lips. She looked like a grad student trying to recall the exact location of the Khan Tengri. "Of course," she said with a bright smile. "It was May, nineteen seventy-five. Carl was just graduating from law school. You do know that he graduated from Stanford? He was amazing even then. He paid for his entire education by himself by working in his father's garage five hours every single day. I remember how embarrassed he was about the grease under his nails, but it was good, honest work and it made me even prouder of him."

She was a journalist's dream. Serious, courteous, quotable. She made me want to puke. "Stanford's pretty expensive. He must have made a pretty penny."

She flashed me an indulgent smile, as if I were a child asking why the grass was green. "He did get a small scholarship, too. But you have to remember that mechanics make a good living."

I nodded and jotted down a few notes to feed her superiority complex. She struck me as the type who would speak more spontaneously to someone whose intellect she held in low esteem. "How did he build up such a successful practice in such a small time?"

"Fate," she said, shaking her head in wonder. "Fate and talent. He was hired by Anderson and Winney, the top law firm in Los Angeles. I hope I don't sound too braggardly, but he simply dazzled them. In six years, they made him a partner. That was almost unprecedented, and the press ate him up."

She started swinging one foot like a pendulum. I crossed my legs to avoid being kicked in the shins.

"He's incredibly photogenic. Have you seen him on television?" she asked. I shook my head. "Well, he makes Kennedy look like Don Knotts. He has so much charisma."

"When did he leave Anderson?"

"In 'eighty-three. He was hired by the D.A.'s office here in San Francisco. That's when he really made his mark."

His political ambitions must have been pretty damn strong for him to voluntarily take a pay cut like that, I thought.

Jackie suddenly stood up and strode over to the filing cabinets. She knelt down and opened one drawer. "I get so many interviews about Carl that I keep a press file in my office." She was speaking to me over her shoulder. "Ah. Here it is." She walked back to the desk and handed me a photocopy of an article that had appeared in the *San Francisco Tribune* back in 1985. The headline read, "Lawrence Wins Another Victory Against Crime."

"You can read that later. Basically, Carl was responsible for breaking two big prostitution and drug rings that had been plaguing the city for years.

I think the city was brokenhearted when he left the D.A.'s office to open his own practice. But he's stayed very active in city politics, helping the police track down some of the city's sleazier characters. And he's a great friend of the press. As a matter of fact, he does a lot of *pro bono* work for the *Tribune,* reviewing articles, providing leads . . . even helping out with some of the staff's personal affairs."

"I understand that he was good friends with a reporter who died recently," I said, keeping my head down so that she couldn't detect the heightened interest in my eyes.

"I'm not sure I know what you're referring to . . ." she answered hesitantly.

I looked up. "Mary Oswell. She was a financial writer for the *Tribune.*"

Her stare sent a shiver down my spine. "I'm sorry . . . I'm not all that familiar with Carl's newspaper friends."

The chill in her voice warned me that I could lose her if I didn't shift gears. "Well, it doesn't matter really. Tell me, why do you think Carl focused on fighting prostitution and drugs?"

"As opposed to what? Jay-walkers?"

I met her patronizing smile with one of my own. Obviously the real Jackie Dolan was starting to tear through the facade.

Just then, her intercom buzzed. She whipped around the desk and pressed a lever. Immediately a voice squawked into the room. "Jackie, we've got a problem down in pedes. A kid just died and one of the new nurses got into a fight with the mother. It's

142

a mess." I could hear someone wailing in the background and another voice shouting obscenities.

"I'm on my way," Jackie spat into the intercom. She turned toward me with a heightened air of self-importance. "Sorry, we'll have to cut this short."

"Do you mind if I wait for you to return?"

"I'll be a while."

I looked at my watch. "Well, if you're not back in five or ten minutes, I'll let myself out."

She looked doubtful. I grabbed her right hand with both of mine. "You've been a great help. Carl's a lucky man."

"Thank you," she said uncertainly.

"You know what they say — behind every great man hides a great woman. Well, duty calls."

I felt like one of those cheesy cocktail-room entertainers, the kind Bill Murray plays, but the act worked on Jackie. She gave me her best press smile and darted out of the office.

As soon as I was alone, I peeked around the office door to make sure no one was coming down the hall. Then I took off my heels, tucked them next to the door, and tiptoed to the desk. The center drawer was a mess: nail polish remover, a nail file with a tortoiseshell handle, hairspray, blush, a palette of eye shadow in a clear plastic container, a small vial of mouthwash, a bottle of white-out, paper clips, two pens, rubber glue, a checkbook, and a memo pad.

I flipped through the checkbook stubs. The woman had expensive tastes. There were four or five checks to jewelry stores, one to a fur dealer, two to an exclusive hair salon in the Mark Hopkins, and at least ten to different department stores. I did a quick mental calculation. All together, she had spent close to $6,000 in a two-month period. Pretty rich for a hospital employee.

I was about to drop the checkbook back into the desk when a thought hit me. The two check stubs to the hair salon were dated right before and right after Mary's death. I jotted down the number.

Next, I took out her notepad and rubbed a pencil over the top page the way I've seen them do in the movies. I raised my eyebrows in amusement when a telephone number appeared. That shit really works, I laughed to myself. I tore the page off and tucked it into my jacket pocket.

The next drawer had correspondence and personnel files. I flipped through them just to make sure I wasn't missing anything. At the back of the drawer was a sealed manila envelope. A yellow stick-um note was tacked to the upper right-hand corner: "Babe, please mail this certified under your *secretary's name*. Kisses, C.L." I smiled when I saw the address on the envelope.

The seal was coming unglued anyway, I rationalized as I slipped Jackie's nail file under the flap. Inside was a list of names. Some of them looked familiar. There was also a handwritten note:

Thanks for contributing to my political success. Here are some names you can tap for your fund-raising efforts. Sorry I can't deliver this in person, but times are hard. I know you'll understand.

P.S. Thought you'd want to know that some

friends of mine are planning to drop into your store for a little business. Probably next Wednesday, around 11:30. Wear your best clothes.

I glanced at the photocopier. Damn convenient, I thought. I made two copies, slipped the originals back into the envelope, took out the bottle of paper glue and smeared a thin line onto the flap, resealing the envelope with a keen sense of satisfaction.

Jackie had been gone a good fifteen minutes and I decided to not press my luck. I looked around the office to make sure there were no telltale signs of my illicit search. Suddenly I noticed the copier light was still lit. I switched it off, my heart thudding and my skin on fire. It was a strangely exhilarating sensation. I felt like James Bond. Maybe a tall, seductive Asian woman was waiting for me by the car.

I walked out of the hospital with a spring in my step, softly singing "Nobody Does It Better."

* * * * *

It was just after two when I pulled up near American Country Gardens where Sharon Goodman worked.

The door tinkled as it closed behind me. I felt like I was suddenly transported to the greenhouse in the Brooklyn Botanical Gardens. A wave of steamy air tickled my face. Thick vines dangled from baskets hung on ceiling hooks. The narrow store was lined with tiers of flowers resting in buckets of murky water. It took about three seconds for my sinuses to go haywire. By that time, Sharon Goodman had

145

climbed on top of a small ladder about two feet away from me.

She was easy to recognize. She was wearing a silver metallic sweatshirt with holes artfully cut out around the midriff. Her leather mini skirt covered little more than her buttocks. She had on black stockings dotted with lace roses. Her purple leather boots stretched over her calves and stopped at the knee.

"Can I help you?" Her voice surprised me. It was almost musical, each word pronounced with a soothing lilt. If I closed my eyes, I could pretend she was Julie Andrews.

"My name's Robin Miller. "I'm investigating the death of Mary Oswell."

She laughed. "Sam told me about you. Said you looked like a dyke. Are you?"

My, she was endearing. "Yes. Does it matter?"

"Hell yes. I don't deal with straights. Mary should've been straight." She climbed down the ladder and stuck her thumb into the dirt of a potted marigold. She pulled it out and licked the dirt off, her eyes fixed on me the entire time. "She didn't deserve to be gay. Uptight bitch. Sam was gaga for her. Don't ask me why. How'd you get involved?" She talked fast, like a New Yorker, but her inflection reminded me of friends who lived in New Orleans.

"Look . . . I just want to ask you some questions . . . okay?"

"Shoot. Ha! Do you carry a gun? Sam has one, but she doesn't carry it with her. Makes her nervous. Can you believe it? A tough-looking dyke like her scared to carry a gun?"

146

Excedrin headache number nine. How the hell do you question someone like her? I felt like I was in the ring with Joe Frazier. "Slow down, huh? I understand you weren't fond of Mary."

"You think I did her in." Fresh!" she said, sounding delighted. "I could have, you know. She got under my skin. But I didn't."

"Why would you have wanted to?"

She stuck her tongue between her teeth and smiled. The expression reminded me of one of my cats. "You new at this shit?"

I blinked twice, feeling amazingly off balance. "What? No. I've been in this business a few years."

"You're green, you know. I can tell. See, I'm an actress . . . damn good too. I study people. You. You're no fucking P.I. Too timid. Polite. Can hear it in your voice. You lie and your voice goes up an octave. What are you really . . . a reporter?"

Damn. She was sharp. I hadn't expected that. I took a deep breath and tried to shift gears. "It doesn't matter who I am or what I do —"

"It does to me. Was Mary your lover?"

"What?"

"You heard me. I bet she was. But not recently. You're from New York, right? You have a little accent, not too bad though. Why do you think I killed her?"

"What? I don't think that. I'm just asking questions."

She picked up a bottle and started spraying the jungle-like vines. "Even if I did kill her, how would you find out? You think asking people questions is going to work? Where was I the night Mary died? I was fucking my brains out with Sam. You want to ask her to collaborate my story? You can. The phone's right behind the cash register."

"No. That's not necessary. Do you know how Mary died?"

"Yes." Her smile was sweet. "Poison. Something like that. Was she good in bed? I bet you had to pry her legs apart. You wouldn't have to do that with me."

At the moment, I could think of few prospects more frightening than sex with this woman. I started fiddling with a leaf on an azalea.

"Bet there are a lot of suspects. Mary was the kind of woman who rubbed people the wrong way." She turned and sprayed me with the lilac-scented water. I sneezed instantly. "But I could have killed her, that's for sure." She smiled again as she clipped a dead leaf off an African violet with the tip of her nails.

I told her to contact me if she had anything else she wanted to tell me, then I walked back to the car and turned on the radio. I sat there dazed, listening to a Liszt concerto for about fifteen minutes before the impact of Sharon Goodman started to fade. I realized that if Carl wasn't the killer, I might have to grapple with Sharon. The thought made me weak in the knees.

* * * * *

On the way back to the hotel, I stopped at an electronics store and purchased a miniature tape recorder, and some electronic masking tape. I wrote the purchases into my business diary, adding a note to ask my sister if there was any way I could deduct the expenses on my tax return. Then I stopped into a deli and picked up a hero sandwich and a bottle of Yoo-Hoo.

When I got into my hotel room, the light on my phone was blinking. I dialed the message desk. I had received three calls. My friend Tom wanted to know if I had finished my novel yet. Apparently my publisher was getting a little antsy. My housemate Dinah had left the message, "ET phone home . . . or else," and Cathy had called a few minutes earlier asking if I was interested in dinner.

I returned all three calls, receiving in turn Tom's secretary, Dinah's answering machine, and Cathy's assistant. I set the phone aside and kicked my pumps into the closet, peeling off my dress and panty hose with a sigh of relief. I changed into a pair of faded Levis and an old University of Colorado sweatshirt I picked up on a business trip a few years ago.

It was 4:10 and I had a few more hours of work ahead of me. I took a bite from my ham and cheese hero and followed it with a belt of Yoo-Hoo, all the time quietly revising the day's agenda. I finished lunch in about six minutes flat, tossed the remnants into the trash and checked my watch. I figured it would take me about twenty minutes to walk to the medical center where Mary's impersonator had picked up her prescription. Which reminded me of Jackie's salon appointments.

I dialed the number for Jacque Pierre Hair Stylists and introduced myself to the receptionist as a friend of Dolan's. The woman was more than happy to refer me to Arno, the "magician" who had done such a marvelous hair-coloring job with his

149

"favoreet" client. Just as I had thought. Apparently, Jackie visited the salon at least twice a month. According to Arno, "Jackee" had been experimenting with hair styles and colors for the past year. "She is trying to discover her true color complements," Arno explained with a flourish.

I made an appointment I never expected to keep, and hung up with a distinct sense of satisfaction. Jackie had just jumped up a notch or two on my suspect list.

But I didn't have time to gloat. I still had to stop at the medical center. Afterwards, I planned to hit the pharmacy where the prescription for penicillin had been filled. And sooner or later, I would have to check out Mary's city apartment and the house in Big Sur.

I pulled out a pair of socks and sat down on the bed. I yanked one sock on and then grabbed the phone and dialed Patty. As the phone rang, I slipped the other sock on. Maybe I should teach a course in time management.

After two rings, Patty's gentle voice sang into my ear.

"Hi Patty, it's Robin."

"Hello." Her voice hardened.

"Look, I'm sorry about this morning. It was irresponsible. Hope you're not too angry."

I heard the refrigerator door open and close and then the sound of running water. "I just got worried, that's all. I could care less what Cathy does with her free time, I just don't appreciate getting frantic phone calls from her coworkers."

"I understand."

"What do you want now?"

"I need directions to the house in Big Sur."

"Ouch." Something clattered in the background. It sounded like silverware dropping onto tile. "Damn. I just cut myself. Stop by tonight around seven. I'll write them down for you. I can't talk now."

"Fine." I put the receiver back into the cradle. My dress jacket was slung over the back of the desk chair, a slip of paper dangling from one pocket. I reached over and pulled the page out. Why not, I thought. I dialed the number that Jackie had written on her memo pad.

The phone rang twelve, thirteen times. Just as I was about to give up, a man answered. "This is a fuckin' phone booth, man! What the fuck do you want?"

I learned all at once what it means to be shocked into silence. "Who . . . who is this?" I stammered.

"Who's this?" He sounded drunk and surly. I pictured one of the Bowery bums that hover around street corners in New York, waiting to wash your windshield for a quarter . . . or spit on your hood, depending on the mood. I said the first name that came to mind. "Patty. I was supposed to call a friend at this number."

"No one here but me, asshole." My friend belched into the phone with obvious delight.

I had a thought. "I gotta talk to Spider," I whined in a heavy New York accent.

"Who is this?" The quality of his voice changed subtly.

"Man, don't shit around with me. I was supposed to meet this guy and I lost the address. Spider's gonna kill me if I fuck up."

"I don't know a Patty." He sounded uncertain, confused. I decided to push harder. After all, I was safe and sound in my hotel room and he was . . . where was he?

"I don't know you either, pisshead. Now, will ya tell me where the hell this phone booth is?"

"You don't know?"

"Fuck it, man. If I knew I'd be there."

"Mission and Eight," he slurred. "You really one of Spider's girls?"

"Ask him. And when he burns your tongue out, give me a call." I slammed the phone down. Well, well. This was getting interesting.

I left a message for Cathy and headed out toward the medical center. The building was about two blocks away from the *Tribune*'s office. From the outside, the center looked as if it had been built with Lego blocks. No windows, just a series of interlocking white cinderblocks. The door was steel gray with rust pockmarks. Mary would have died before using a medical facility like this.

The inside decor was not much better. The waiting room was painted pale gray, with rows and rows of hard-back seats. It reminded me of a bus terminal. A card table on the far wall was littered with dog-eared issues of *Life, Good Housekeeping, Road and Track, People,* and some children's magazines.

Most of the patients were Hispanic. A woman who looked sixteen at most was wiping the nose of a sniveling three-year-old while simultaneously bouncing a newborn on her lap. In the far corner, two men were huddled in an intense conversation. Something exchanged hands.

The triage window was just to the right of the magazine table. I walked over and tapped on the glass. No one was in the room. I pressed my nose to the glass and peered in.

"She's taking a pee," someone muttered behind me.

I turned around and found myself staring at an elderly woman with silver hair matted to her scalp. She smelled faintly of urine. She had on a man's wool overcoat with grease stains and torn elbows. The wrinkles on her face were caked with dirt. She smiled at me with surprisingly intelligent eyes and then shuffled to the door.

This place made the hospital look like a vacation resort. I tapped the window again impatiently, this time noticing the thin, crisscrossed wires. Great. Bullet-proof triage windows. How comforting.

Finally, a heavy-set black woman around thirty-five strolled into the room. She had on a well-worn nurse's uniform, dark pantyhose with an ace bandage around her ankle, and a large silver cross swinging back and forth on her ample bosom. Her smile was dazzling. "Sorry honey. I'm the only one here right now. Every time I got to go to the bathroom, I feel so damn guilty I wait till I'm ready to explode." She pulled over a metal stool and sat down. "What can I do for you?"

"I'd like to see Dr. Harrison."

She chuckled. "Yeah, a lot of people want to do that. If he were black, I'd jump his bones myself."

"No, I didn't mean . . ."

She slid the glass panel open and patted my hand. "Of course you didn't, honey. I'm just playing with you. I got to entertain myself sometimes."

153

We stared at each other a few seconds and then she nodded, as if she had sized me up and decided I was okay. "You look fitter than most of the medical staff here, so I'd bet my paycheck you got questions that ain't exactly medical."

"You're good."

She winked at me.

"Hey man, what about me? You two gonna gab all day?" I turned to find a middle-aged man with a bandage across his forehead.

The nurse leaned forward. "Ray, that you? Now, don't start busting my chops first thing. Sit down and I'll call you in turn. Now go on."

Ray mumbled something to himself and flung himself into the nearest seat.

"They pay you what you're worth?" I asked.

Her laugh was rich and deep. "Sure. Didn't you see the Mercedes out front? Okay girl, we better get down to business before they start throwing beer bottles at us. What do you want with Dr. Harrison?"

I looked into her eyes and decided that this time I'd try the truth. "A friend of mine died recently. She had an allergic reaction to some penicillin that Harrison prescribed for her. But I know her, and she wouldn't have allowed him to prescribe something she was allergic to." I hesitated. "I think she was killed. That someone came here pretending to be her." I felt the energy draining from me, as if I had sprung a leak somewhere. Lying was easier.

"Dr. Harrison's the fourth door on your right. He's just finishing lunch, but you tell him Marsha said he'd better see you or she'll trash his office."

Her eyes were moist. I wanted to put my head on her bosom and sob. Instead I shook her hand.

The hallway was lined with yellowed posters of sports figures and entertainers. Most of them had started to buckle away from the wall. The door was ajar, so I poked my head in. Dr. Harrison was sitting on an examining table cross-legged, eating an overstuffed tuna fish sandwich on doughy white bread. I liked him instantly. He had short, spiky hair the color of hot butterscotch and freckles sprinkled over the bridge of his nose. His eyes were coppery and his smile mischievous.

"Can I help you?" he asked with a mouthful of food.

"Marsha said you better see me or she'll trash your office."

"Better come in then," he said, wiping his chin with a paper towel. He stood up and extended his hand toward me. "Dr. Harrison, believe it or not." I shook his hand. He had wide, spade-shaped palms with stubby fingers. I could quicker imagine him milking a cow than examining patients.

"My name's Robin Miller."

He laughed. "I've been waiting for you to show up here." He took another bite of his sandwich, then tossed the rest into a trash can under a side table. "Detective Ryan stopped by to ask me some questions about a patient of mine. Asked if you had been to see me yet. Said I should expect a visit from you." He ripped off the tuna-stained paper covering the table and replaced it with a fresh sheet.

"When did he stop by?"

"Early this morning." He patted the table like an old dog and faced me. "I'll tell you what I told him. I don't remember her."

"Did he show you a picture?"

155

He tucked his hands into his jacket pockets, narrowing his shoulders. His expression grew serious. "Yes . . . Ryan told me the connection between you two. I didn't tell him this, but I'm gay too." He sat down on a metal folding chair and clasped his hands between his knees.

"In the past two years, I've had eight friends die . . . one of them was the first man I ever slept with. A physics professor. One of the most brilliant, generous people I've ever known." His voice faded. Then his eyes snapped back to mine. "I know what it's like to lose someone you love. How out of control and furious it makes you. If I could help you out, believe me, I would. After Ryan left this morning, I spent twenty minutes staring at my records for that day. April sixth."

He stood up and started pacing around the table. "This is what I remember." He looked down at his feet. "Your friend — or someone who looked like her — came in here with a sore throat. She worked in the area and was in a rush. I don't remember her face, what she said, or what she wore. I saw thirty-eight people that day. Thirty-eight." He stopped and stared at me. "I'll tell you one thing, though. I never prescribe medicine without asking about allergies. Never. If I prescribed it for her, I must have been damn sure she had taken it before and knew there wasn't a problem."

"Dr. Harrison, do you remember anything unique about her appearance?"

He closed his eyes, his concentration deepening lines of fatigue I hadn't noticed before. He shook his head. "I'm sorry."

I gave his hand a small squeeze. "Me too. Thanks."

* * * * *

Jack Day's pharmacy was another three blocks away. I asked who had been working on April 6. The cashier went into the back, clucking her tongue like a chicken. A thin, elderly man with five o'clock shadow and a suit like a mortician came out with her.

"Hello. I'm Jack Day. Is there a problem?"

"I'm working with SFPD on the death of one Mary Oswell," I said in a cold monotone, trying to sound like Joe Friday. It's amazing how many personalities lurk inside my head.

"Yes," he said, waiting for the punch line.

"We have reason to believe that the murderer obtained a prescription for penicillin from this pharmacy and used the victim's name."

He looked round the store with a salesman's eye. "We better discuss this in private." He swung a panel aside and escorted me into a small, brightly lit office. Barbra Streisand was singing in the background about finding a place somewhere. "What's the victim's name?"

"Mary Oswell."

He started nodding even before I said her last name. "Yes. I remember now. The police were in here a couple of weeks ago asking if I recognized her from a photograph they had. I don't remember them asking specifically about the penicillin though."

"They originally thought she had reacted to

clams. Apparently, no one knew she was allergic to penicillin."

He raised his eyebrows. "Nobody mentioned that to me," he said defensively. I could tell that he was already calculating the possibility of a lawsuit.

"We think that was deliberate. The murderer knew about her allergies and obtained the penicillin for the express purpose of killing her."

His face muscles relaxed. "Kind of an odd way to kill someone. How did he force her to take a pill?"

The question caught me off guard. I hadn't even thought about that part. "We're not sure yet."

He put his legs across his desk. His pants hiked up and his hairy, knobby ankles poked out. There was a pleased, contemplative look on his face that made me suspect he was a heavy duty Columbo fan. "I guess he could have forced her at gunpoint, but then he could have just shot her. Or maybe he drugged her and made her swallow the pill while she was still dopey." He was tilting his chair further and further back. "Or he could have pretended the pill was an aspirin or something benign like an antacid." He was on a roll now and totally oblivious to my presence. "The best would be just crushing the pill into something the person loved, like vanilla ice cream or —"

"Yogurt!"

"What?" He was startled to hear my voice.

"Yogurt," I said, slapping my forehead. "Mary ate yogurt every damn night before going to bed. It was a ritual with her, like brushing your teeth."

"Bet I'd make a great detective," he said smugly.

"Okay, what do you remember about the woman who came in for the prescription? She was here

April sixth." My adrenalin was pumping and I wanted answers fast.

"Let's see. I'll have to look at my records." He left and returned with a card. "She was very attractive, that much I remember." He slipped his hand under his suit jacket and scratched his armpit like a baboon. As long as it helped him remember, I wouldn't have cared if he started combing his arm hair for bugs. "Okay, okay. It's coming back." He leaned toward me. His breath smelled like sour cream. I shifted my chair to the side. "She didn't look sick, which made me think that the penicillin was for a social disease. You know, V.D., something like that. It kind of amused me."

Great sense of humor.

"We started talking. She had a little movie-star cough. You know, that heh-heh type. Like she was too rich and too sophisticated for the real thing. She had shoulder-length blonde hair. I couldn't see her eyes 'cause she had sunglasses on. The real dark ones, like the ones Cruise wore in that movie, you know?"

"Was the color natural? Did it look like a dye?"

"What? The hair? Sure . . . I guess so. I didn't look that close. It wasn't a guy though, that much I know."

"What?"

"You think it was a guy dressed up like a woman?"

Earth to Mars. "No. I think it could have been a woman whose hair had been recently dyed," I said slowly, as if I were talking to someone from another country.

"Right. Well, I don't know about that. If it was a

dye job, it was a damn good one." He opened the top drawer of his desk and pulled out a pack of cigarettes. "Mind if I smoke?"

I did, but I didn't want to antagonize him. "No, go ahead. What else do you remember?"

He lit the cigarette with a yellow Bic lighter and sucked at it greedily. "We talked about that oil tanker business."

"The Exxon Valdez."

"Right." He exhaled into my face, making my eyes water. "She was real upset about that. She said she'd seen a picture of an otter coated in oil and it made her cry like a baby."

So the murderer was as animal lover. Or an excellent actress. Suddenly, Sharon Goodman popped into mind. Damn, this was confusing. "Anything else?"

"She bit her nails. I notice that kind of thing."

Jackie and Helene McNeil both had long nails. But they could be fake. I tried to envision Sharon's hands, but all I could remember was the sight of her sucking dirt off a fingertip.

"What about her height?"

"Not sure. We have a platform behind the counter. It makes all of our customers look kind of short. I guess I'd say she was a little shorter than you."

"How old do you think she was?"

"Age is a funny thing on a woman. She could have been twenty-five and she could have been forty. She had a great figure."

Frustration gathered in me like a fever. So far, his description could almost fit Jackie, Helene, or

Sharon. "Did she look like she might have been drinking?"

"I didn't smell her breath, so I couldn't say. But she wasn't real steady on her feet, so it's possible."

Or she might have been teetering on high heels. "Look, if you remember anything else, call me." I took out a piece of paper from my back pocket and wrote down my name and hotel number.

"Sure thing." He picked up the paper and squinted at it through a haze of smoke. "You think you're gonna need me to do an ID?"

"Maybe. I'll keep you posted."

As I left the room, he was still staring at my note.

Chapter 10

By the time I walked back to the hotel, it was after seven. I made a quick phone call to Cathy, whose huskily whispered dinner invitation made my heart beat faster. Then I headed to Patty's house.

She answered the door wearing a red "Happy Cooker" apron. Her hair was pinned up and her face was flushed. On her left shoulder was a tattered pink blanket that looked as if it had been burbled on recently. Her feet were tucked into furry slippers that reminded me of sea otters. Sometimes it amazes me that she was ever gay.

"Here are the directions," she said, lifting my hand and curling my fingers around the slip of paper, her lips thin with distaste.

"Patty, I don't want there to be bad feelings between us."

"Bad feelings?" She looked at me the way my cats do when I tell them they can't walk on my dinner plate. "Oh . . . you mean this morning. Look, I am sorry about that." She stepped toward me, carefully closing the door behind her. It was damp outside and her fur slippers started to droop. "You know Cathy and I were involved ages ago?"

I nodded, wondering why ages sounded a lot longer ago than five years.

"I guess I still have some residual feelings about that whole scene." Her voice dropped to a whisper. I had to lean forward to make out her words. "It was the absolute worst time of my life. A nightmare. And when that woman from her office called this morning . . . it threw me back. I suppose I overreacted." She paused, waiting for a response.

"It's okay. Like I said earlier, we made a mistake." I extended my hand. She looked at it for a moment as if it were a snake and she was trying to detect whether or not it was poisonous. Finally, she gave it an indifferent squeeze.

"By the way, a lot of the stuff in Mary's apartment has been cleaned out. The day of the funeral I went over there with her aunt. I hope you don't mind."

"Actually, I'm relieved," I said, a dull ache awakening in my temple. "I'm not looking forward to this."

"Maybe you should ask someone else to handle this stuff."

"No . . . I have to do this. I've postponed it long enough." My stomach was tossing sour bubbles into my throat. "What did you get rid of?"

"Nothing of value. I wouldn't try to cheat you . . ." she said defensively.

"Come on, Patty. That's not what I meant."

Her expression turned sheepish. "Mostly her clothes. Her aunt wanted to save some of her dresses. I guess it's some bizarre habit of hers." She smiled awkwardly. "Apparently, she still has some dresses that Mary's mom used to wear. Also, the landlord wanted to buy some of her furniture, so I went ahead and sold a few pieces. The money went right back to the estate."

"If you want, I can arrange for the rest of the furniture to be sold." She paused. "Robin, you're not up to this."

Her words were like a slap in the face. My eyes met hers. "You're wrong about that. I'm up to this because I have to be. It's as simple as that. Mary took a piece of me with her and the only way I'm going to get it back . . ." My throat closed. I turned on my heel and strode to the car. I pulled out at top speed, stopping abruptly two blocks later. Then I put my head on the steering wheel and sobbed.

* * * * *

As I rang Cathy's doorbell, a wave of garlic curled over me. The familiar smell made me smile.

"Hi . . ." Cathy opened the door with a four-star smile that flitted across her face and died instantly. She grasped my hand and pulled me into the hallway. Without hesitation, she wrapped me in her arms and cupped the back of my head with one palm. I clung to her, the events of the day overwhelming me.

Cathy ran her hands over my back, cooing soothing words. After a few minutes, she took a step back and looked into my eyes. "You need cucumber."

I snorted and sniveled at the same time. "What?"

"Cucumbers. For those bags under your eyes." She kissed both eyes and then steered me into the living room. "Sit there." She propelled me onto the couch. "I'll be right back."

She disappeared into the kitchen for a few minutes and returned with a plate of delicately sliced cucumbers. "Head back, gorgeous." She lifted my chin and covered each eye with a cool circle of cucumber. "Doesn't that feel good?"

I warbled something that sounded like "Oh yes" and sunk deeper into the couch. She lifted my legs and carefully placed my heels on the coffee table.

165

That minute, I realized how much I missed living with someone. The tears started to build again and I squeezed my eyes tighter.

"If you don't stop frowning, you're going to develop ugly worry lines right here." Cathy pressed a finger between my eyebrows. She began massaging my temple, her fingertips drawing slow circles.

"You're good at this caretaking stuff." I grinned. Her lips brushed mine, her breath sweeping over me like an early spring breeze. "You smell great," I murmured.

She licked my lips. I lifted my hand to remove the cucumber slices, and she caught it in hers. "No," she whispered. "Just be still." Slower than the tick of a clock, her lips fluttered over my face, neck, hands. Seconds passed before I realized that I had stopped breathing. "Lie down," she said, gently pressing my shoulders into the couch pillows.

A minute passed without any sound or movement except for the intake of my own breath. Then she eased her hands under my sweatshirt and pushed it up. As she leaned over me, wisps of hair brushed the side of my waist. Her hands stroked my skin with the lightness of a feather. I reached up for her and she pulled back.

"Just for you," she cooed into my palm. Her tongue flittered between the fingers of my hand. A sound like a growl rose in my throat. I heard her chuckle as she began to softly suck the tip of my index finger. Her tongue felt like cool velvet.

Her mouth skimmed my ear, sending chills down my spine. "Keep your eyes closed," she sighed into my ear. She took the cucumber from my eyes with her lips. There was another pause, and I could feel my body rising to find her hands.

Carefully, she rolled my shirt over my head and then slipped a hand behind my back, snapping my bra open with a deftness that sent a bolt of jealousy through me. And then her lips closed on me, and thought evaporated like ocean spray on a sultry midsummer day.

* * * * *

I awoke stark naked beneath a creamy cotton sheet. Mr. Tubbs was squatting on my belly with half-open eyes.

"I seem to have this strange effect on you," Cathy sniggered from the other side of the room.

I turned around. She was wearing a Chinese black silk robe, her slender calves just visible beneath the hem. She had a yellow terry cloth robe draped over the back of one arm. "This should fit," she said with a smug smile.

"How long have I been sleeping?"

"Just an hour or so. But I refuse to spoil another of my dinners on account of your inexplicable fatigue."

I nudged Mr. Tubbs off my stomach and he flung me a quick hiss just to show how displeased he was with my decision to move.

"You look much more relaxed now," Cathy said as I shrugged into the robe.

I gazed up at her and wiggled my eyebrows like Groucho Marx. "Can't imagine why." I tied the robe, stood up and started nibbling on her neck.

"Nice way to show your appreciation. Dinner's burning in the kitchen, but do you care?"

I planted a kiss on her lips and headed toward the dining room. "Why, I do believe there's garlic somewhere over yonder," I drawled, sniffing the air like a dog.

Dinner was as satisfying as the appetizer. Cathy had assembled an elaborate Caesar's salad with chunks of garlic, followed by baked artichoke hearts in a parmesan sauce, homemade pasta in pesto, and a side of garlic and broccoli. We held hands between courses and stared into each other's eyes with goofy smiles. I speared a piece of garlic and tucked it into my mouth with a lusty grin. "It's a good thing we fooled around before dinner," I quipped.

"Why, is that it for the evening?" Cathy said teasingly.

"I think so."

Cathy's face dropped. "Why?"

"For one thing, I sleep too well here." I squeezed her hand reassuringly. "Seriously, I have to finish my book before my publisher sends a hitman for me. And I need to think things through. Tomorrow's going to be a hell of a day. I was planning to go through Mary's apartment. Not my idea of fun."

Cathy started to clean the table, disappointment written all over her face.

"Cat, I'm not going to feel at peace till I settle this mess. You have to understand."

Her eyes sparkled with candlelight. "I do. It's just that it's been so long for me . . . since I felt this greedy for someone."

I walked around the table and hugged her. "That makes two of us."

We left the dishes on the table and meandered upstairs without a word. We made love with the desperation of ex-lovers. Afterwards, we curled around each other and slept.

I woke up around one o'clock in the morning and slipped out of bed. Downstairs, I wrote a tender, provocative note, then padded out the door. The night air clung to my car in small, round droplets. In the distance, I could hear the clang of buoys bobbing in the surf. A breeze blew past me, carrying a hint of fish. I paused by the car, tempted to crawl back upstairs and snuggle up to Cathy's warm back. Then I felt Mary's keys in my pocket and slunk into the car.

By half past three, I had written my last chapter and was about to collapse on the bed when my phone rang. I picked it up and growled. "Can't get enough of me?"

"You wanna know who killed Mary, you get your ass to the top of Twin Peaks in half an hour." The voice was gravelly, muffled.

"Who is this?" I snarled into the phone, my limbs turning cold as ice.

"Someone with answers."

There was a click and then the buzz of dial tone.

My pulse was pounding inside my ears. Someone with answers. Without thinking, I grabbed a jacket from the closet and stormed out of the hotel. The fog had grown thicker and there was a peculiar stillness to the air, as if I had cotton in my ears.

169

I picked the car up at the lot and raced toward Twin Peaks.

* * * * *

I know San Francisco pretty well, but on a foggy night it's easy to get lost. I ended up driving in circles, cursing at every stoplight. Finally, I screeched into a spot on a steep incline and pulled out a street map. Damn. I had made two wrong turns.

I swung the car around, skipping over the curb like a drunk. Twenty minutes had already passed. I put my foot on the gas, flying over hills like a stunt diver. I flipped my brights on and the fog bounced back into my eyes. I switched to dimmers, rounding a corner so close I knocked a garbage can into the gutter.

At last, my headlights caught the sign for the cut-off to Twin Peaks. I slowed my pace as I weaved around the hairpin curves. I was breathing so fast I started to hyperventilate. I edged my car into the parking lot and turned off my lights, forcing myself to take a couple of deep breaths. The fog was so thick, I couldn't see the edge of the car.

This is stupid, I said to myself as I unlocked the door and stepped out. The wind blasted me against the car. I'd been up at Twin Peaks on sunny afternoons, when the entire city, from Golden Gate Bridge to Coit Tower, glistens beneath you like a museum model. On the best days, the wind gusts at near-hurricane strength. Right then, it was stinging my skin with bits of gravel and dust.

I shielded my eyes with one hand and tried to

peer through the fog. I couldn't even tell if there were any other cars parked near me. I started to walk toward the front of the car, the wind howling in my ears like a banshee. I kept one hand on the car for support and shuffled along like a blind man.

"Hello?" I screamed into the wind. "Anyone here?" Something flew into my mouth and I spit it out with vehemence, my stomach shifting up toward my chest. Damn.

All of a sudden, I heard a metal chink, like the sound of someone opening a can of soda. I spun around, losing my footing and knocking my shin against the car. "Who's there?" I barked.

Something struck my back and my heart stopped. I pivoted and covered my face with my hands. Nothing. I lowered my hands and squatted. A newspaper. I must be nuts.

I opened the car door. Then I heard it again. A metallic clack, and then a dull rattle, the sound of marbles dropping on wood. My heart thumped.

"You got something to tell me, then come on." My voice trembled. I moved away from the car, my jacket blowing off my shoulder in the wind. "God damn it! Where are you?"

Someone cackled. The wind tossed the sound around so that it surrounded me. I spun in place like a top.

Suddenly, the night split open with a bolt of light. I flinched from the light and stumbled toward the car.

"Don't move," the voice rumbled.

The beam of a flashlight flickered over me, the fog bouncing around me like smoke. I started to move and a blast sparked past my elbow. I dropped to the ground and rolled. Something sharp ripped into my knee, but I kept moving. I dropped below a small hill, clinging to a parking marker. My toes scraped the side of the hill, and stones rolled out from under me. Shit. Twin Peaks is a goddamn cliff. I could be hanging off the edge and not even know it.

I dug my nails into the dirt and started crawling up the hill on my belly. I heard another metal click and the image of my sister's face jumped into my head. The smell of gunpowder hung in the air. I shook my head. Not now, Robin.

In the distance, I could hear someone scrambling around. The flashlight pierced the night with an angle of swirling clouds. The light swung in my direction and I slapped my mouth into the dirt. The light bent around a shape in front of me. The car!

This was my best chance. The car was blocking my position. I got to my knees, ready to sprint, praying that the car was mine and not my assailant's.

I counted to three, rocking on my heels like a racer. From the corner of my eye, I could see the light arcing towards me. I took off like a bullet to where the car should be. There was another crack and something whistled past my ear. I slammed against the car and felt for the handle. Someone was running at me. I swung the door open, diving across the seat and turning the car on while my feet were still hanging out the door. I felt something slam into my feet as I twisted around and crashed into the steering wheel. Another blast, this one shattering the window next to me.

I shifted into drive and spun the car down the hill, switching my lights on just in time to see I was headed off the road. I swerved to my left, ramming into a sign and then angled back onto the road.

Chapter 11

A half hour later, I pulled into a 24-hour
McDonald's and stumbled out of the car. My pants
were torn at the right knee and blood was dribbling
down through the dust on my jeans. I lumbered over
to a phone booth and dialed Cathy's number. The
line was busy. Who the fuck was she talking to in
the middle of the night? I slammed the phone down,
noticing all at once that my left arm and hand were
sprinkled with shards of glass. The left side of my
side felt sticky, like honey. I waited another five
minutes and then dialed again.

"Hello," Cathy yawned into the phone. "That you, Robin?"

"Yeah."

I could hear her fumbling for the light. "It's four-thirty. Did you sleep at all?"

"No . . ." I hesitated. "Who were you just talking to?"

She sounded suddenly alert. "No one. I was sleeping. You must have dialed the wrong number. Are you okay? You sound awful."

I pushed suspicion to the back of my mind. "Cathy, I need you to come get me."

"Where are you?"

I laughed, a bone-tired laugh. "I'm not sure. A McDonald's. Not far from Twin Peaks. Hold on a second . . ." I dropped the phone and limped to the corner. San Anselmo and Claremont. I dragged myself back to the phone booth and slumped against one side. When I picked up the phone, Cathy was screaming my name. For a split second, I forgot why I had called. A stab of pain in my knee reminded me.

"I'm at San Anselmo and Claremont. Get in touch with Detective Ryan." I hung up and lumbered back to the car. I opened the door and flung myself across the seat.

The next thing I knew, Cathy was sitting in the driver's seat, cradling my head and sobbing. Detective Ryan was circling the car, muttering under his breath. He saw that I was awake and leaned in the window on the passenger side.

"Good show, Miller. Almost got your head blown off. What do you do for an encore?" He was trying hard to keep the concern out of his voice. I understood the tactic all too well. I rolled my eyes up at Cathy. "Do I have to take this abuse?"

"You bet you do," she said.

"Can you sit up?" Ryan asked.

"Sure." I sat up and the world tilted to the right. "Whoa." I covered my mouth, fearing the worst.

Ryan lifted each eyelid with his thumb, staring into them like an old pro. "Probably got a concussion." He grinned and shook his head. "You're a pain in the ass. Do you even remember what happened?"

I started to answer but Cathy interrupted. "Shouldn't we get her to a hospital?"

Ryan stared at me as if he expected me to answer. Right then, all I wanted was a cool, clean toilet bowl and five minutes of privacy.

"I guess so . . . Hey Bob!" Ryan yelled over his shoulder to a young man with a scraggly beard and torn T-shirt. "Take care of this car, will ya? I'm driving her to the hospital." Bob waved his acknowledgment and bit into a hot apple pie. I knocked Ryan out of my way and threw up next to the car.

"I should have been an accountant," he muttered as he walked away.

* * * * *

An hour later, I was sitting on an examining table in University Hospital. I was getting pretty tired of medical facilities. I got five stitches above my left eye and another ten in my knee. According to the doctor, a middle-aged Indian man with a soft

176

touch and an impossible accent, I probably fell on a piece of rusted metal. Which means I also got a tetanus shot.

I had little scab marks running along my forearm, and the inside of my mouth felt sore. I felt around with my tongue and discovered teeth marks inside my cheek. Must have happened when I fell.

Ryan stood over me, tut-tutting like a grandmother. Cathy just glowered at me.

"Will the two of you stop it? I feel like a teenager who borrowed Dad's car without permission."

"What you did was a lot less responsible," Ryan said. "Driving up to Twin Peaks in the middle of the night because some asshole tells you to." He shook his head. "You're dumber than I thought."

"It proves someone killed Mary." I pouted.

Ryan exploded. "What it proves is someone tried to kill you. And maybe it's because you're sticking your nose where it don't belong. Like Spider Rose's business."

I stopped, remembering the cackle. I closed my eyes. Was the voice male or female? I felt the first bullet whiz past me again. "Someone connected with Rose wouldn't have missed that first shot. I was a sitting duck."

"The fog was thick enough to throw anyone off."

"No, not at that distance. That flashlight burned right through. Whoever it was had to be as close to me as six feet."

Ryan walked over to the medicine cabinet, examining the contents with a fierce scowl. "You don't know that for sure, kid. You were scared out of your wits." His voice was low. "Look, I want you to drop this. Someone tried to kill you tonight. I don't need that on my conscience."

He turned to look at me. "We'll find out who took a shot at you tonight, and chances are, that's maybe — and I mean maybe — who killed your friend. We already got people up on Twin Peaks looking for spent shells, tire tracks . . . anything that can help. What I'm saying is, I was wrong for letting you get into this in the first place. It's a police matter now . . . so stay out of the way."

Cathy was standing in the corner, one hand over her mouth. I didn't think she had stopped crying yet.

"I can't do that." Both of them stared at me with disbelief.

"Robin, you have to," Cathy wailed. She lowered her eyes, opening and closing her watchband nervously. Then she looked at me. "You can't bring Mary back. She's dead . . ." She paused, weighing her words. "It's not worth dying for. Mary wouldn't have wanted that."

"You're wrong. Both of you. I'm not stopping, especially when I'm this close."

Ryan stalked over to me and cupped his hand under my chin as if I were a bratty four-year-old. "You know what you're close to . . . huh?" He poked a finger into my temple. "You're close to a bullet in your head. Pop!" He spat at me with disgust. "That's it, Miller. Pop. And you're dead, just like your friend." His eyes had that possessed expression, the one he got whenever he talked about his wife.

He must have seen the recognition in my eyes, because he suddenly turned on his heel and stormed out of the room. Two seconds later, the door slammed open. "This is my case now. Mine. I find you butting into my work again and I'm gonna drag you to the airport by the hair." The door banged closed.

Cathy sidled over to me and shook her head. "Why didn't you at least call me first?"

"God, not you too! Look, I did what I had to. Now, if you don't mind, I've got an awful headache and feel like shit. I just wanna go back to the hotel and sleep."

"No, you're not."

"Geez, Cathy . . ."

"Shut up and listen. You're going to spend the day at my place . . . with me and Tubbs. That's it."

I didn't have the strength to argue. Or to wonder why Cathy's phone had been busy when I first called.

* * * * *

Cathy bundled me up in blankets and plied me with rosehip tea. I kept complaining that I wasn't sick, but she ignored me. I figured she had more experience nursing colds than she did glass wounds and concussions.

I watched Regis for about twenty minutes, until the Kraft commercials started getting to me. Cathy was hovering over me again.

"Not more tea?" I cried out.

179

She laughed. "No. I just wanted to check on you."

My mouth curled into a pleased smirk. "Thanks, Mom."

She knelt to kiss me with a trace of last night's passion.

"Are you planning on taking advantage of me?" I asked playfully.

"You're impossible." She tucked the sheets around me. I was stretched out in her queen-size bed. The bedroom was decorated much like the living room, with black lacquer furniture livened by white and red highlights. Even the sheets carried out the motif, with a black and white checkerboard design that had squiggles of vermillion zigzagging across the lines. It made me dizzy.

"I just spoke to Ryan. They came up with zip last night. I'm going down to talk to him and then I'm going to take care of your poor rental car."

"Why are you meeting with him?" I stopped her from fluffing the pillows behind my back.

"He's planning to interview everyone who knew you were staying at the hotel. I shudder to think of how McNeil's going to react."

"But why you?" I asked nervously.

She shook her wrist out of my grasp. "How do I know?" She picked up her car keys from the top of a dresser that shone like wet obsidian. "Do you want me to arrange for another car?"

"If they'll let me have one."

"Promise me you'll stay put till I get back."

"Can I shower?"

She considered the question. "No. You might get dizzy and fall. And you're not supposed to get the stitches wet. And don't go to sleep!"

"Great. So what am I supposed to do? Sit here and smell dirty?"

The tension in her face dissipated. She fingered my lips tenderly. "You smell delicious to me. I'll be back in a few hours. If the phone rings, ignore it. I turned the answering machine on." She blew me a kiss and whirled out of the room.

I picked up the remote and started clicking through the channels impatiently. I was itching to get out of bed, but every time I moved an arm or leg, spasms of pain blasted through me. Finally, I gave in. I threw the remote on the floor and closed my eyes, forcing myself to stay awake.

I was about to drift off when I remembered a dream I had had a few days ago. I was in some park. I think it was Central Park, but the Golden Gate was just beyond the trees. Mary was sitting on some kind of brick wall. She didn't see me. Something happened and all of a sudden, she fell. I ran over. Her leg was twisted out of shape.

The police photograph of Mary's body sprang before me. I sat up.

In the dream, I ran over to help her, but when I got there, she was okay. No . . . it wasn't even her. It was Cathy. And I couldn't find Mary. I ran all over the park looking for her, screaming her name, and then I stumbled over a body and it was Carol . . . Christ . . . it was my sister. And there was blood everywhere.

My body was sodden with sweat and my hands tingled. What the hell did it all mean? Mary sitting on some wall like Humpty Dumpty. Then it clicked. In spite of myself, a small smile flickered over my lips.

And all the Queen's men couldn't put Humpty Dumpty together again. Dinah would have a ball with this one. Once again, I was trying to make amends with the past. This time, through Cathy.

I threw my feet over the side of the bed and wobbled into the bathroom. Every fixture was antiseptic white. It reminded me of the hospital. One glance into the mirror made me realize how close I had been to landing on a slab in the morgue. Maybe they were right. Maybe I *was* in over my head. I splashed my face with water, brushed my teeth, and then ran my fingers through my hair. I took a second look at myself. That's better, I thought.

I stumbled back into the bedroom, picking up my notepad on the way. All I had to do was hold on a little longer. The answer was lurking right around the corner, I could feel it. I folded myself into the sheets and started mentally shifting through the pieces of the puzzle.

Chapter 12

About eleven o'clock the next morning, the wail of a nearby fire engine woke me. I had fallen asleep with my notes scattered around me. I straightened up and crossed to the bathroom. I sat on the edge of the tub and sponged myself off like an invalid, vaguely aware of the departing sirens. False alarm, I thought. And then I had a brainstorm.

I rummaged through Cathy's closets and found a simple shirtdress that fit me a little too snugly around the boobs, then I popped a painkiller and called a taxi.

I stopped at the hotel for a few items, including a pair of low-heel pumps. I dumped my sneakers into my briefcase and headed downstairs. The taxi driver was just revving the car as I stepped out of the doors. I slipped him a five to keep him happy. We made two quick stops in Chinatown and then drove to Carl Lawrence's office.

His offices were on the tenth floor. I stepped out of the elevator and took a deep breath. My arm was throbbing from the tetanus shot and my knee felt like someone was prying it open with a screwdriver. Luckily, no one was walking in the hallway. I took a quick survey of the ceiling and found a fire alarm about five feet away from a staircase. I eased the door open and stepped inside.

I opened my briefcase and withdrew three packets of sparklers, five packets of punks, and box of modeling clay. Feeling a little bit like a junior MacGyver, I molded the clay into a series of clumps and then stuck in the sparklers and punks. I took out a book of matches and checked my watch. I'd have ten minutes at the most.

*　*　*　*　*

The alcove to Carl's office was about ten by fifteen, with waist-high mahogany panels on the walls. His male secretary was seated at a rolltop desk tucked into a corner of the room. He looked a lot like Greg Louganis. He was taking a phone message and acknowledged me with a small nod.

I sat in a chair that consisted of black leather and chrome piping. I felt homesick for my apartment. Santa Fe hues of pink, rust, and teal. R. C. Gorman prints lining the walls. The thick, cotton pillows of my favorite chair, the color of dawn.

"Miss Miller, right?"

I glanced up. The secretary was stalking me. "Paul Evans. Mr. Lawrence's assistant."

I shook his hand, noting his carefully manicured nails. "Is Carl in?"

"Yes, but he's on the way out. He has a fund-raiser in Santa Cruz."

"Do you think I could see him for a minute or so?"

Paul flashed his capped teeth at me, his eyes skipping over the bandage on my forehead. "Sure, Miss Miller. I'll be right back." He knocked on Carl's door and then slipped into the office with an air of familiarity.

I checked my watch. I had about six minutes before my plan went into effect.

"Okay. He'll see you."

"Paul, do you think it's possible to get a can of seltzer? I'm taking this medication that's making me a little nauseous. The only thing that seems to help is seltzer and lime."

Anxiety flickered over his face. I could see him weighing his options. Did he keep his post or satisfy a client and potential voter? "No problem. I'll just run up to the conference room. Would you tell Carl?"

"Certainly. You're a wonder. Thanks." I sounded like a grade-A phony, but he didn't seem to notice. I clicked open the office door and hobbled in.

"Jeesuz . . . what's happened?" Carl darted

185

around his massive desk and swept me into his arms. If I didn't know better, I would have assumed his concern was the real thing.

"I had a car accident last night. It looks worse than it is."

"Sit down."

I was more than happy to oblige him considering that my legs were starting to give way. "I still owe you some papers." I dug into my briefcase and pulled out a sheaf of legal documents.

"You should have called me. I would have picked these up myself." He dropped the papers onto his desk without a glance, shaking his head with an indulgent smile.

"I also wanted to talk to you about the house in Big Sur. How do I go about selling it?"

"You shouldn't even think about that option till you see the place. Besides, you're in no shape to be making financial decisions."

"Maybe you're right." I stood up and limped over to the picture window behind his desk. I moved the curtain aside and gazed outside as if I were thinking deep thoughts. "This is all so painful . . ."

Carl moved behind me, draping his palms over my shoulders. My body stiffened involuntarily. I forced my muscles to relax. "Have you heard from your doctor yet?" he whispered into my ear.

I nodded yes while scanning the wall behind his desk for an outlet. Sure enough there was one just to the left of my knee. I put my hand to my head, emitted a breathless gasp and swooned. Carl leaned over, lifted my eyelids and called for Paul nervously. For the first time in my life, I was grateful to Suzy

Penelow for showing me how to roll my eyeballs back into my head.

Just as he scampered out of the office, the fire alarms went off. Perfect timing. I almost smiled. Carl whirled back into the room, cursing under his breath. "Damn, damn . . ." He felt my pulse and then slammed out of the office. I pulled a screwdriver out of my pocket and took off the outlet cover.

I hobbled over to my bag, whipped out my brand-new voice-activated tape recorder, hit the "on" button, and tucked it between the wires. The fire alarm stopped, meaning time was running out. I quickly spun the screw back into the plate. Carl and Paul stamped into the alcove just as I was rearranging myself on the floor.

"Call Medical Services," Carl was saying as the door opened. He stepped over to me and put his fingers under my nose. I couldn't resist. I started coughing wildly.

"Whoa, whoa." He stepped back to avoid my hacking breath. I sat up, hoping I looked dazed and helpless.

"Are you okay?" Carl helped me to my feet.

"I guess so. What happened?"

"You passed out and then the fire alarm went off. I tried to carry you out, but I was afraid I'd injure you more. I ran out and found Paul instead."

How noble. "Thanks. Do you mind if I just sit here for a bit?"

He checked his watch. "I'm late for an appointment, but Paul will help you downstairs. You sure you're okay?"

I clasped his hand. "Yes. Thanks."

"About the results . . ."

"I'm okay."

His face brightened. "Good. We'll have to get together soon. Real soon." He called Paul in and then squeezed my hand goodbye with what I supposed was a seductive gaze.

I turned my attention to Paul, who looked extremely uncomfortable. He was probably the type that considered illness to be an unforgivable form of bad taste. "What can I do for you?" he asked with distaste.

"Just let me sit here, okay?"

"Sure. Here's your seltzer." He returned to his desk eagerly, leaving the office door open.

I was aching to search through his files, but decided I had pressed my luck further than I should have. I took a sip of seltzer and did a visual survey. The walls in here looked even darker than those in the alcove. The paintings didn't help much. Somber portraits framed by walnut and gilded leaves reminded me of El Greco's moodiest work.

The file cabinets were oak, with brass handles. I took another look at the desktop. Clean as a whistle. A black rubber blotter with an antique inkwell and a brass business-card holder. The rug was tightly braided, in industrial gray. It looked as if it were vacuumed every hour on the hour. I could even see the vacuum tracks. I hobbled into the alcove.

"Thanks, Paul, you've been very helpful."

"Can I accompany you downstairs?" he asked reluctantly.

"No, thank you. I've imposed on you far too much already."

I ducked into the staircase again, swept the clay and burnt-out punks into a garbage bag, hauled it into my briefcase and got out of the office building as quickly as I could.

* * * * *

Cathy was squatting on the roof edge so I knew I was in trouble right away. I paid the driver with the few dollars I still had in my wallet and slunk to the front door.

"Gee, why don't you take a quick jog while you're at it," Cathy sniped as she opened the door.

"I had some things I needed to take care of . . ."

"How about your health, or doesn't that count?"

I was torn between being touched by her concern and pissed at the inquisition. To make matters worse, I *was* feeling pretty wobbly, and my stomach was threatening to heave-ho.

"That's my dress," Cathy said all of a sudden. Her eyes smiled. "I was wondering where you found clothes." She gave me quick hug and then pulled back. "Come on," she said with mock sternness. I followed her up the stairs like an obedient dog.

Once I was back in bed and tucked into fresh sheets, Cathy's disposition improved markedly. I told her about my trip to Lawrence's office and the fire alarm scheme. She raised her eyebrows but otherwise remained silent. When I was done, she ambled over to the window and stuck her head out. She inhaled greedily. For a moment, I worried that I was starting to smell. Damn the stitches, I was going to shower.

"Ryan wants me to personally reign you in. He

189

thinks you're more likely to listen to me than to him." Her voice drifted into the room like a stray breeze. "I think he overestimates my influence."

"Cat . . ."

She turned toward me briefly and then looked away again. "You must have loved her a great deal."

"I did."

"If I tell you I'm afraid you're going to get yourself killed before we ever get to really know each other, you wouldn't drop all this . . . would you?"

I wanted to say yes, to throw the sheets aside, stride over to her and kiss her neck, whisper soft assurances. But I couldn't. I kept seeing Mary's face, hearing Mary's voice. "I don't expect anyone to understand this . . . but I owe it to Mary." My words sounded hollow. All at once, the truth struck me. "I need to do this . . . for myself."

Something in my tone alerted Cathy. She spun around and stared at me.

"Mary loved me the best she knew how. And it wasn't enough." I closed my eyes, seeing Mary's face as if she were sitting across from me. I remembered how she would curl around me each night, kiss my earlobe and murmur, "You're my best dream." Then, she'd kiss my back and fall asleep, clinging to me.

"When my father died and she didn't comfort me the way I wanted, I started to close down . . ." My voice cracked. "I made it hard for her to love me, and I blamed her for that. Whatever she did just wasn't enough. I got so I refused to tell her what I needed because I wanted her to figure it out herself. To know. Just know. As if that would make the difference. Convince me she really loved me."

Cathy sat down next to me and covered my hand. I flinched. I felt like a deer paralyzed by headlights. I braced for the collision.

"When she told me about the opening at the *Tribune*, I hardly reacted." My throat clamped down, shredding my voice into thin strands. "Said it was too good an opportunity to pass up. And when she accepted, I blamed her. For abandoning me. Failing us."

Tears broke through unexpectedly. "I didn't give her a chance. Not really. I was so angry at her for not being everything I wanted her to be that I pushed her away."

Cathy opened her arms and waited. I looked at her through a wave of tears — suspicious, hungry, ashamed. I wanted her to be Mary, searched her features with a desperation that frightened me.

Then something inside me broke, and my grief and guilt split the air like the wails of new widows. I collapsed into her arms and, with deep wracking sobs, I told Mary how much I loved her and how sorry I was for letting her go. And then I said goodbye.

Chapter 13

We spent the rest of the day huddled in bed like teenaged girlfriends, talking about our pasts. Cathy told me about growing up in the Napa Valley, how she and her best friend used to play hide and seek in the vineyards. She also talked about her parents. Her mother worked as a masseuse in Calistoga and was a new-age mystic way before mysticism became popular. Her father had been a reporter for a local newspaper. Cathy's voice crackled as she described him.

"He used to sit at the typewriter in his office

with a bottle of Scotch at his side. You know that scene in *Julia*, where she tosses the typewriter out the window? He did that once. Hurled it right through. I was outside playing. It grazed me."

She lifted her bangs to show me the faint scar. "Didn't stop him though. Next day he tossed an empty bottle of Dewars out the same damn window. After that, Mom made a point of keeping the window open." She laughed bitterly.

Her parents divorced in the early seventies. By that time, Cathy was at Berkeley, driving a motorcycle and looking for love in all the wrong places. She told me about her inexplicable crush on Tom Jones, her six-month marriage to a college boyfriend, the first woman she slept with, and the last few years with Patty. I talked about growing up in Brooklyn, coping with Carol's death and the impact it had on my other sister Barbara and my baby brother Ronald, who talks to me about six times a year.

Sometime around eleven o'clock, we clomped down to the kitchen, unexpectedly ravenous. We made popcorn and tuna sandwiches and popped open an ice-cold beer. Mr. Tubbs followed, waiting for us to drop a scrap his way.

Two hours later, we were back in bed with bellyaches. I did my Gomer Pyle and James Mason impersonations, which made Cathy laugh so hard she said her sides hurt. Then the two of us took turns remembering theme songs from old TV shows. At one point, we simultaneously burst into Mary Tyler Moore's opening song, both of us tossing our pillows into the air at the same exact time. We laughed ourselves to sleep.

When I woke up in the middle of the night, Cathy was still curled around me. I kissed her palm and felt myself smile. "I won't make the same mistakes this time," I whispered as she nuzzled against me.

The alarm clock woke us around five. Cathy slipped out of bed, shook her shoulders and, amazingly enough, launched into exercise. I pretended to sleep, my eyes open just a crack so I could watch her stretch her tightly toned limbs. But when she bent over to touch her toes and her nightshirt lifted above her firm buttocks, the temptation was simply too much. I eased my still aching body over the edge of the bed and leaned forward to kiss a cool cheek. Cathy jumped.

"You scared me!" she shouted with delight, and then she tackled me.

We tousled in bed until my knee somehow hit the headboard, making me see stars rather than fireworks. Cathy sobered up immediately. "You need to rest, and I need to get ready for work." She kissed me square on the lips and rearranged me on the bed as if I were her favorite teddy bear. "I guess I can't make you promise to stay in bed all day."

"No."

"Will you at least let me know where you're going?"

"To Mary's co-op on Sunset," I said, bracing for a lecture. I could see her considering whether or not it paid to argue with me.

She must have decided not to because all of sudden she turned around and headed for the bathroom. A few minutes later, she returned in the yellow terry robe, her hair freshly washed and her skin glowing. She opened the ties and let the robe float to her feet. I gasped. She tossed me a sultry smile and opened a dresser drawer. I watched her with the sheer lasciviousness of a voyeur.

"Put on that pink satin chemise," I said suddenly, pointing to a carefully folded item in her lingerie drawer.

She looked at me with surprise. "For God's sake, Robin, I'm going to work."

"I know," I said, making my voice husky. "All day, I can imagine you darting around the office in your carefully tailored tweed suit while underneath, the satin rubs against your skin, reminding you of me . . . my touch." I slid my palm along the back of her thigh.

Cathy looked flushed. "You're making it difficult to be responsible."

"That's the point."

She looked at me for another second or two, trying to figure out whether I was serious. I was. The nasty gleam in my eye must have convinced her because she unfolded the chemise, shook it out, and proceeded to shimmy into it with all the skill of a seasoned stripper. By the time she closed the last button on her suit jacket, I was practically panting. "Serves you right," she said, punctuating the remark with a little bump and grind.

I reached for her and received a little slap in return.

"You asked for it, now suffer."

"C'mon Cat . . ." I whined.

She laughed, her eyes sparkling with play. "You could be addictive."

The remark made me uneasy. Cathy must have

recognized the look because she immediately closed down. "I'm running late already," she said, checking her watch. "If you get a chance, call me later so I know how you're doing."

She gave me a cursory kiss and then snatched her briefcase from a corner of the room. "By the way, I won't be home till late tonight. I have a screening to attend. You can come back here if you like . . . it's up to you." She tossed back her hair, the coppery highlights catching the early morning light like the back of a red fox darting between trees.

"I want to be with you, Cat," I said, trying to make up for something I didn't even understand.

"Just let me know what you decide," she said as if she didn't hear me.

I listened to her skip down the stairs. A few minutes later I heard the solid click of the door lock. The sound echoed inside me.

I didn't let myself dwell on what had happened. I couldn't. I stood up and stretched. My limbs still felt stiff, but the pain was a lot duller than it had been yesterday. And my stomach felt steadier.

I was determined to take a full-body shower before I stepped one foot out of the house . . . stitches be damned. I opened the linen closet and immediately burst into laughter. Talk about fastidious. Cathy had a stack of six or seven shower liners, all of them still in their store packages. Her towels were arranged by color and size. She had one entire shelf devoted to Crabtree and Evelyn soaps and shampoos, with a heavy emphasis on fruit scents. I took a deep whiff and felt lonesome for her. Sometimes I can be a complete ass.

I gingerly extracted a thick bath towel and headed for the shower. The hot water felt like heaven on my skin. My bruises throbbed under the jet of water, but even the pain felt okay. There's a lot to be said for simple pleasures, like being alive and clean.

I slipped on a robe and glided downstairs. Cathy had left a pair of old jeans, a faded polo, two sets of keys, and a short note on the table near the front door.

I know you'll need these. Also, I've left you keys to the house and to the rental car. It's a red Nissan. Hope that's okay. See you tonight.

P.S. I think staying in the hotel is a waste of good money, but it's your call.

She's something else, I thought, smiling to myself.

Mr. Tubbs chose that moment to announce his presence with a heart-breaking cry. I knew immediately what he meant.

I made Tubbs and myself scrambled eggs with cheese. I dropped his serving into a gray ceramic bowl decorated with cats scampering in all directions. He slapped his tail against my ankles in appreciation, then sidled over to his bowl guiltily. Cathy would probably kill me for feeding him this, I thought as I forked the remaining eggs onto two slices of wheat toast. As a matter of fact, she probably wouldn't be so keen on this either, I mused, biting into my breakfast with gusto.

A little while later, I checked out of the hotel,

wincing involuntarily at the bill. I stopped at a Cirrus bank to check my account and withdrew several hundred dollars. Mary's money would come in handy, but even if I never earned another cent, I could live pretty comfortably on the royalties from my books. I'm still somewhat cautious about money, having been raised on meatballs, hamburgers, sloppy joes and other budget incarnations of ground chuck.

My parents were strictly working class — my father a postman and my mother a checker for A&P. She used to sneak home bags of Oreos that other customers had ripped open during their frenzied shopping sprees. "We can't sell 'em anyway, so I can't see that it matters much," she'd explain as she lifted her booty from the bottom of her bag. Those unexpected treats were one of the highlights of my childhood. Mary used to tease me about being sentimental about supermarkets.

I pulled up to Mary's building. It was a four-story Victorian with a pale pink cupola on the roof that reminded me of a wedding cake. There were four rows of three windows, the middle window being a small stained-glass pane.

I jangled the keys in my pants pocket, and then gingerly removed them. Mary's mailbox was unmistakable. The white gum label had been peeled off. Her apartment was on the second floor.

I plodded up the stairs, wishing I hadn't been so adamant about doing this by myself. I hesitated in front of her door, then inserted the key, flexing my neck till it cracked. As the tumblers fell into place, I broke into a chill sweat.

The apartment smelled musty, like an unfinished basement used for laundry and storing old clothes.

All the blinds and windows were closed. Probably Patty's idea, I thought, sweat beading up under the edge of my bra straps. I was standing in a narrow foyer. To my right was an entrance leading to a kitchen. On the left was a large living room. I went into the kitchen first.

I don't know why Patty had said the apartment had been cleaned out. The room looked strangely complete to me, as if the owner had just stepped out for some milk and eggs. A cork board was screwed to one wall, notes and appointment reminders stabbed to the board with bright, multi-colored push pins.

Her butcher-block table was a replica of the one we had owned together. So were the spindle-back chairs. A framed Chagal print hung over the table. I smiled and opened the refrigerator. The inside glistened and smelled faintly of Ajax. So this is what Patty had meant by "cleaned out."

I crossed to the window and yanked it open, sucking air like a fish. My heart had begun to race and my legs felt like wax held too close to a flame. I pulled over a chair and sat down. After a few minutes, my head began to clear. I rose slowly and walked to the cork board. My eyes filled as I scanned the notes written in Mary's tight, typewriter precise hand.

"Confirm dinner plans with Pete."
"Cancel Thursday's interview."
"Buy baking soda and kumquats."
"Talk to publisher about McNeil."

I ran my fingertips over the scraps of note paper, my fingertips tingling. Maybe she was planning to oust McNeil.

There was a postcard pinned to the corner. I pulled it off and took a closer look. The front was a picture of the Mormon Tabernacle Choir. I flipped it over.

There's no place like home . . . literally. Pete and Miriam are outside with my folks, so I snuck up to my old room. I felt like a teenager again. They even have that old teddy bear sitting on my squeaky twin bed. Miss you terribly. We'll be back next week. Till then, keep singing, Patty."

With a start, I realized that Patty's loss wasn't much less than my own. I had been treating her as if her sole purpose was to act as my personal informant. I carefully pinned the card back in place, as if I were afraid Mary would come home and be angry at me for having read it.

In the living room, I saw that most of the furniture was already gone. The rug was a deep mauve pile. A dark rectangle by the far wall told me where her couch must have sat. Above it, a dusty outline indicated where a picture must have hung. I felt my body sway and I reached for the wall for support. All that was left in the room was a bentwood rocking chair, an antique blanket box that must have served as a coffee table, and a knobby pine serving table that Mary had inherited from her grandmother. I wobbled around the corner into the bedroom.

Her bed was untouched. Dusty rose comforter, pillow shams and bed ruffle. I remembered the set from the days when we lived together. It was my least favorite and for four years it had sat in a plastic zipper bag. Whenever we did our spring cleaning, Mary would tug it out and try to reopen negotiations. "I could live with it now," I whispered into the stale air.

Her dresser drawers were totally empty. So was her bedroom closet, except for a pair of ragged suede slippers I had bought her for Christmas the year we split up. I picked them up and held them to my chest, my breathing becoming as thin as mountain air.

"What a pretty picture."

I whirled around. Carl Lawrence was leaning against the doorjamb. He was wearing tight black jeans and a black chamois shirt. He looked like a cat burglar. I dropped the slippers into the closet and backed away, my heart thudding in my ears.

"Surprised to see me, I bet." He leered at me. "Why don't we have a seat," he said in a cool voice. When I didn't move, he pointed to the bed. "Sit."

Dumbfounded, I sat down. This is it, I thought. How ironic, to die here in Mary's bedroom. My eyes darted around the room for a weapon. There was a thick crystal vase on top of the heavy oak dresser at the foot of the bed.

"You don't seem very happy to see me," he said, stroking the side of my cheek with his index finger. "Why is that?"

How fast could I swing over to the dresser? Maybe I should just dive over and spear the vase at his head. My thoughts were running like wild fire.

"Could it be you're frightened of me?" Carl was leaning over me now, his breath teasing the outside of my ear. He smiled with one half of his mouth.

"What are you doing here?" I squeaked out. He threw his head back and laughed.

"I followed you from the hotel. I thought for sure

you'd notice me when I parked right behind you, but I guess you were otherwise occupied."

He straightened and crossed to the dresser, his wide hand sweeping the vase up and hefting it like a hammer, his eyes smiling at me. Then he shrugged. "Too much temptation." He opened a drawer, dropped the vase in, clucked his tongue once and slammed it shut. "Looks like no one's home."

He turned around and hopped onto the dresser, the oak groaning under his weight. He must have registered the distaste on my face because he lifted an eyebrow with satisfaction, kicking his heels onto the foot of the bed. "Am I being disrespectful? Sorry, darling."

He paused to stroke his thighs as if he were working out a cramp. "But don't you think it's a little disrespectful to go prying into someone else's life?" He stood up suddenly and went to pull something out of his back pocket. My muscles tensed, ready for battle. "This," he said waving my tape recorder at me. "This is unforgivably disrespectful. Imagine how I felt when I got back to my office to make a few phone calls. I open my mouth and I hear this little click somewhere behind me . . . like a whore smacking gum. I shut my mouth, there's another click."

He pulled his bottom lip with his thumb and index fingers. "Incredibly rude. So was interviewing Jackie under false pretenses." He tossed the recorder onto the bed.

Shit. I glanced over to the bedroom door. If I could make it in two steps I'd have a chance of reaching the apartment door before he did.

Carl followed the direction of my eyes and

strolled to the door casually. "Maybe we need more privacy." The door closed with a tortured squeak. He leaned against it with his hands folded behind him.

"Now, why don't you tell me what the *fuck* you're up to."

The word *fuck* struck me like a fist. I decided to throw my cards on the table. I didn't see that I had much to lose. "Mary thought you were connected to Spider Rose. I don't know how or why. But I know she did."

He pursed his lips thoughtfully. "Does this mean our pleasant dinner was a ruse as well? As well as your famed medical test? Could you be that dishonest?" He seemed unfazed by my mention of Rose.

"What's the connection, Carl?"

He smiled generously. "Do you really expect me to hand this shit to you? How naive." He sauntered back to the bed and gazed down on me. "You know being alone with you like this is a real turn-on. I keep imagining you and Mary grinding away on the bed. Did the two of you ever do it here?"

I lowered my eyes. He was standing toe-to-toe with me. I balled my hand into a fist and stabbed at his groin. Carl moved like a boxer, arching backwards and hooking my wrist with his right hand.

"The dyke fights back," he snickered. "Do you know how many men find resistance exciting?" He pushed my hand against his crotch. His penis was hard and straining against his pants. "Have you ever sucked a man, Miller?" he asked with a growl in his throat.

"You want to add rape to your other crimes?" I

spat up at him. My fingers were splayed against him. I expected to hear them snap.

"What other crimes? Honey, I am the epitome of responsible citizenship, and don't you forget it," he said with a sarcastic sneer. "Now, what do you know about Rose and me?" He squeezed my hand around his balls and then slapped it away.

"Nothing."

I felt the wind before I felt the back of his hand across my jaw.

"Bitch!" He stabbed his hands under my arms and lifted me like a rag doll. My feet were about six inches off the floor. "Remember how much you admired my muscles the other night?" he asked. His lips were dry and cracked.

Adrenalin coursed through me. My lips pulled back across my teeth as I kneed him in his balls. He tossed me across the bed, doubling over and howling like a cat whose tail's been stepped on. I scampered across the bed and made a beeline around him. He caught me by the back of my head, wrapping my hair around his knuckles.

"You know what I've wanted to do since the moment you first walked into my office?" He grabbed my breast roughly. "This." His eyes flickered and he groaned. When they opened, they had an almost maroon gleam. "I bet you're a screamer," he moaned, yanking my head backwards.

I stood still as a statue, using every ounce of willpower not to cry or wince. "Carl," I said, straining to sound calm, rational. "I'm not worth losing your career over."

He twisted my breast till I cried out, tears streaming down the sides of my face. "Good," he said, flinging me onto the bed. "That much you're right about. You're not worth a career. Neither was Mary." He opened the bedroom door. "Take this as a warning. Back off."

I crawled up the bed and wrapped myself in the comforter like a cocoon. Carl's footsteps receded. I held my breath until I heard the door close. And then I fell apart.

Chapter 14

I drove myself back to Cathy's house, shooting
past red lights and honking my horn like an
ambulance with a cardiac patient aboard. When I
finally arrived, I panicked that Carl had followed
me. I turned the car around and headed over the
Golden Gate Bridge. Sheer terror propelled me to
drive off random exits through fast food drive-ins
and back onto the highway. Finally, I crossed the
bridge and drove to the police station where Ryan
worked. I was vaguely conscious of a string of horns

and cursing drivers following me. But there was no Carl, and that was all I cared about.

I sat outside the station, watching cops drag perpetrators in and stroll back out with blue paper cups of steaming coffee. Gradually, my breathing slowed and my legs stopped trembling. About then, I remembered Ryan's last tirade and decided to spare myself the indignity of confessing my latest miscalculation.

I cruised back to Cathy's, this time at a snail's pace. I sat in the car craving a cigarette — which was odd, since I've smoked only one cigarette in my life and that was when I was fifteen. I don't know how many hours passed before I finally mustered the strength to open the car door.

Tubbs was howling at me before I had climbed the first step. I had trouble getting the key in the lock, and his desperate meowing was making the hair stand up on the back of my neck. When I finally slammed the door open, the vase on the side table crashed to the floor. Tubbs and I flattened ourselves to the door. If I had a tail, it would have bristled like a porcupine's back . . . which is exactly what Tubbs' tail did.

I swept him up, smothering him with kisses. He looked too stunned to protest. Besides, I think he remembered his breakfast treat. I crashed on the couch and didn't move for hours. Tubbs made a nest for himself in my lap, and the two of us lay there till Cathy came home, which was sometime after ten.

She took one look at me and shook her head. She tossed her keys on the table, took in the shards of vase and rose petals scattered on the floor, and gave me a startled double take. I hadn't remembered the vase until that look. Then I started to cry.

She was pretty good. She didn't lecture me until I had sobbed myself dry. But then she tore into me with a vengeance. When she was done, I felt about four years old. All I could do was snuggle into her arms, muttering apologies and occasionally gasping for air.

She held me without a word.

* * * * *

"Here's the best comfort food I can think of. Oreos and ice-cold milk. Will this do?" Standing in the doorway in white silk pj's and her hands full of treats, Cathy reminded me of an angel. We smiled at each other with the comfort of old friends. "Well, move over, kid."

I sidled over and fluffed her pillow up.

"Did the bath help?" she asked, twisting an Oreo apart.

I nodded. "Especially the apricot suds."

She handed me the split cookie and a glass of milk.

"How'd you know I like it like that?"

She pointed to her head and winked. "Mind reading."

We gobbled half a row of cookies and then drifted back to the subject we both wanted to avoid.

"Will you press charges?"

"I don't think I can."

Cathy shot me an impatient look. "Of course you can. Attempted rape."

I flinched at the word. "He walked out on his own."

"Sexual molestation, then. There has to be something."

"I'm not sure, Cat. Besides, I want Ryan to press on the bigger charge. Mary's death. If I go after him on this, I'm afraid he'll clean house too well."

Cathy started playing with the edge of the blanket. "You're not going to stop, are you?"

I covered her hand with mine as an answer.

She simply nodded. "So what do you do now?"

"I still have to get down to Big Sur."

"Okay. We'll drive down there this weekend."

"No . . . I'm driving down tomorrow."

Her head snapped in my direction. "Jeezus . . . what does it take to slow you down . . . a steamroller? You're not safe, Robin. And that ride can be treacherous. If you have to go, fine. But I'm coming along."

I squeezed her hand, but she whipped it away. "No, that won't do it. I swear, sometimes I think you're trying to get yourself killed."

"I'm not. But I don't have time to sit around. Carl's pissed now. He knows I'm on to him. Even if he didn't murder Mary, he's hiding something. The longer I wait, the longer he has to cover his tracks. Besides, right now he doesn't know I'm staying here. Which gives me an edge I can't afford to lose. I'm leaving first thing tomorrow morning."

"Damn you," she sputtered as she kicked out of bed. She picked up the tray and stomped out of the room. I was afraid she wasn't going to come back, and I desperately needed her warmth next to me. I pulled back the blanket, pivoted off the bed, and slid into the slippers she had loaned me. Just then she appeared by the open door. She had a gun in her hand. My skin went cold.

"Will you take this with you? Will you do that much for me?" She walked into the room, holding the barrel between two fingers like a dead mouse that might still have some life in him.

"I can't take it, Cathy," I said, relieved but still uneasy. "Where'd you get that?"

She dropped the gun on the bed between us. "I bought it last year when we had a series of robberies in the neighborhood."

My eyes fixed on the muzzle. In my head, I heard that crack, the thunderbolt that tossed me back against a stack of shoe boxes. Saw the mushroom of gray smoke, felt the gunpowder sear my nostril hairs. Heard my sister wailing my name . . . and then the awful silence. The stickiness of her blood, like honey on my fingers.

"Robin, oh God, I'm sorry. I forgot."

I couldn't feel Cathy's arms around me. The bedroom had disappeared. It was as if I held my sister Carol in my arms, and for the millionth time, the rattle in her chest shook the marrow in my bones.

* * * * *

The moon splashed a powdery blue beam across the bed. Cathy's head was tucked under my chin, her arm flung across my waist and her leg straddling my calves. Her snore sounded like a cat's purr. I lifted her hand and kissed her wrist. She cuddled closer, mumbling contentedly. She had to be innocent, I repeated inside my head like a mantra.

Her skin looked as smooth as a starlit lake on a still night. My fingertips glided over her arm. She responded by kissing my shoulder. Her eyes opened, their brilliant blue dappled with flecks of moonlight. "I want you," she said. There was a question in her voice. I stilled her doubts and my own by turning toward her, outlining her lips with my tongue.

"Mmmmmm." She sucked and nibbled at my neck. A groan rose in me like a wave. "I want you," she whispered as she tenderly eased me onto my back. She lifted my nightshirt over my head, my body instantly beading with goosebumps. Gently, she circled my breast with the edge of her palm. I could feel the bruises where Carl had dug his fingers into me. I raised my hand to stop her, but then her breath fluttered over my nipple and my protest melted into a sigh. It was easier to give in, to let my body still my mind.

A few hours later, I slipped out of bed. Cathy mumbled in her sleep. I bent over to kiss her forehead. Cathy was the only thing keeping me grounded. I had to stop doubting her, I warned myself as I slipped into the bathroom.

By the time the alarm clock rang at five, I had showered, dressed, mapped out my trip, and packed an overnight bag.

"I guess it's too late to lure you back into bed," Cathy said, letting out a classic yawn.

"Yup. But I have an assignment for you."

"Oh goodie. You're going to drag me into this mess with you. How considerate."

"Would Tonto say that to the Lone Ranger? Would Lacey begrudge Cagney a small favor?"

Her face brightened. "Okay, pardner. Shoot."

"There was a note in Mary's apartment about a meeting with the newspaper's publisher. She was going to discuss McNeil. I need to know if she really was angling for McNeil's job. If so, McNeil may be a more serious suspect than I realize." And I may be way off base with Carl, I thought.

She wrote a note to herself. "Done. What else?"

"I need to know just how jealous Sharon was of Mary. Talk to Sam. Find out if she thinks Sharon could have had anything to do with Mary's death." I looked down at my notes. "And ask her if she was with Sharon the night Mary died. You might also try to find out if she and Mary had anything going."

"Are you serious?"

"Yeah. Look, I may be missing the obvious." I caught myself staring at her, my eyes searching for any signs that she was keeping something from me. She looked up at me with a puzzled frown. I turned my head away. I couldn't let suspicion poison my feelings.

She rose up on her knees and draped herself around my neck. "Be careful out there. I don't want anyone but you admiring my sweet, syrupy blossom," she cooed in that Southern lilt that drives me nuts.

"Not fair," I said, extracting myself from her arms with difficulty.

"Wrong. All's fair in love and war . . . and this is war." She leaped into my arms and plastered me with kisses, till I rolled onto the bed shaking with laughter. As soon as I hit the bed, she jumped up and started running in small circles, singing the Rocky theme.

"You're nuts."

"Sure enough," she said, helping me to my feet. "Now git before I get a mind to whup you good." She propelled me out the door with both hands, cackling like Minnie Pearl.

I opened the door to a chill breeze. Morning was spreading itself over the horizon in a strip of melon haze. Above me, the sky was the color of blue topaz. Birds were cheeping in a sycamore across the street. I took a deep breath and my nostrils tingled.

One thing about being an insomniac, you get to enjoy that delicate moment before dawn, when the wind is crisp and tickles your skin with dew, and the air's so quiet it feels like you're swimming underwater. I could even hear the shush of my own breath.

I started the car and glanced up through the moist windshield. Cathy was standing near the bedroom window, one hand parting the milk-white curtains. I waved up to her and backed out of the driveway.

I drove around the block and pulled up by the corner. I stepped out and looked around, listening for the sound of another car motor, a door slamming, feet shuffling through leaves or gravel. Nothing.

I got back in the car and turned the radio on. I found a station dedicating its morning program to Bach's Brandenburg Concertos. I took it as a good omen.

Chapter 15

The route I had planned took me straight through Gilroy, the garlic capital of the world, and it had taken me a little over an hour to get there. By then, the sun was burning off the mist that dusted the golden fields running along the road. I could tell Gilroy was close just by tasting the air. The garlic hit my taste buds first, then a subtle hint of tomato. The combination brought an instant recollection of every Italian meal I had ever consumed. Twenty minutes out of Gilroy, I was still salivating over the vision of steaming lasagna and bubbling garlic bread.

I popped a cinnamon Certs into my mouth and focused on the highway. Every now and then I passed a family of cows nestled against a wire fence near the road, grassy stalks dangling from their mouths, the slant of early morning light painting their hides a rich cocoa brown. I slowed down and mooed at the first group, but they just stared at me with bulbous eyes till I started feeling foolish.

The field grew narrower, the road dipped and climbed, and soon I was hugging the hillside, a sheer drop off my right, the swish of the tide rushing up the cliff like smoke. Offshore, a storm was brewing. You could see the line of battleship gray clouds colliding at the base of the horizon.

I thanked the powers that be that the fog was dangling far in the distance. The coast ride is magnificent, but in the fog, it's about as much fun as walking a tightrope blindfolded. In other words, you pray a lot.

I rolled my window down, turned up the radio, and began accompanying Bach with my own inventive trill. He was probably stuffing moss into his ears. I was having a grand old time ta-ta'ing in time with the brass, till the road buzzed closer to the mountain and started hairpinning around steep ravines. Then I remembered why they sometimes call Route 1 "Dramamine Road."

I rattled onto the first vista point I could find, my nostrils flaring and my stomach doing little flip-flops. I opened the door and flopped down on a rock near the cliff edge. I was desperate to focus on something straight and stationary. Unfortunately, my eyes tripped over a metallic flash at the bottom of the gully.

A car had apparently skipped off the side of the cliff and crashed upside down on the rocks. Waves were lapping at its back tires. It reminded me of Harry, a turtle I had when I was six. One day I found him feet up under the radiator, dust and iron flecks coating his belly.

I closed my eyes and tuned in to the roar of the surf. Better, much better. The salt air tossed my hair like a playful lover. The sun settled on my shoulders, the length of my back. I smiled. This is my first and best love, I thought. One of these days, I'm going to have a house by the sea.

And then I remembered where I was going.

I wiped dirt from my backside and slid into the driver's seat. I stopped in Carmel for a quick lunch, gas, and a bag of miniature Hershey bars. An hour later, I was edging into Mary's driveway, my stomach muscles in a knot and my breathing as ragged as a homeless woman's skirt.

It took me a good fifteen minutes before I could even glance at the house. Then my eyes shot to the spot where the police had outlined her body. The chalk markings were still faintly visible. They reminded me of the lines in a coloring book. My eyes filled in the details.

I turned my back on the house and looked out to the ocean. The view was magnificent. I could still see the clouds broiling in the distance, but close by the skies were clear and the water bright turquoise. Mint-green sea foam lathered a string of boulders just offshore and the air was crackling with the sound of seagulls and terns.

The house was set off from the cliff edge by

twenty feet at most. I walked over to the holding wall, a collection of weather-worn charcoal rocks that reminded me of the ruins of an ancient fort. I hopped on top and sat down Indian-style. For some inexplicable reason, my usual vertigo had receded. I gazed down a hundred-foot drop into the roiling whitecaps and felt wonderfully giddy. Pelicans were fishing for a mid-afternoon snack, and every now and then I caught a glimpse of sea otters peeking over the waves. I don't know how long I sat there, but by the time I finally moved my legs were numb and my cheeks wind-burned.

I jumped off and did a quick set of stretches. Except for the stitches, most of my aches and pains were fading into a dull memory. I was bent over, touching my toes and humming Pachelbel's Canon through clenched teeth, when I heard footsteps behind me. I spun around into a crouch, my fists balled and ready to strike.

In front of me stood a middle-aged woman with silver-white hair pinned up in a Grace Kelly bun. She jumped back and covered her mouth with one hand. "I am sorry," she said with newscaster enunciation. "I didn't mean to startle you." She extended her hand. "I'm Martha Sparks."

Martha smelled like new dollar bills. She wore a white blouse with a Peter Pan collar and a blue paisley skirt with gardener gloves that looked like kid leather tucked into the pockets. She didn't look like a killer, but then neither did Jean Harris.

"Robin Miller," I said, shaking her hand. Her clammy palm made me think of wet lasagna noodles.

"I hope you don't mind my asking . . . but just what are you doing here?" Her voice was nasal.

"I've inherited this property." I waved in the direction of the house without moving my eyes from hers.

"Oh." Her face shut down. "Well, I *am* sorry about your friend. It was an awful accident. Were you very close?" The question didn't seem casual.

"We used to be . . . years ago. To tell you the truth, I'm surprised she left it to me."

She smiled as if this last piece of news somehow increased my worth. "It's a glorious home," she cooed. "Do you plan to sell it? I've had my eye on this property for years . . . even before Mary bought it."

How much did you want the house, I mused to myself. "You're the one that found Mary."

"Yes." She walked over to an old beer barrel planted with impatiens. "These need to be watered," she murmured distractedly. "It was extraordinarily unpleasant . . . do you mind?" She strolled over to the wall, hopped on top with surprising ease, and crossed her legs ladylike. "My feet are simply killing me. I've spent the entire morning fine-tuning my garden. Trimming branches, snipping off discolored leaves."

For an instant, I envisioned her conversing with Sharon Goodman about garden techniques. The image was startling.

"Gardening is such dirty work, you know," she cooed.

You couldn't tell that by looking at her. For someone who had spent the day gardening, her clothes were impeccably clean.

She must have noticed the look in my eyes because she chuckled in an upper-class way. "I wear an apron while gardening. Good Lord, I'd be an absolute ruin otherwise. I even wear a kerchief to cover my hair. One must remain presentable, you know."

I was wearing my scuffed sneakers, wrinkled chinos, and an oversized L.L. Bean rugby shirt with bold black and peach stripes. She made me want to hide behind a bush.

"I've been stopping by the house on occasion to make sure that no new-age hippies or meandering hikers decide to camp out here. My house is just about a hundred yards up the road."

"I see."

"I'm sure you do," she said uncertainly. She readjusted her skirt so that the hem fell exactly below the knee.

"Do you mind if I ask you some questions?"

She arched one penciled eyebrow. "Of what sort?"

"Questions about Mary. People who visited her. How often she stayed here."

"May I inquire as to why?" Her tone was getting more and more nasal and I suddenly realized she probably had sinusitis. I smiled to myself.

"Bad day for allergies, isn't it?" I asked with a clipped British accent. Limey, I was turning into a veritable chameleon.

"Oh quite. I have the most awful headache." She dug a finely manicured nail into a spot above her right eye.

"You should try massaging your sinuses. It works wonders." I reached over and started rubbing her temple with the balls of my fingers.

"Well, that does feel wonderful. Mmmmm."

"There's also a spot right above the ear . . . if you don't mind?"

"No . . . not at all."

I moved my fingers to her ears and drew infinitesimal circles.

"Heavens . . ." she sighed.

Silently I thanked my friend Amy for her lessons in sinus relief. Years ago, I spent a week with Amy and some other friends in Puerto Rico. I spent the first two days snorting and wheezing until Amy convinced me that sinus massage really works. I've blessed her fingers ever since.

"So would you mind helping me out?" I asked in the type of voice people use when whispering to each other during a performance at the Metropolitan Opera House.

"Of course not, my dear."

I increased the pressure slightly and almost immediately her shoulders slumped. "Did Mary come to the house often?"

"Whaa . . . oh, yes. Every weekend, I suppose. I made a point of visiting at regular intervals. I firmly believe that one should know one's neighbors . . . uh, do you have a tissue? I'm afraid my sinuses have begun to drain."

I dug a tissue out of my back pocket and handed it to her as if it were a silk handkerchief purchased in Paris. She accepted it with the same air, then brayed into the tissue. I returned to her ears with a restrained smile. "Did she work out here?"

"Work?" she asked, as if it were a foreign concept. "Well, I can't say I ever hear her mention work. She wasn't terribly talkative. To be candid with you, I often felt that she viewed my visits as a bit of intrusion."

"How unneighborly."

"My sentiments exactly. I'm glad we understand each other," she said with a wink. "Could you lower you left hand a bit . . . ah. Perfect. You know, you could do this for a living." She uncrossed her legs, her head falling against my hand like a bowling ball.

"Did she ever have company?"

Martha straightened up, a flash of anger in her eyes. "Frequently. Perhaps you didn't know this, being a friend from her past, but she was, well . . ." She glimpsed over her shoulder, apparently worried that a low-flying seagull might overhear us. "She was a homosexual." She pronounced the word ho-mo-sexs-u-el.

I raised an eyebrow as she expected me to. "I find that hard to believe. We used to double date when she lived in New York."

"I'm sorry to be the one to tell you this, but it's true. She had all types of visitors in and out of the house. It was quite distressing. Once I brought my grandchildren over . . . they were selling Girl Scout cookies . . . and right there on that deck . . ." She pointed behind me. "Two absolutely horrid men were sitting and holding hands. Well, I never."

I bet not. "Did she have woman friends over as well?"

She nodded, her nose flaring with distaste. "One woman in particular. Long, blonde hair. Amazingly feminine. Good figure. It was shocking."

"Do you know her name?"

"No. Mary was always shooing her out of the room, like a miscreant dog. Whenever I saw her, she'd dart around a corner. The last few months were absolutely disgraceful."

"Do you remember any other physical details?"

"She was a poor dresser. Her clothes were cheap." She checked me over and decided to rephrase her statement. "Not that one must always wear fine clothes. I mean, your outfit is perfectly functional. I expect you were planning on cleaning the house."

I wanted to tell her these *were* my fine clothes, but instead I smiled appreciatively.

"I don't remember much else about her. She wasn't very memorable."

"How about Carl Lawrence?"

"That handsome attorney? Good God, no. Why would he be here?" A pained expression crossed her face. "Don't tell me he's a homosexual too. Well, I suppose I should have known . . . he's simply too beautiful to be a real man. That darling Jackie Dolan must be a front. How awful . . ."

"Actually, as far as I know, he's perfectly straight. He just happened to be Mary's lawyer. In fact, he's handling her will."

"Whoo. That's a relief. One hates to have one's idols knocked off their pedestals, you know."

"Do you know Jackie well?"

"Not very. I met her at a crafts show in Carmel. She's quite lovely."

"Did she and Mary know each other?"

"What?" She chuckled indulgently. "I doubt it."

"Did Mary seem particularly agitated near the end?"

"Agitated?" She looked puzzled. "On the contrary,

she was disgustingly euphoric. She and that . . . that woman would lie here, lounging around in ridiculous outfits, giggling and whispering like silly adolescents."

"Did she have any enemies you knew of?"

"Enemies? Why . . . don't tell me you suspect her death might have been intentional?"

"Some people think so."

"Well, perhaps some people just got sick and tired of her flaunting perversity in their very own backyards."

My jaw dropped.

She tapped my shoulder with one finger as if I were the Pillsbury Doughboy. "Don't misunderstand. I would never hurt a fly . . . no matter how irritating the fly might be. But others aren't as tolerant as I am."

"Yes. I'm quite aware of that."

She slid off the wall and rolled her shoulders. "I feel marvelous now. You will let me know if you plan to sell." With a bright grin she caught my hand and squeezed it.

"A few more questions, if you don't mind."

She hesitated. "Not at all. I'm all ears."

"Was anyone visiting her the day she died?"

"That Saturday? Let me think . . ." Her eyes practically crossed with the effort. "No, not that weekend. But she did have company that previous Saturday. Her woman friend."

"How do you know?"

She lowered her eyes coyly. "I had stopped by to inform Mary that her outdoor lights had burned out

. . . but then I heard them . . . on the deck. The sounds they made . . ." Her hand fluttered to her neck.

I decided to change the subject. "What did you do when you found her?"

"Found her? Oh. The day she died. Well, I screamed, what else?" She laughed at her own joke. "Seriously, at first it was so dark, I couldn't tell it was a person. Then I thought she had just fallen down. She was wearing these Royal Stewart pajamas . . . I think I've seen them in an Eddie Bauer catalog. Anyway, I knelt down and turned her over. Do you have any idea how heavy a dead body can be?"

I winced, but Martha continued on gaily. "I knew she was dead as soon as I saw her face. She had the most ghastly expression, like this . . ." Martha contorted her features into a gnarl of pain. My stomach flip-flopped. Behind Martha, a pelican was gliding on a breeze. I focused on its flight, words drifting into my ears as if from a great distance.

"She was all bloated and had spots of vanilla yogurt splattered over her pajama top. It was horrid."

"I'm sure," I whispered.

"I ran inside and called out, but no one was there. So I called the police."

"You called the police from here?"

"Of course."

The police report had stated that the phone was found off the hook. "Did you hang up afterwards?"

"What an odd question. Do you think I'd leave the phone dangling? That's . . ." Fear crossed her face. "Well, maybe I did leave it off. It's hard to recall. I was under stress, you know. I don't remember what I told the police." She started to back off toward the driveway.

"What time was it when you came by?"

"Time?" Her focus had drifted. Something wasn't right here. "Well, I don't rightly know. In the morning. Early morning. Around seven-thirty."

"But you just said it was too dark to see?"

"It might have been earlier."

"Earlier than seven-thirty?" I tried to keep the disbelief out of my voice.

She checked her petite gold watch. "Why, yes . . ." She was fishing for an answer. "She used to go for a run quite early in the morning. I wanted to join her. Now, you must excuse me, but I have to interrupt our meeting. My manicurist is due in a few minutes. Maybe you can drop by for some tea sometime?" The invitation was more polite than sincere.

"Thanks. Maybe later tonight."

Her eyes widened. "Oh. Not tonight. But soon. I'll give you a ring. It's been very nice chatting with you."

"Same here. I'm sure we'll be speaking again soon."

As soon as her butt wiggled around the bend, I wiped my palms against my pants. The woman had lied through her teeth. I was going to have to find out why.

Chapter 16

When Martha's footsteps faded away, I turned to face the house. Grief, rage and suspicion evaporated like steam from a teacup. My mouth slanted into a grin and I shook my head. "You sure had taste, Mary," I whispered into the gathering wind.

The house had three levels, each one with its own deck and angle. It reminded me of a Rubric's cube with each layer of cubes set at a different position. The shingles were the color of driftwood. There were so many windows, I lost count. Wilting geraniums and impatiens bloomed in clay pots that lined each deck. A faded rainbow flag hung from the top deck, the flag clapping in the breeze like a lone admirer.

I stepped up to the front door. Police tape was crisscrossed over the frame. I ripped it off with unnecessary vehemence. Enough, I thought.

This time I was prepared to hit the wall of stale air, but as I opened the door the sea air followed me in. The foyer smelled like roses and vanilla, with a hint of saltiness. I spun around, disoriented by the lovely scent. On a pale beech table I found the source: a bowl of potpourri.

The foyer opened into a space that reminded me of a New York loft. There were no walls. To my right was a beech frame sofa-bed supporting a futon covered in a peach, flowery fabric. Three matching chairs faced it. In the center was a coffee table consisting of a pale green marble slab on a base of driftwood. Mary was always a sucker for furniture that looked as if it had been built in an arts and crafts shop. Plants were scattered in all four corners, most of them withered now. Hanging from ceiling hooks were six or seven air ferns, all perfectly positioned. The room had windows on all four sides. I was surrounded by a border of trees, bushes, and ocean. It was glorious.

The kitchen was at the back of the house. Every General Electric appliance you could dream of was interspersed among a row of floor-to-ceiling windows. As I shuffled closer, I noticed that the top window panels were open. Beyond them, rose bushes were just beginning to blossom and small yellow and black birds were bouncing on the branches like gymnasts. This is heaven, I thought.

I circled the room like it was a museum, noting every knickknack on each shelf, the magazines scattered on the table, the bowlers and cowboy hats hooked on a wood post at the center of the room, the antique typewriter arranged artfully in a child's red wagon. I knelt down and looked under the handle. Sure enough, there were our initials. We had bought the wagon the summer we rented a house on Fire Island. One night, after hours of playful lovemaking, we pulled out a pen knife and carved our initials onto the wagon. "This is ours forever. RM & MA." I ran my fingers over the ragged edge, and realized my lips were curled in a tight smile.

Near the door leading to the deck was a wicker table. On top was the phone and answering machine. I flipped the lid up and found the answer tape missing. I stared at the machine a few hard seconds and then pressed the memo check button. Mary's deep, sexy voice flowed into the room:

"I'm not here at the moment. The sunset was just too beautiful to resist. Please leave your name and number, as if I didn't know it already, and I'll call you back as soon as the night falls. Look forward to talking with you."

The beep whined into the suddenly chill air. I found myself shivering. This was a special message for a special person. The night she died, Mary was expecting to hear from her lover. All at once, discovering who that person was became incredibly important to me.

I plucked the tape out, slipped it into my

briefcase, and headed toward the spiral staircase near the back of the house.

The second floor was almost exactly like the first with one primary difference. A set of pine stairs on the left-hand wall led upstairs to the third level, which reminded me of a balcony in a theater. A low pine railing ran from wall to wall. The pitched ceiling consisted of honey-colored knotty pine beams.

Apparently, Mary had never got around to fully decorating the second floor. In front of the windows facing the ocean were three pink futon couches forming an open triangle. Against the back wall was an expensive, matte-black stereo system. The only other furniture was a knee-high bookcase off to my right and a simple oak desk positioned just two feet away from the door leading to the deck. I touched the rough grain top of the desk and smiled. Mary's father had owned a used bookstore near the university in Provo and had worked at this desk until three weeks before he died. I was pleased she had kept it.

Outside, the wind had picked up and was moaning around the house. I unlocked the door and stepped outside. I walked to the railing and looked out. The cloud bank had shifted closer to shore and the air had an edge to it. I hugged myself and closed my eyes. The roar of the surf warned me that the storm was a lot closer than it seemed. A shiver of excitement shot through me.

"Come in, you goose!" Mary calls from the doorway of our Fire Island rental house. A salmon-colored summer down quilt is wrapped around her like a cocoon. "It's freezing out there."

I grin at her over my shoulder, my hair whipping against my head. "We could remedy that."

She shuffles onto the deck, a glimpse of her bare shoulders sending a shiver down my spine.

"You are simply glorious." I sigh.

"And you're nuts. You heard the radio. They're expecting a bad storm."

"I know. Isn't it exciting?"

Mary burrows into my arms. I can feel her naked body trembling.

"You are cold."

She lifts her puppy-dog eyes to me and shakes her head. "Not any more." She slips her hands under my robe and clings to me. I kiss her forehead. In the distance, thunder rumbles. "Let's go inside," she says, her firm breasts pressing against me, her lips quivering.

I lock the deck door and turn to find Mary standing on top of the quilt, her arms reaching for me. Together, we float to the floor, and as the storm's fury hits the shore, we soar against each other like birds.

Raindrops pattered against the decking like fingers tapping a table top. I wiped the tears from my cheeks and moved back inside.

According to the clock on Mary's desk it was just after two. I sat down and picked up the phone. There was a smear of lipstick on the mouthpiece. I made certain my lips didn't touch the surface.

"Ms. Chapman, please."

"Can you hold a moment?" her secretary snorted.

There was a short pause and then Cathy was laughing into the phone. "I'll finish the story later," she said to someone apparently leaving her office. "Hello, Cathy Chapman here," she announced in her business voice.

"It's Robin."

"What's taken you so long?" she asked, her tone becoming younger, deeper.

"I collided with one of Mary's neighbors."

"The inimitable Martha Sparks, I assume. I didn't think rich people could be that nosy. I can't tell you how many times we had to shoo her out of the garden like a stray cat."

A suspicion crept into the back of my head. "Were you down her a lot?"

"Often enough. Do you blame me? It's an incredible house."

My breath skipped.

"What's wrong?"

"Were you here the week before Mary died?"

"I don't remember. It may have been the weekend before that. Why?"

I took the plunge. "Were the two of you having an affair?"

The line fell dead.

"Are you there?"

"Yes."

I could hear her breathing into the phone.

"Why are you asking me this?"

"Mary was involved with someone. I need to know who."

"Why?"

I wasn't really sure, but I knew that answer wouldn't suffice. "It's important to me, Cathy. I can't go into all the details."

"We slept together once. More than a year ago.

She didn't like the merchandise," she said, her voice hard and distant. "Do I pass? Was that the right answer? Or did you want me to tell you different?"

"Forget it, okay?" Suddenly, I felt guilty. I was doing it again, letting my doubts and insecurities chase someone away.

"No. Not okay. I'm tired of getting quizzed by you."

"I'm sorry. Can we change the subject?"

"Sure."

"I've decided to spend the night here."

She smothered her voice. "I'll be right with you, Mark. Why don't you go ahead to the conference room."

"I'll call back later," I said.

"Fine." The phone clicked in my ear.

I paced around the room, trying to rid myself of my nagging doubts. But the questions kept needling me. Why did Cathy become so agitated whenever I questioned her? Was she trying to hide something from me? And if so, why? I tried to recall everything I had been told about Mary's mysterious lover. The description could easily apply to Cathy. But the secrecy didn't make sense. Mary was private, but not to the point of hiding her relationships. And how did all of this connect with Carl?

Jackie Dolan. I remembered how her skirt hiked over her knee and the carefree way she dangled her leg under my nose. Bisexuality was certainly not out of the question, and it would explain Mary's secrecy. And it might mean Carl had yet another motive for getting rid of Mary.

The only other possibility was Sam. But then I thought of Mary. Unless she had undergone horrific personality changes since moving out west, I could not imagine her finding Sam's thickly muscular body attractive. I started to dial Patty, then had second thoughts. I had bothered her enough. I pulled out a sheet of paper and made a note to call her later on, after I had finished looking through the house.

The third floor was basically a wide platform overlooking the edge of the bluff. A seagull was perched on the deck rail. We stared at each other like old friends. A futon bed with peach seashell sheets was positioned against the far wall, six or seven pillows in various pastel hues tossed artfully against the headboard. The sheets were slightly rumpled, the outline of a body faintly visible in the shape of the mattress. A book lay open on one side of the bed. A small oak cube served as a night table.

I knelt down and fingered Mary's reading glasses and her watch. How could death be so casual? She must have been getting ready for bed, pulled her glasses off, put the book down, and lumbered downstairs for her cup of yogurt. I knew the ritual well. The bed was still waiting for her. I could almost feel her body heat. I moved my hand over the bed like a magician levitating a body.

All at once, I realized what I was doing and stood up abruptly. Back to earth, Miller.

I walked down the stairs, each step wheezing a little under my feet. The rain was slashing the windows and, strangely, my mood had lightened. I walked over to the stereo and reviewed a rack of CDs, my smile widening with each title. Mary had adopted my rather eclectic musical tastes.

When we first met, she used to tease me about my Mel Torme and Frank Sinatra tapes. Now, there were at least six or seven compact disks by each artist. I selected a Sinatra CD and popped it in. As soon as Frank started crooning about the summer wind, the last knots in my neck unwound.

I was about to turn my attention to the desk when I noticed a row of videotapes with handwritten labels. Mary and I shared a passion for photography, but somewhere along the line her tastes shifted to video while mine stayed with the traditional print format. She drove me crazy with the camcorder, filming me typing, eating, sleeping, and occasionally catching me in more compromising positions.

I scanned the labels: "Thanksgiving '88," "Birthday Party with the Gals," "First Weekend in Heaven: MY NEW HOUSE!" and "Favorite Moments." I picked the last one, popped it into the VCR, pulled over one of the oversized pillows dotting the house, and plopped down with the remote.

The fuzz flickered into row after row of faces, mouths open in song, flashes of purple and turquoise in the background. Mary's voice narrated the scene.

"Gay Pride '88. It reminded me of the March on Washington . . . the camaraderie . . . the unity. This was the first time I had agreed to attend a march in my own city. In the past, friends, lovers have tried to coax me, convince me of the importance of standing up for myself. But I have been afraid of the TV cameras . . . the slack-jawed on-lookers . . . the blue-haired women gasping with shock."

The camera drifted to a group of anti-homosexual protesters, a small group of people whose faces were contorted with anger and fear.

"But this time, I strode up to the gathering throng of cowardly bigots and stared at them . . . with this camera eye and with my own. Hard. Long. And when they faced my own courage and pride, they averted their eyes. I could only hope it was with shame."

I freeze-framed the picture on the screen: a line of marchers screaming "Shame!" at some unseen target, their hands raised in fists, their fingers pointing like rockets ready to explode.

Good for you, Mary, I thought. I could feel myself beaming at the screen. Damn, I wish I had been there.

During the next fifteen minutes of tape, I watched Mary, Patty and Liz saunter through a safari park, Miriam drooling and giggling at lions, Liz and Mary licking cotton candy off their fingers, Patty bent over the baby carriage in hysterical laughter. Spite shot bile into my mouth. How could Mary had been that happy without me?

I fast-forwarded through other scenes of Mary playing guitar for a gathering of unknown friends, stopping only long enough to see if anyone matched the description of her mysterious lover.

At some point, I got up to rummage through my overnight bag for the half-empty bag of Hershey bars. Thus fortified, I returned to the television. By now, the sun had begun to set and the ceiling and walls were tinged orchid pink. I settled myself on the pillow and pressed the play button.

I freeze-framed on a picture of Mary and Sam playing in the lifeguard chair down by Laguna Beach. Sam was wearing cut-off shorts and sleeveless

T-shirt. Mary had on a black and white bikini that didn't leave much to the imagination. Christ! What if Sam was the mystery lover? I pressed the fast-forward button. But there were no more scenes of the two of them together.

During the last few minutes of tape, Mary was sitting crosslegged in front of this very television set, a news program on how the Exxon spill devastated the Alaska shore droning on behind her back. Mary was talking about growing up as a Mormon, her face animated, her hands gesturing. After a few minutes, she cocked her head at an angle. "Your turn," she said, standing up with her customary ease.

The camera wiggled and then swung around to focus on Patty. Mary must have attached the camera to a tripod.

Patty tapped the edge of a ragged nail against her front tooth and then smiled. "Okay," she said with a sly look. She then proceeded into a hilarious monologue of what it meant to be a Mormon during the radical sixties.

She laughed so hard, her eyes began to tear and then unexpectedly she was sobbing, her body heaving with each gasp. "It was so easy to be excommunicated back then. Everyone was doing —" She laughed through her tears. "Sometimes it seemed you could be excommunicated just for watching the Beatles or the Stones. I mean, we were in great company. But then the eighties rolled around, and all of a sudden everyone was returning to the church. I started worrying that my best friends wouldn't be where I was headed. So I got back in the fold . . ."

She smiled into the camera like a Miss America

candidate. "Now I'm heading straight for the pearly gates, Pete and Miriam in my arms." She stared up at Mary through swollen eyes. "Don't you ever worry what will happen to you when you die?"

From off-screen I heard Mary's tight voice. "God, Patty, don't be so morbid. It gives me the willies. Besides, I've got plenty of options. If the Mormons don't want me in their heaven, I'll just knock next door at the Buddhist stronghold."

Patty's jaw dropped in shock. Mary stepped into the picture and tousled her hair. "I'm just joking. Here's what I really think . . . when I die I'm going to be buried. And if I'm *really* lucky, some small part of me — call it soul or energy — is going to surface again in a new baby with pink cheeks, or maybe a wide old oak tree, or a deer or an elephant, and that's more than I could ask for."

The lump in my throat started to choke me. I clicked the set off, the picture of Mary's gently teasing face etched into my memory, and gave myself up to a good twenty minutes of sniveling. Afterwards I curled up on the pillow like a fetus, my muscles limp and my eyelids like lead weights.

I must have dozed for a few hours because when I woke up the house was pitch black except for the blue-gray glow of the television. Rain was lashing the house and the wind moaning. I straightened myself and shuffled to the bathroom. My cheeks were blotchy, my eyes puffy and circled with shadows, and my eyebrows pulled together in worry. Frightening.

I opened the medicine cabinet for aspirin, but the police must have cleaned it out. I settled for a quick shower and a warm robe. I dug through my bag for my pj's, my nose curling at the slightly acrid smell emanating from the bowels of the bag. I balled the contents up and tossed them into the washing machine downstairs. While the contents beat a tin pitter-patter, I dialed Cathy.

"Robin?"

"Good guess."

A sucking sound wafted through the phone.

"Are you smoking?" I asked, puzzled.

"Can you believe it? I haven't smoked since Patty and I broke up."

"Why now?" My face felt hot.

"You. You're driving me nuts. Passion, accusations, accidents . . . I feel like a spinning top."

I was clenching the phone so hard, my knuckles went white. "Cathy, I'm not doing this *to* you. For God's sake, you wanted to be involved. I can't help it that questions come up." My voice was tight with impatience. I could hear her blow out smoke with a tiny whistle.

"You're right. But I don't have to like it." She took a deep breath. "What's happening down there? You miss me?" She shifted gears like a Grand Prix winner.

"Sure," I said, hating the fact that I felt obliged to say yes, that the suspicion still lingered. "The rain's pretty bad down here," I added for no particular reason.

"Have you found anything?"

"Some videotapes. I haven't had time for much else. Right now I'm washing some desperately dirty clothes."

She laughed — an honest, open laugh. I started to cool down.

"Guess what I'm doing?" she asked.

"What?"

"Washing the rest of your clothes. Next time you take a trip, try overpacking."

"Good advice."

"By the way, my phone's been jumping all night. I received calls from your sister Barbara, someone named Dinah, and even Carl Lawrence himself."

"Carl?" I asked, startled.

"He was terribly charming. Made me want to barf."

"What did he say?"

"He said, and I quote, 'Just tell her I've been looking for her.' End quote. Sent chills up my spine."

"Mine, too. What did my sister want?"

"Apparently she just got back from a trip."

"A conference in the Bahamas. It's a hard life."

"She's furious at you. Told me I should say . . . now, let me get this right . . . Robin, you're a 'selfish, ignorant, hard-headed slut' and she's disowning you."

I let loose a belly laugh. "Thanks for the message. It sounds like Barbara. What about Dinah?"

"Dinah was pleased to make my acquaintance, if only by phone. She hopes that you and I will be very happy . . . or else. Oh yes, she also said I should use my feminine wiles to coax you on a plane headed back to New York."

I lifted the lid of the washing machine to pour

some softener over my clothes. I was laughing so hard, I splashed pink gook all over the floor. I ripped off some paper towels and cleaned up the floor. "Sorry about the deluge. But what can I say? I'm a popular gal."

"I've never doubted that. By the way, I spoke to Albert Dassler, the publisher. He was real candid . . ." She paused, and I knew instantly what was coming. "Mary was trying to get McNeil fired. She had documented every single indiscretion committed by McNeil over a three-month period. She had even followed her to bars and noted the number of drinks she had during lunch hours. It was pretty ugly. Albert's planning on hiring a new editor within the next few months. I guess her plan worked. Or almost worked."

I had a sick feeling in my stomach. The thought of Mary maneuvering to destroy McNeil was hard to take. "So McNeil had a legitimate motive," I said disgustedly. "Anything more on Sam and Sharon?"

"If Sam and Mary slept together, she's keeping mum."

"I found a videotape of the two of them cavorting down in Laguna."

"Yeah . . . last summer. A bunch of us went down to the beach for a weekend. If they fooled around that weekend, it's news to me."

"Does she think Sharon could have hurt Mary?"

"No. She was adamant about that. She said Sharon's all bluster, she's gentle as a lamb, a real pussycat. I didn't buy it, but I couldn't get her to say anything different."

I was trying to fit all the pieces together in my head, but they kept falling apart.

"Now let's get to the important stuff. Are you coming back tomorrow?"

"I plan to. Probably late in the day. I still haven't sorted through the desk files."

"All right. I'm looking forward to seeing you . . . and Robin?"

"Yes?"

"I really am sorry about how I acted earlier. It's been so long since I cared about someone that I'm all over the place. Try to be patient, okay?"

I smiled into the phone. "You bet. I'll call you in the morning." I set the phone down with a shrug. There were plenty of suspects without me trying to weave a web of deception around Cathy.

When the washing machine clicked off, I tossed the clothes into the dryer and made my way upstairs. After all these years, the desk still smelled a little bit like used books. I circled the desk. A floorboard bowed under my heel. I bent down. And then I saw that little secret compartment I had almost forgotten about.

On the side of the desk near the floor was a faint rectangular outline, with a fine notch near the top edge. I inserted a fingernail under the lip and tugged. Sure enough, the board lifted up on a hinge no wider than a toothpick. The scent of coffee wafted over me. This was where Mary's father had hidden his secret coffee cache from his wife, caffeine being off limits to strict Mormons.

Inside the compartment was a stack of dog-eared legal pads, a videotape, an envelope marked "photos," and a cassette tape.

I plopped down next to the desk and chuckled for a long time.

Chapter 17

I settled back in front of the television. Almost immediately, the picture focused on an empty street corner. The gutter gleamed like wet coal under the streetlights. A small breeze tossed crumpled papers and an empty Budweiser can around the curb.

Suddenly, a car eased up to the corner. A man in a khaki overcoat stepped out, glancing over his shoulder nervously. For a shocking second he stared right into the camera's eyes. I flinched involuntarily. Carl. He snapped open the hood of his car and started fiddling with some wires. With another furtive turn of his head, he signaled to someone off camera. A few minutes later another man walked over, mumbling under his breath. Carl straightened up with a thick envelope in his hand.

The other man, wearing a maroon leather jacket and jeans so tight you could see the outline of his balls, took the envelope with a laugh. He leaned close to Carl and gently slapped the envelope against his cheek. They stared at each other for a few frozen moments and then the man in the leather jacket nodded, almost imperceptibly.

A gold Mercedes sailed next to Carl's car. A woman stepped out. I recognized her immediately. Selma. She clip-clopped over to the two men on four-inch heels the color of split pea soup. She handed Carl another envelope and immediately slunk back to the car. Carl fingered the envelope warily, his eyes searching the face of the other man — who had to be Spider Rose — with fear and vulnerability. For a split second, he had my sympathy.

Spider pursed his lips, as if he were about to blow a kiss, a hard sparkle in his eyes like the glint of a sharpened knife. He bopped around Carl, his shoulders swinging like a dancer's. Carl whirled around and shouted after him. Spider stopped in his tracks, his body turning instantly rock hard. You could almost see his hairs bristle.

He spat out a reply that made Carl blanch. In the streetlight, his face looked almost ghostly, his skin blue-white. He seemed to be pleading for something. Spider sneered across the street and then said something to Carl that made his face flash red. He started yelling at Spider with an angry desperation. Spider coughed and spat some mucus across Carl's shoe. Then he strode over to the driver's seat of the Mercedes, opened the door, and ducked into the car and screeched away. Carl slumped against the bumper of his car, his head falling into his hands.

The screen went black. I fast-forwarded, but the rest of the tape was empty. Not that I needed any more evidence that Carl had more than enough motive for killing Mary.

But how? That's what I still needed to find out. How did he know that Mary ate yogurt every night, or that she was allergic to penicillin? And how did he get access to this house? My thoughts drifted back to Mary's unknown lover. Maybe Carl had set her up with someone. If not Jackie, maybe one of her friends.

I felt so close to cracking this case, I could taste the victory: sweet, powerful, intoxicating. Shocked at my response, I shook my head and stood up. I wanted to dash out and head back to San Francisco, smash into Carl's house, and tug him out of bed by the hair. I paced the room in tight circles. Calm down, I repeated to myself like a mantra. You have to stay cool. I made myself a cup of coffee, discovered an old frozen muffin that I revived in the microwave, and then climbed back upstairs calm and clearheaded.

I slipped the cassette into the stereo, depressed the "play" button, sipped my coffee and waited. When I heard Mary's voice, my nerve faltered and coffee sloshed over my feet. I wiped it off with a napkin, my ears tingling as I listened to Mary confronting Carl. He laughed as Mary accused him of working with Spider.

"C'mon, kid, this is ridiculous. I'm as clean as they come, you know that." I could almost see him slapping her on the back with a patronizing wink. "Mary, we go back a long time. I've helped you and your paper break more stories than either of us can count. As a matter of fact, I may be one of the best friends this city has."

"You're also one of the biggest shits. I have a videotape of you and Spider making an exchange."

The tape rolled in a hissing silence. Finally, Carl cleared his throat and responded, his voice flat and thin. "I thought we were friends, for God's sake. How could you do this to me?"

"I'm a reporter, Carl. And I have standards. You might remember what that word means."

"It's not what you think. Look, this is a bad time for me to talk. I've got clients in the hallway, an interview scheduled for two o'clock. Why don't you come back later and we'll talk then. Is that okay?"

Mary hesitated. Say no, I muttered to the tape.

"Well . . ."

"Christ . . . I'm not about to skip town. I swear . . . come back later and I'll lay my cards on the table." There was another pause. "Look. You're right. Spider and I do have a connection. We exchange information. But there's some numbers missing in the equation. Come back later and I guarantee you'll see this whole situation in a very different light."

"Okay. Here's my number. Call me when you're ready. Just make it today."

"No problem. And thanks, Mary. For being so fair."

"I just hope I don't end up regretting my generosity."

"Never. See you later."

Again, the rest of the tape was blank.

I heaved a bone-shaking sigh. Damn. What happened in that second conversation, and why didn't Mary tape it? I picked up the stack of notes on the desk and rummaged through them for answers.

After twenty minutes, I was bleary-eyed and frustrated. Nothing new. The only vital piece of information was tucked in the back of the last legal pad. On April 5, slightly more than a week before her death, Mary had written a two-page summary of what she knew about Carl.

Several years ago, Carl had one of his apparently regular encounters with a prostitute. Spider filmed them in action. At first, he used the tape to blackmail Carl for money, but as Carl's career took off they made other arrangements. According to her notes, Carl offered to help Spider's "business" by eliminating his competition. He'd also warn Spider any time the cops were planning to sniff at his door. In exchange, Spider would supply Carl with information about imminent drug deals and prostitution rings.

The deal worked better than either man anticipated. In a few years, Carl's career had taken off like a rocket. When he set his sights on the political arena, Spider was his most enthusiastic supporter. Not only did he keep him posted on the activities of his competitors, but he also started filtering funds to Carl's political coffers through some fairly legitimate business contacts.

Mary's notes were filled with indignation and fury. She had believed in Carl. He was an active supporter of every cause she believed in: fighting crime, assisting the homeless, supporting gay rights, battling drugs, cleaning up the environment. Her disappointment was raw.

On the last page of her notes, dated two days later, she wrote simply, "Get videotape from Carl's office safe. The ass uses his birth date: 9-15-50."

Chapter 18

I checked my watch. It was just after midnight. I hesitated for a split second before dialing Ryan's home number. The same woman who answered the last time picked up the phone. She groggily explained that a cop had been shot near the wharf. Ryan was heading the investigation, which meant he wouldn't be calling home any time soon. I left a message anyway, then tried the station. I gave up after the sixth busy signal.

I couldn't wait for Ryan.

It didn't take me long to figure out what my

next step had to be: breaking into Carl's safe. There was still plenty of time to head back to San Francisco and break into the office. I didn't know how I'd do it, but I didn't let that stop me.

I changed into my jeans, still slightly damp, and black sweatshirt, which felt toasty from the dryer. While my body tried to adjust to the two temperature zones, I packed up a few things. I dumped the videotape, cassette, and notes into the shoe box and sealed it with masking tape from Mary's desk.

I bit the inside of my cheek as I calculated my driving time back to the city. If the rain let up, I'd be able to make it in three or four hours. I nodded, satisfied that the timing would work, then I sat down at the desk to make a quick search through the drawers.

Wedged in the back of the bottom file drawer, behind a musty copy of Webster's, I found a bundle of letters tied with a red ribbon. I didn't have to open the ribbon to know what I had found. Mary had kept all my love letters in the same way.

Sure enough, the envelopes contained sheets of perfumed stationery with ocean scenes. The first thing I did was flip through the letters, looking for a signature. No luck. They were all signed with some sentimental pet name: Teddy Bear, Dynamo, Wild Woman, Tsi-Tsi.

I stared at the handwriting, butterflies bumping against the walls of my stomach. The neat curls and angles looked oddly familiar. I closed my eyes and searched my memory but every time I came near to the image, my mind darted in another direction.

I didn't have time to sit there and play

calligraphy recall games, so I started scanning the words.

Darling, the days I spend without you are like days spent in a cave with no air. I dream of being with you in our glorious bed by the sea, the waves rocking the air the way you rock me with your tongue, your moans.

My cheeks flushed. Jealousy and embarrassment swept over me. I finished reading the letters, then retied them with the ribbon and dropped them in my briefcase.

Outside, the rain was blowing from four directions at once. I flipped up my collar and barreled into my car. With the lights on, the rain looked like silver tinsel. "Great night for a drive," I muttered as I flipped on the wipers and radio. The road was slick and banked in a fog so thick my lights bounced back into my face. My palms were sweating on the wheel. It took me a full three hours to get to Gilroy. By then, the rain had turned into a heavy mist. I put my foot down on the gas.

I parked across from Carl's office at a few minutes past four. I sat watching the building, my heartbeat stamping its imprint against my chest. Now that I was here, I didn't know what the hell to do. I glared at the locked office door for close to two hours, frustration making my blood boil.

Around six, a figure flickered at the end of the block and my antenna shot up. A slim black woman in her twenties was walking down the block with a Walkman plugged into her ears. Her gray raincoat was open and underneath I spotted a crisp, white dress with a small tag pinned above her bosom. She stopped in front of Carl's building and started digging in her bags for keys. I jumped out of the car.

"Excuse me!" I hollered across the street.

The woman flashed a startled look at me and then dug into her bag with a fury. I ran across the street and she lurched against the door, a can of mace in her hand. "Back off or I blind you, bitch!" she shouted.

"Christ, you're good," I said between wheezes.

"You crazy?" she asked, lowering the mace with a puzzled look.

"Look, how would you like to make a quick five hundred dollars?"

She dropped the mace in her bag and shot daggers at me with her eyes. "I'm a cleaning woman, sister, not a whore."

I shook my head. "I didn't mean that." I had to come up with the right lie. "It's my boyfriend. I think he's cheating on me. I need to get into his office and check his files. You got to help me out. I'm desperate."

"Desperation scares me. Find someone else." She singled out a key and unlocked the front door. My teeth were chattering from cold and impatience. I snapped out my wallet and pulled out nearly all of my cash.

"Here," I said, shoving the bills under her nose. "All of this is yours. Just help me out. I swear I'm legit. Please . . ." I mooned at her like a basset hound.

She snatched the money and stared at it, then me, then the money. Back and forth three times. "No man's worth this trouble, honey."

"So you'll help me? I swear to God I won't steal anything. I just want to get up to the tenth floor, check out his office, and slink back out."

"I can't afford to lose my job."

"If that happens, I'll move hell and heaven to get you a new one. All I want is your keys and the dress."

"My dress?" she shouted.

"We can switch clothes in my car. As a matter of fact, I'll even leave you the car keys."

I could see the scales tilting in my direction. She puckered her lips and nodded. "All right. But you get caught and I'll swear you mugged me."

"It's a deal. By the way, what's your name?"

"Sandra."

"Thanks, Sandra."

We shook hands enthusiastically and jogged over to the car. Minutes later, I was stepping out of a supply closet with a mop and pail, my short hair tucked into a white handkerchief. I meandered up to Carl's office with studied casualness. It took me a few seconds to realize I was humming the tune to Michael Jackson's "Bad."

I paused in front of his door, my ears set on radar. Convinced I was alone, I pulled out Sandra's keys, unlocked the door, and pushed against it with my hip. It whined open. I clenched my teeth, the hairs of my arms standing up like porcupine quills.

A dull light shone from underneath the crack of the inner door. My heart thumped. I started to back out of the office but just then I heard the elevator down the hall thudding to a stop. Damn. I closed the door behind my back, my skin sizzling with nerves.

Footsteps approached in the hall. I spun around, the mop angled at the door like a spear. Just a few feet away, someone stopped in a fierce coughing fit. He sounded old, sickly. He stamped his feet and then started to move away. I didn't move for a full five minutes. Finally, I lowered the mop with a sigh. Fine weapon, I thought. I could just see the headlines: Woman Fights Off Attacker With Dirty Mop.

I leaned the mop against the wall, tiptoed to the second door, and pressed my ear against the cold metal. Nothing. I slowly turned the knob.

A small banker's lamp on the desk threw a pool of yellow light around the room. I glanced at my watch. I had already wasted fifteen minutes, more time than I had to spare. I surveyed the room, looking for a safe. I had watched enough television to assume that it might be hidden underneath the paintings hung on the wall. I circled the room with a cocky air, tugging at the corner of each frame. They were bolted to the wall. So much for the years of *Columbo*.

I stared into the dark corners, my thoughts moving at break-neck speed. All of a sudden, my eyes settled on the file cabinets, and I half grinned. Why not?

I opened the file door and swept the files to one side. Sure enough, at the back of the cabinet was a cut-out square — and beyond that, a safe door. Now, let's hope Mary was right about the numbers, I thought. I leaned in and spun the dial. 9-15-50.

The tumblers clicked into place. I reached in and slipped out two videotapes. I walked back to the desk and held them under the light.

All at once, the door swung open. My head snapped up. I recognized the silhouette immediately.

Chapter 19

"You're an idiot, Miller." His voice was a monotone, empty even of threat. There was a letter opener on the corner of the desk, hidden in shadow. I slipped it into my hand and moved out of the light. "I guess we need to have another talk," he said, dead calm.

He flipped on the light switch. I blinked my eyes.

"Sit down." He gestured at one of the thickly cushioned chairs in front of his desk. I shook my head and edged my way to the door.

"I said sit. Or would you rather I call the

security guard down the hall? It might be amusing to hear how you'd explain that ludicrous outfit to the police."

Breaking and entering is not something I'd like on my permanent record. I sat down on the edge of the chair, the letter opener digging into my palm. He shuffled some papers on his desk casually. Then he looked at me with dead eyes. "Why don't you hand me the letter opener?"

For a split second, I thought about slicing it across his face and running. "I think I'll hang onto it for a while longer. You want to talk? Fine. I'm listening."

He narrowed his eyes. "How'd you know about the videotapes?"

"Sheer luck."

His nostrils flared. "You're not that lucky, Miller." He rounded the desk, loosening his tie with one hand. "Do you know what's on them?"

I stood up, rage making the muscles in my arm ripple like electric cables. "I know your whole fucking career has been built on the back of one sleazebag pimp."

"How self-righteous," he spat. "As if fucking prostitutes is any more deviant than what you do."

The letter opener was burning a hole in my hand. "It's a lot different, Carl, but I don't expect you to understand. But maybe you'll understand this . . ." I stretched my body taut, my lips inches away from his freshly shaven chin. "The police are going to be all over your back by this afternoon. And I'm going to be sitting on the side laughing my head off."

He walked around the desk, a spark of amused

interest flaring in his eyes. He sat down and steepled his hands in front of him as if he were posing for a political ad. "You're very naive. It's almost touching. You think you can skewer me because of a few careless moments. You obviously don't realize how powerful I am."

I leaned over the desk, my breath steaming. "And you don't realize the power of the press. What do you think this city's going to do when they find out you killed a woman?"

Surprise flickered over his face. "What are you talking about?" His voice had lost its smooth tones.

"I know you killed Mary, and I'm going to make sure you rot in jail for it."

He stood up and snarled into my face. "What the fuck are you talking about? Mary's death was an accident."

"Bullshit. You killed her and I have the proof."

He cut around the desk and clutched my shoulders. I pointed the letter opener at his gut, ready to smash into him at the first wrong move. "Back off," I said quietly.

He dropped his hands and took a step backwards. "You're off base, Miller." His face looked drawn. "I may have some unsavory friends, but I am not a murderer. That is way out of my league."

"Then you had Rose arrange it for you."

He cocked his head at me, a question in his eyes. Then he laughed. "Whew. You had me worried for a while. But you're just shooting blind." He switched off his desk lamp. "Look, I'm not saying her death wasn't convenient. It was. But I didn't do it." He picked up the videotapes from the desk and walked over to a half circle of chairs in the corner of the room. "Come on, have a seat over here," he said, suddenly congenial. He opened a wall panel, revealing a sophisticated entertainment system and a small wet bar.

I sidled over to the seating area, my eyes riveted to his hands. He poured himself a shot of Chivas and then inserted one of the tapes into the VCR. "You're right about Mary knowing about me and Spider Rose. But we had a deal."

The videotape started to roll in silence. Carl pumped up the volume, his eyes gleaming with contentment. "The bitch — excuse me, Mary — made me make a taped confession."

In the videotape, Carl was sitting in a cream-colored swivel chair in a room that I remembered instantly as Mary's city apartment. "Are you ready now?" he sneered into the camera. Off camera, Mary muttered yes, her voice thin with disgust. Carl looked up at the camera with an impish grin. He flipped a sheet of paper out from his pocket and started to read in a schoolboy's voice. "First of all, this confession is not made under duress." He laughed. "And if you believe that —"

Mary's voice broke in. "Carl! You want to play around, fine. We can forget all this and just let the pieces fall where they may." Her voice had an edge to it I didn't recognize.

"Your ex was a hard one," Carl commented to me.

In the videotape, Carl proceeded to read his confession, admitting to an allegiance with Spider Rose that went back almost eight years. At the end of the tape, he looked up with moist eyes and smiled. "In exchange for Mary's generosity in not reporting this story, I have agreed to cut my ties with the past and start anew. From now on, I will refrain from any contact with Mr. Rose, whose threats over the years have led to much misconduct on my part . . . misconduct I deeply regret."

He stared into the camera soulfully for another second or so, and then stood up abruptly. "Now let me get the fuck out of here," he blurted off camera.

Carl ejected the tape and then emptied his glass in one gulp. "So you see, Mary was no longer a threat to me. And neither are you." Carl poured himself another shot then raised it to me as if in a toast. Apparently, he was quite pleased with his taped performance.

"Why'd you agree to make the tape?"

"It was the only way to make sure she'd keep her mouth shut."

I sauntered up to him and stared into his face. "Mary wouldn't make a deal like that."

He threw back his head and laughed. "I was waiting for that. God, this is fun." He spun around and popped in the second tape. "See, I had something on Mary as well. We both agreed to keep quiet under certain conditions." He stepped back to give me a full view of the screen. "It seems that one day Mary and a friend of hers got so hot and bothered they checked into a hotel not far from here."

The camera focused on a queen-sized bed. Off-screen a door slammed and I could hear two women giggling. I closed my eyes. Carl's hand clamped down on the back of my neck, his fingers digging into my tendons. "Come on. Don't get squeamish now. This is the good part."

I jabbed the letter opener into his thigh. "Touch me like that again and I'll cut out your fucking eye!" My blood was pounding in my ears.

Carl blanched, rubbing his thigh. "Firecat," he said, his eyes boring into mine. And then the gleam shifted. His eyes snapped to the television screen. I followed his gaze. Mary had moved into the picture. She was wearing a white linen suit, her skin flushed, her eyes flashing. "This is nuts," she tittered.

"I can't wait any more, Mary. I need you now." The voice sounded familiar, but I couldn't concentrate. Heat rose to my head. I felt almost faint. I sat down and breathed through my mouth.

"This is the dull part," Carl said. He pressed fast forward. "Ah, this is it."

Mary was bending between the other woman's legs, her head bobbing up and down, her naked back filling the screen. I shot up and slapped Carl out of the way. I picked up the bottle of Chivas and smashed it through the screen, then I whirled around and stuck the broken edge of the bottle under his chin. "I could kill you and not even blink." My lips were quivering with fury.

Carl glowered at me.

All of a sudden, the door burst open. An old man in a security guard uniform stood there, a gun shaking in his hands. "Trouble, Mr. Lawrence?" he asked, his voice quaking.

I lowered my arm and tossed the broken bottle on the chair behind me.

"No problem here, Roger," Carl said, his eyes riveted to mine. "But why don't you just wait outside for a bit."

"Sure thing, Mr. Lawrence." He backed out of the room, his face red. He's probably about to go into cardiac arrest, I thought.

"Let's try to be calm about this," Carl said, gloating over my rage.

"Sure." I whipped the kerchief off my head and stuffed it into my pocket, along with the letter opener . . . just in case. "I'll be calm when you're in jail . . . now if you'll excuse me." I stormed toward the door. Carl cut me off.

"I'm not done. I got that tape from Spider Rose. Mary had been fool enough to pick one of his hotels for her rendezvous." He shook his head at the joke.

My anger started percolating again. I had to get out of there before I did something that would land me in jail.

"I borrow tapes from him on occasion, for a bit of amusement. You can imagine my delight when I got this gem."

"Carl, I'm warning you . . . let me out now." The words fell from my mouth like burning wood.

"Just one more minute. I got that tape a full month before Mary approached me with her information. It ended up being my bargaining chip. We checkmated each other. She was supposed to keep the taped confession and I was supposed to keep this . . ." He tilted his head toward the smashed screen. "Under wraps. Except I loaded the dice. I had an old client break into her apartment and steal the tape. So I was sitting pretty. In other words, although I was pissed enough to kill her . . . I didn't. I had no reason to."

He paused. "And, by the way, neither did Rose. He didn't give two shits about saving my ass. That's another reason I was willing to bargain with Mary. And I would have kept my side of the deal too, if she hadn't died." He was gritting his teeth now. "Now, I've got another trump card. This one's good enough to stop you."

He blew sour-whiskey breath over me. "You open your mouth, and your career is over. I'll make damn sure every paper and every news program in this country announces the fact that Laurel Carter is a dyke. Do you understand me?"

"Are you blackmailing me?"

"No, honey, I'm asking you on a date."

I put a quiver into my voice. "You wouldn't really do that to me, would you? That's my whole life. What would I do if you exposed me?"

His face contorted into an ugly grin. "Starve."

I looked down at his feet and nodded. My shoulders slumped with defeat. "Okay, Carl. You win."

He lifted my chin with his hand, a move he had made the night we had dinner at Gaylord's. I tried to deaden my eyes.

"Don't be too upset, huh? I really am a good politician. Wait till I'm mayor. I'll impress the shit out of you."

I recoiled and broke away. "Go fuck yourself."

I stamped out of the office, remembering to wink at the security guard on my way out.

When I got downstairs, I found Sandra pacing around my car angrily. I ran across the street and started apologizing.

"Forget 'I'm sorry.' What happened up there?

You're as red as a beet. And you smell like a goddamned drunk."

"It's too long a story. Let me get out of these clothes."

It was about 7:35 a.m., and the streets were just coming alive — which meant changing in the car was out of the question. I grabbed some items from the car and then we ducked into a 24-hour coffee shop around the corner and switched clothes.

"Great. I go to work in this and I'll be fired for boozing," Sandra wailed. Her dress, which had been as crisp and sterile as a nurse's, now had whiskey stains all over the front and dirty gray stripes from where I had slapped my hip with the mop.

"Then don't go to work," I said wearily. "Here's a check for another two hundred dollars. If you get any grief, call me at this number." I gave her my publisher's number in New York. I slopped water onto my face from the bathroom faucet, my eyes focusing on copper-green rust circling the drain cover.

"Shit. You look worse than me," Sandra said with a smile. "Did you at least find what you wanted?"

I lifted my head and shook it like a wet dog. "I guess so."

We stepped outside, sat down at the counter, and shared a cup of coffee and an assortment of high-cholesterol breakfast foods — my treat. Afterwards, Sandra headed home and I jogged back to my car with purpose.

It was close to nine when I pulled into Cathy's driveway. She was gone already, which was fine with

263

me. My head was spinning and my stitches itching. I crept upstairs and ran a bath, spilling in half a bottle of lemon bath salts. I stripped in the bathroom, balling my clothes up and kicking them out of the room like a football.

The bath felt glorious. I closed my eyes and let my head sink below the water line, the warm water flowing into my ears. I drowsily remembered that I wasn't supposed to get my stitches wet and lazily adjusted my leg so that the wounded knee popped out of the water. The sound of my heel against the floor of the tub sounded like a car screeching to a stop. I lifted my head and breathed deeply.

I had come to a dead end. Carl was guilty of a lot of things, but not Mary's death. His argument was just too convincing. I also doubted that Spider Rose had dirtied his hands to save Carl's reputation. The only other possible suspect related to Carl was Jackie. And that didn't make much sense either. Unless she was the other woman in the videotape, the woman who was so horny she dragged Mary into some sleazebag hotel. The videotape images came back to me in haunting detail. I shook the picture of Mary's naked back from my mind.

Maybe Carl had asked Jackie to seduce Mary and bring her to the hotel so he could arrange for the videotape. But why would they then kill her?

Think straight, I urged myself. The pieces have to fit somehow. I kept reviewing the equation in my head, but each time the numbers didn't add up. The only way Mary could have been convinced to hop into a cheap hotel was if she was crazy in love with someone, the way we had been at the beginning. And Jackie just didn't make the grade. I doubted she could mask her bitchiness long enough to fool Mary. Besides, the other woman's passion had sounded real, urgent. Desperate.

My thoughts zeroed in on the mystery woman.

I jumped out of the tub, soapy water gurgling over the side. I towel-dried myself and scurried down the hall. I threw some clothes on and then sat down at Cathy's desk to reread Mary's love letters. Maybe I had missed something the first time.

I smacked my lips in distaste and started from the beginning. Almost all the letters were the same, describing the wonder of their lovemaking, their secret tumbling in the garden, their midnight phone calls. Nothing indicated her identity. I tossed them aside in disgust.

The only people who seemed to know about Mary's lover were Liz and Martha Sparks. That seemed odd in itself. From Martha's description, the lover must have looked enough like Mary to have passed for her in the clinic and pharmacy. And she would have undoubtedly known about Mary's allergies and her ritual of eating yogurt before going to bed.

If the lover was innocent, why hadn't she come forward after Mary's death? If they had kept their relationship quiet simply for the sake of privacy, then she had no reason for staying anonymous once Mary died. Unless she had something to hide. I grabbed my address book, looked up Liz's home number, and dialed feverishly.

She sounded sleepy, and I waited for what felt like hours before she left her bed and picked up the extension. "Hi. What's up?"

"Were you at Mary's funeral?"

"Of course," she said, offended.

"Who else was there?"

"Christ, Robin, how would I know? I was sobbing my eyes out half the time. If Candice Bergen, Jamie Lee Curtis, and Elizabeth Taylor had been sitting in front of me, I wouldn't have noticed."

I laughed despite myself. "Come on. Not even Candice Bergen?"

"Well, maybe I'm exaggerating."

"Look, Liz, it's important. Was there any woman there you didn't know?"

"Absolutely not. I am personally familiar with every straight and gay woman in the San Francisco Bay area. Robin, be sensible. She had friends from the paper I had never met, relatives from Utah, neighbors from her building. Maybe I knew five or six people, at most."

"Who were they?"

"Me and my mouth," she groaned good-naturedly. "Okay, there was me, Patty and Pete, Cathy, Sam and Sharon McNeil . . ."

"McNeil was there? Mary's editor?"

"Yeah, why?"

"People don't usually attend their enemy's funeral."

"Depends on how sick you are."

Exactly. "Anyone else?"

"Let me see. Her friend Pam from the newspaper . . . she sells ad space, then there was . . ."

I cut her off. "What does Pam look like?"

"Not your type, I'm afraid. Very straight. Kinky

266

hair, lots of jewelry. Cellulite on her knees. *And* she's a whiner. Other than that, she's a great gal."

"Is that it?"

"Nothing like being drilled early in the morning. Let me see . . . well I guess there were others that looked familiar, but I can't think of their names."

"Think, dammit."

"Whoa. What do you think I'm doing . . . shaving my legs?"

"Sorry." I felt properly chastised. "Look, you know this mystery lover you told me about?"

"Yeah?"

"I'm starting to think she may have had something to do with Mary's death."

"What happened to Carl Lawrence?"

"That theory didn't pan out."

"Sorry to hear that."

"Did anyone seem especially sullen? Self-absorbed?"

"Now you're getting crazy on me again. I was grieving, remember?"

I felt a pang of embarrassment. "Sorry, Liz. I'm just grasping for straws."

"It's okay. If I remember anything else, I'll call you."

"Thanks." I slam-dunked the phone. Christ. What if this was another wild goose chase? I had a frightening image of me still running around in circles three years down the line. Just like Ryan, I realized suddenly. My heart sank.

When I left the house, I had on April-fresh

chinos and an ironed polo, all thanks to Cathy. I
stopped for gas and a bottle of Yoo-Hoo. I needed
the energy. Then I drove over to the police station.
Reporters were swarming the front steps. I barreled
through them, hoping to find Ryan in his office.

He frowned dramatically as soon as he spied me
down the hall. "Not now, Miller."

"It's important." I wagged a large manila
envelope in front of his bulbous nose. "One minute.
That's all I'm asking."

He stretched his neck and checked out the scene
at the front door. There were so many flashes going
off, the hallway looked like there was a strobe light
going full speed.

"For chrissake." Ryan tugged me into his office.
"I got a good cop with a bullet in his lung, and the
damn city's breathing down my neck. You got five
seconds. Make it good."

"I got the dirt on Carl. It's all in there. Mary's
notes, a videotape, a cassette. Everything you need."

"Did he kill her?"

"Doesn't look that way."

Our eyes met. "Sorry." He put the envelope down
on the desk and started leading me out. "Don't give
up yet. When this is over —"

"Two more questions . . ."

He glanced down the hall. Someone had managed
to get the press outside the building. "Okay, but
fast."

"There was a tape missing from Mary's answering
machine down in Big Sur. Do you have it?"

"No." He rolled his head to one side and cracked
his neck. "We never found it. Since her death was
ruled an accident, we let it go. When you're in the

business as long as me, you expect a few loose ends. I'm not saying that's right, but it happens. Next question."

"When was Mary's body found?"

"You're a royal pain in the ass." He crossed his desk, checked the file. "Around eight-twenty a.m. The neighbor called the local station about fifteen minutes later."

I nodded to myself. "Did she say where she called from?"

He flipped through some pages. "According to these notes, she ran back up to her house and called from there. Why?"

"She told me a different story."

He raised his eyebrows. "So she's lying." He drummed his fingers on the desk. "Doesn't mean she's the killer. But she's hiding something." He almost smiled. "I'd say it was time for another visit."

"Yeah, that's what I thought too."

His face stiffened. We stared at each other for a moment. Finally, he broke the silence. "I won't be able to take care of this for a while . . ."

His eyes told me he knew I wouldn't wait that long.

Chapter 20

Sam stiffened when she saw me exit the elevator. I gathered that my interest in Sharon had soured her taste for me. I pointed at the door leading to Mary's old office. "Do you mind? I'm looking for Cathy."

"Wrong place to look. She just went down to the lobby for a coffee."

I pushed the Down button by the elevator. "Thanks. Look, I know she talked to you about Sharon . . ."

"Sharon didn't do anything."

I leaned over the desk. "I know how important she is to you . . ."

"Don't pull that 'best friend' bit with me." She crossed her arms over her chest.

"I'm not pulling anything. I'm just trying to find the truth. I think we all owe that to Mary."

For a moment, she reminded me of Ryan, her eyes revealing the battle between her need to be tough and her desire to be fair. Finally, she shrugged.

"If you have anything else to tell me, you can call me at Mary's house in Big Sur." I wrote down the number, handed her the slip, and jumped into the elevator.

"Maybe you should check out McNeil . . ." she yelled suddenly.

I jammed my hand against the elevator door. "What?"

"McNeil's on vacation in Big Sur. Probably drying out again. Why don't you try questioning her? If you're looking for suspects, she's a prime candidate. She had motive . . . and she had opportunity."

"How do you know?"

"A package came for her the Friday before Mary died. Her secretary had to overnight it to her in Big Sur." She paused for effect. "She was down there the night Mary died."

Her tone made it clear that she thought she'd be a lot better at investigating than I was. Maybe she was right. I let the elevator door close before she could read the doubt in my face.

When I got downstairs, Cathy was just paying for her coffee. "Hey, stranger."

She turned to me, startled. Then she broke into

a 200-watt grin. She swept over to me and took me in her arms. "What are you doing here?" She kissed me and then held me at arm's length. "You look awful. Have you slept?"

I tried to remember. "I don't think so."

"Then get out of here. Come on," she said, shooing me out of the office building with her free hand.

"Stop, Cathy. We need to talk."

"Not again." Her face changed tone the way the sky does when a storm blows in. "What do you want to know now? Did I kill my mother? No. Do I rob banks in my spare time? No again."

"Do you know who Mary was sleeping with when she died?"

Color drained from her face and she looked away. "We did this one before. Mary and I slept together once. Period."

"That wasn't the question."

Her eyes focused on me, a dark glint sending shivers down my spine. "Do you still think it was me?"

I hesitated. "I'm not sure what to think."

"Then I guess you're on your own." She spun around on her heel and tapped away.

I got back in the car and drove around for a half hour, reviewing every detail of the case I could remember. After a while, I started passing red lights and threatening innocent bystanders. It was then I decided that sleep was my first priority. I drove to Cathy's house, feeling like an intruder as I slunk up the stairs and crawled into bed.

A neighbor down the street was mowing his

lawn. Great. So much for my nap. It was the last thought I had. I woke up five hours later, my disposition greatly improved. I skipped downstairs and made myself a cheese sandwich with extra mayo. My arteries were probably caked with the stuff. I bit into the sandwich and headed upstairs to Cathy's office.

My notes were scattered over her desk. For a fleeting moment, I considered shredding them into confetti. Then I sat down and read them for the hundredth time. After a while, my eyes started to blur. Time for a break.

I picked up the phone and dialed Patty. "Patty, it's Robin. I know I've been a pest, but it's paid off."

"How?" She sounded anxious.

"I got Lawrence. Mary had one hell of a case against him . . . a pimp's been financing his career. You'll probably hear about it on the news."

"What a relief."

"He's not the murderer."

Her voice faltered. "What do you mean? You sounded so sure."

"It just didn't add up, that's all."

"So you're back to square one?" Miriam was wailing in the background. "That's awful." The fatigue in her voice was almost palpable. "Can you hold on? Miriam has a cold and she won't stop crying."

I closed my eyes while I waited for her to return. It must be great to be a baby, someone waiting on you hand and foot.

"So where do you go from here?"

I went over my list of suspects, with Cathy's

name tactfully omitted. "I think Martha Sparks is hiding something. Matter of fact, I'm driving down there today to talk to her."

Patty made a cooing sound to Miriam. "Well, look, I really have to go. Call me as soon as you know something, okay?"

I went into the bedroom to pack my bag for my trip back down to Big Sur. This time, I was going to sleep over. A full night of sleep. By 5:20 I was locking the front door. Cathy had just pulled into the driveway.

"Leaving so soon?" She stretched her long legs. A pang of regret thumped against my stomach wall.

"I'm headed down to Big Sur."

Cathy locked the car door, her back as erect as a telephone pole. "Were you planning on calling me?" she asked over her shoulder, her voice fiercely casual.

"I left you a note."

She turned and sneered at me. "How kind."

My temples tightened with impatience. "This isn't a kiss-off. I just need to take care of this business."

She crossed her arms over her chest, tapping one high-heeled foot like a crazed woodpecker. "Even though I may have killed Mary. Or is this some kind of set-up?"

"Christ, Cathy, I haven't accused you!"

"You've come pretty close. What happened to all your evidence against Carl? Or am I just a more appealing suspect?"

The conversation was setting my teeth on edge. "Carl's still in the picture," I lied, surprising myself. "But there's another lead I have to follow."

She lowered her eyes and nodded, her lips

pursed. "Why don't you want me to come tonight?" she asked petulantly.

"Do you want to come? Fine. How fast can you get ready?" I practically spat the words.

She raised her eyes and we stared at each other. We could have started a fire. "I have a premiere to attend tonight," she said. "I can't miss it. As it is, I'm in trouble with my editor. He says I've been 'preoccupied' the last few weeks. What an understatement."

She swept past me and unlocked the door to her house. "This is not an auspicious beginning to our relationship," she said with a dramatic snap of her head. The door slammed in my face.

Fine. I stormed into the car and pulled away at fifty miles per, the smell of burnt rubber trailing me for blocks.

* * * * *

The sun was angled over the water by the time I pulled up to the house in Big Sur. The normally gray shingles glimmered pale lilac in the fading sunlight. The air was crisp and cool, the fog rolling in like loose strands of pink cotton candy. I climbed out of the car and grabbed my overnight bag, briefcase, and a bag of groceries from the back seat.

I unlocked the door with a sense of coming home. How odd. The house seemed so familiar, so comfortable to me. I strolled over to the refrigerator and unpacked the groceries. Nothing elaborate. A Swanson TV dinner, two apples, a quart of milk, a six-pack of Yoo-Hoo, a box of Ritz crackers, peanut butter, a loaf of bread, a carton of eggs, and a pint of French vanilla ice cream — the kind with the black specks. I'm a firm believer that there's nothing like a well-stocked refrigerator to make you feel safe.

I popped the frozen dinner into the microwave and changed into my sweatpants while fried chicken molecules flipped magnetic orientation right before my eyes. Modern technology astounds me. I tugged my sneakers on just as the buzzer rang.

I tossed the plastic tray onto a real plate to alleviate my shame at eating frozen food and then dug into my meal with gusto. For a moment or two, I felt like Henry the VIII, tearing skin off a drumstick with my front teeth. I finished the dinner in less time than the microwave took to zap it. If my metabolism wasn't on fast-forward, I probably wouldn't fit through the front door.

I wiped my hands on a paper towel, dumped the remains of dinner into the empty grocery bag, and looked up Martha Sparks' phone number. She was just finishing dinner when I called. Her reaction to my suggestion that I stop over for a chat was less than enthusiastic — that is, until I mentioned selling the house. She quickly asked me to drop by around ten. I checked my watch. I had about an hour to kill.

The sun had already set, but the western sky was still glowing: a thin strip of melon, a wide band of pale green, and a spectrum of blues that faded into navy behind the house. The only sounds were the cry of seagulls and the crash of the waves beyond the bluff. I decided to go for a quick run to clear my head.

I jogged off to the right of the house, the ground rutted and sloping toward the sea. My knee was throbbing, but the sea air felt delicious against my face. I slowed my pace and narrowed my eyes to see better in the approaching dark. Within a few minutes I hit a tangled fence. There was a mossy boulder near a torn section. I crawled around it and slipped through. It was getting too dark to see clearly, but it didn't take long to find a moldy sign on a spindly stake. Mary's house abutted a nature reserve.

I wasn't crazy about the idea of getting lost in a thick pine forest with the growl of raccoons and the stink of skunks stalking me. After all, I am a city kid. I backtracked to the broken stretch of fence, chased by swirls of fog.

Just as I was about to squeeze through, a deer appeared in the deep shadows of a cypress. Her fur was golden brown with white markings and her eyes jet black, the color of the sea on a night without stars. But then, all of a sudden, there was a spark deep within her gaze. It caught my vision and held.

After endless seconds, she lifted one leg and held it aloft, her eyes reaching into mine, and then she stamped it once, her ears flared in my direction. I sat down on the cold, wet ground, damp moss squishing between my fingers. Eye to eye, we stared at each other till I felt the color draining from my skin.

With unexpected power and grace, she leapt away and bounded into the forest. In an instant, she had disappeared.

I stood up, my legs wobbling beneath me, and traced my way back to the house on pure instinct, my eyes still seeing the spark in her eyes, my skin still goosebumped. The inside of the house had an eerie cobalt blue glow. I ranged through, flipping on every light switch I could find. The encounter in the woods had spooked me beyond reason. I felt as if there were a message in the deer's unwavering gaze, and I wasn't sure I wanted to be the recipient.

*　*　*　*　*

Martha's "sitting room," as she dubbed it, was disturbingly tasteful. Scattered throughout were delicate crystal vases holding miniature rosebuds almost too perfect to be real. Antique chairs and tables were arranged in discrete "conversation circles" set off by coordinating Chinese rugs. The tassels looked combed.

Martha directed me to a Queen Anne's chair upholstered in ornate Oriental fabric. I sat down and was surprised to find that my feet barely reached the ground. Martha eased into a nearby settee, a small smile letting me know she had noted my discomfort.

Between us stood an elaborately carved mahogany table with the kind of silver tea service I associate with old English films. A hand-painted porcelain bowl held a variety of unblemished fruit, beaded with moisture. It was like being transported into a still life painting. I started to squirm.

"I am delighted you decided to drop by," she beamed at me. "My husband is away on business, but I can certainly discuss preliminary bids on the house. Have you met with a real estate agent yet?"

"No."

"Well, you really should. We fully intend to offer you a competitive price —"

"When did you find Mary's body?"

Dumbstruck, she stared at me in incomprehension. Then her face tightened in distaste. "It was my understanding that you wanted to discuss the sale of your house."

"Maybe another time. Right now, I want to know why you lied."

"I did no such thing." She stood up and straightened her skirt. "When you are ready to discuss business, I will be more than —"

"A friend of mine double-checked the case files. According to the police records, you found the body after eight in the morning. But you told me it was so dark you could barely make out what was lying in the doorway. You also said you ran inside to call the police . . . but the records say you called from here." I stared up at her. "So what's the truth?"

"I didn't tell you it was dark," she blurted out defensively.

"I know what I heard."

"So I made a mistake. Big deal."

"It is now. The police are reopening the case . . . and a mistake like that might interest them. Do you see what I'm saying?"

She sat down and poured herself a slow stream of tea. "All I know is that I reported her death in a timely fashion. And I would hardly call poor memory a crime." Her voice was thin, controlled, and an octave too high. She was lying through her teeth. And scared that I knew it.

"Let's try this again. When did you arrive at Mary's house?"

"I have no intention of answering your question." She spooned sugar into her tea with the precision of a chemist.

"Well then, you leave me no choice." I stood up abruptly. "May I use your phone?"

"Whatever for?" She suddenly looked more alert.

"To call the police, of course. If you won't cooperate with me . . ."

She tapped the spoon on the edge of the cup harder than she had anticipated. A small splash of tea landed on the rug. She swore under her breath. Then she closed her eyes and sighed. "Perhaps you should sit down."

I did. On the settee next to her.

"I will tell you exactly what happened . . . under one condition. I don't want you talking to the police about me." She studied my face for acquiescence. I kept silent.

"For heaven's sake, I didn't kill the woman. You want the truth? I found Mary on Saturday night. A little before eight. She was already dead by then, but her body was still quite warm. It was rather astonishing —"

"You left her there all night?" I jumped.

She glared at me. "May I proceed?" She waited for me to ease back into my seat. "I ran into the house to call the police. I even picked up the phone . . . but when I saw the answering machine, I panicked. I had called earlier in the day and left a . . . rather unpleasant message. About her . . . friend. The woman had been there the previous night and when I stopped by to check the house, she had practically attacked me —"

"Physically?"

"Well, no. But she wouldn't open the door, and she called me all sorts of horrible names. So I left a message telling Mary that she and . . ." She was selecting her words with such excruciating care that her upper lip curled with the effort. "That woman . . . were not . . . welcome in this neighborhood. But I was not that polite." She leaned over and rubbed her index finger into the spot where the tea had splashed, a pained expression on her face. "I was afraid the police would misinterpret the message. Perhaps suspect that I had something to do with her death. So I ejected the tape and came home."

Angry and exhausted, I rubbed a hand over my face. "Is that it?" I asked, exasperated.

"Don't look at me like that! I am not devoid of feeling. As a matter of fact, I couldn't sleep at all that night. The very next morning I called the police."

I stood up, towering over her. "I want the tape."

"I destroyed it."

I startled myself by slapping the back of my hand across the teapot. Martha gasped. The teapot landed upside down on the edge of the rug. She watched the tea soak into the weave with thin-lipped horror. "My God! Look what you've done —"

"You left a woman dying in her doorway —"

"She was dead — she must have been . . ."

Shock coursed through me. "You said you felt for a pulse!"

"I did! The next morning —"

"Christ." Blood was pounding in my ears. I strode across the room, fury making my hands shake. "She could have still been alive . . ."

"She looked dead . . ."

I spun around, my eyes settling on her with disgust. "Were there other messages on the tape?"

"Heavens . . . how can I remember?" She scampered to the teapot and lifted it off the rug like it was a torn off limb from a child. "This is just awful."

I stood behind her, my voice threatening. "Were there other messages? You have one minute to remember. One."

She plopped down on the rug and stared up at me with unexpected vulnerability. "I don't remember." Fear crossed her face. "Do you really think she was still alive? I never —" She stood up suddenly. "There were three messages. One from someone at the newspaper. A woman. Very agitated." She was walking in ragged circles, wringing her hands. "I can't remember what she said." She stopped, her eyes squeezed tight in concentration. "Oh . . . I can't recall."

She opened her eyes. "There was another message, from a friend whose wife was drinking too much. And a third message. That was the most peculiar. There was music playing and a woman screaming obscenities in the distance. It may have just been one of those things adolescents do for fun . . . I mean, they never even said Mary's name."

"Do you remember what the message said?"

She blanched. "Think of every four-letter word you know and you'll be close."

"Did you recognize any of the voices?"

"I didn't make a habit of listening to Mary's messages," she answered wearily. "Now, I've answered your questions and you may have destroyed a valuable Oriental rug. I think our business is through."

I realized I had pushed her — and myself — as far as I could. "Let's just say it's over . . . for tonight."

Her eyes burned through me as I backed out of the room.

* * * * *

I sat down on the back steps and breathed in the damp night air. I was still not convinced that Martha had told me the whole truth, but I had already gathered more information than I could digest. I needed some time to clear my head.

After about fifteen minutes, I slumped upstairs, punched the stereo "on" button and dropped in a big band CD. Better. The bright, brassy notes of Benny Goodman's "Sing Sing Sing" pumped through the house. I stood in front of the speakers, the sound vibrating inside me, my head bobbing in time to the beat until I started to feel grounded again. Okay.

Now what? I went to the desk and took out my notes. With Carl out of the picture, I was left with several possibilities: Helene McNeil, Sharon Goodman, Martha Sparks, Jackie Dolan, Cathy, and the mystery lover. Who could be almost anyone.

I found myself absentmindedly drawing a circle around Sharon's name. She had a motive . . . or at least I thought she did. And that phone call luring me up to Twin Peaks had come just hours after my conversation with her. Ryan still didn't have any news on that episode. I skimmed through my notes. Sharon had access to Sam's gun, so she could have been the one who shot at me.

I leaned back and tried to imagine her pulling a trigger at point-blank range. It was far too easy. And it was just as easy to imagine her calling Mary and leaving an obscene message. Just for kicks.

Could she have posed as Mary? Possible. No. It was more than possible. Sharon was an actress. Pretending to be Mary would have just been another role. The only other person who could have realistically impersonated Mary was Cathy. And she also had access to a gun. Damn, I was going in circles again.

I also had to consider the unknown factor. The lover who had gone to such great lengths to keep her identity a secret. Why? Either she was ashamed of being gay . . . or she was involved with someone else. I spread the love letters over the desk and reread them. Nothing.

Frustrated, I stalked over to the stereo to change the CD. And then it hit me. What if Sam *was* Mary's lover?

My eyes snagged on the row of videotapes. Had I missed something. One after the other, I plugged them into the VCR. I replayed Mary's "Favorite Moments" tape and freeze-framed the scene where she was sitting cross-legged in front of the TV talking to Patty. God, she was beautiful.

All of a sudden, the screen flickered behind Patty. There was a picture of a sea otter coated in black oil. The Exxon Valdez disaster. When did that happen? I closed my eyes and concentrated. I had been on a business trip when the Valdez ran aground. That was March something. I strained my memory. March 24. Just three weeks before Mary died. Something tugged at my memory.

I ran over to my briefcase and dumped out my notes. I snapped through them to the first pages. What had Patty said? I found what I was looking for and sat down on the floor with a heavy thump. According to Patty, the last time she visited Mary in Big Sur was at Christmas, Pete and Miriam in tow.

Why had she lied? I fast-forwarded to the part where Patty launched into her comic monologue about growing up a Mormon. Her cheeks were flushed, her eyes glittering.

Could she and Mary have been lovers? I stared at the still frame till my eyes hurt. Then I shut the set and stood up, bewildered.

Patty and Mary? The pairing didn't make sense. They had been best friends for years. Why would they have started a romantic relationship now, so late in the game? I sat down at the desk exhausted, shuffling the letters to one side and dropping my head on my folded arms.

I scanned the desk blotter, the tightly formed characters of one love letter jumping off the page. "Love, your wild woman." Patty? A wild woman? Suddenly, I sat bolt upright. The note that had fallen from the book in Cathy's office. Hadn't it used that same wording? "Love, your wild woman, Patty." Dammit.

All at once, the pieces started clicking into place like one of those corny domino designs. Tap the first block and the rest just clack over, one after another. The postcard in Mary's apartment. The same handwriting. Patty's "Miss you terribly," she had written.

I slammed my hand against the desk and plunged through my own set of notes again. All the clues were there. Her anxiety that first night, her irritation at my calls, her reaction when I asked for the directions to Big Sur. Startled by my request, she had cut herself. I felt like an ass.

But could Patty have killed Mary? And if so, why? If they had become lovers after all those years of friendship, why would she have killed her? There had to be a motive.

My notes blurred in front of my eyes. I remembered the night at Twin Peaks, the bullet whistling by my head, the car window exploding near my elbow. Patty? My head was spinning. I couldn't imagine Patty shuffling into a store and buying an automatic.

Then another thought struck me like a lightning flash. Pete. What about Pete? God knows, as a military man, he had access to a gun.

What if he had found out about the affair — or worse, the videotape? Maybe he forced Patty into murdering Mary. I remembered the way she bit her lips nervously right before he came home, how her whole demeanor had changed in an instant. The fear in her eyes.

The scenario had a crisp logic. No wonder she was so edgy about my phone calls, constantly trying to coax me into leaving things alone. Even her insistence that Mary's death was a suicide made sense.

She must have been so relieved when I started

sniffing after Carl. I scooped the letters into my briefcase and picked up the phone. It was 11:20.

Cathy answered on the second ring. "I feel miserable about our stupid, petty argument," she said.

"Me too, but that has to wait . . . I have some bad news."

I heard a chair scrape across the floor. "Okay, I'm sitting down. Have you been hurt?"

"No. But I've found out who Mary's lover was." There was an uncomfortable silence on the other end of the phone. My eyes narrowed in suspicion. "Christ. You knew all along, didn't you?"

"She means as much to me as Mary does to you."

My head swung to the side with the impact of her words. "You did know! Why the hell didn't you tell me?"

"She doesn't have anything to do with Mary's death, so why should I betray her trust?"

My chest was tight with fury. Scenes flashed into my head. Cathy's moodiness, her quick temper whenever I questioned her about Mary's mysterious lover. "Because I almost got killed trying to find Mary's killer and you had the damn answer all the time!"

"What are you talking about?" Cathy bellowed into the phone.

"Pete's the killer . . . or are you trying to tell me you haven't figured that out?" My mouth was so dry my lips dragged across my teeth.

"Look, I'm not saying that the thought didn't cross my mind, but I just don't buy it. He's one of the gentlest people I know. So's Patty. Believe me, if I had any reason to suspect that one of them had killed Mary, I would have said something. But I don't. All I've tried to do is protect two people that I care a great deal about. That's it. I don't know why you're acting like I'm guilty of some heinous crime."

I gritted my teeth and counted to ten before answering. "Did you ever stop to think what might happen to me if your assumptions are wrong? If Pete killed Mary, don't you think he'd be capable of doing the same to me . . . to keep me quiet?"

"Pete didn't kill Mary."

"Then who did?"

"Why not Carl? Or has this latest revelation about Patty wiped his slate clean?"

I suddenly realized that Cathy didn't know about what had happened with Carl. I wiped my hand across my eyes.

"Carl's out of the picture. It's a long story." And it had been a long day. All at once, I felt like a hot air balloon punctured by a jet propeller. I was plummeting fast.

"Thanks for keeping me posted," she said sharply. "When did all this happen?"

"Last night . . . this morning. Right before I came to see you at the office. I found a bunch of tapes that prove he's guilty of obstructing justice and a lot worse than that. But not Mary's death."

Once again I replayed the lurid videotape in my head. The woman who had dragged Mary into that hotel was Patty. My stomach started to churn. "Did Patty ever mention a videotape to you?"

"What kind of videotape?" Her words were clipped, but I was beyond caring.

"A videotape of Mary going down on her."

She wheezed into my ear. "Jeezus, no. Who . . . how?"

"Carl had it. Apparently, the two of them made a mistake of slipping into one of Rose's hotels. He videotaped the whole damn encounter."

I could hear Cathy's breathing quicken.

"Mary was supposed to have had the tape," I added. "If Pete knew . . ." The words froze on my lips. Another image slipped into place. The note on Mary's refrigerator door: *Confirm meeting with Pete.*

"Robin, are you still there?"

"Yeah," I said absentmindedly. "What if Pete asked Mary for the tape and she refused? Don't you think he could have been angry enough to kill her?"

"I don't know what to think any more," she said tentatively. "You're sure Carl's not guilty?"

"Yes," I said reluctantly. "I wish it were that easy. By now, I'd be fast asleep, a smile on my lips."

For a few seconds, neither of us spoke.

"Do you still want me to come down?" Her voice had softened, but I felt like a piece of driftwood battered by hard surf.

"I don't know."

She sighed heavily. "I see."

"Cathy, I'm really beat. Why don't we talk in the morning. Maybe we'll both feel better by then."

I hung up and stared into space. I was swimming in quicksand . . . and sinking fast. I closed my eyes and rotated my neck till it cracked, my vertebrae clacking into place like a stack of dishes. What do they say about staying afloat in quicksand? Don't fight it. Stay calm, still.

I stood up and stretched, my bones snapping. I

289

bent over to touch my knees and heard another crack. Funny. I straightened up, my ears alert. A dull rattle. I walked onto the deck. The fog had banked against the house. But there was no wind. I walked back into the room and headed for the stairs.

Just then the lights went out. I lurched against the bannister and held on for dear life, my thoughts scattering like a split bag of marbles. Should I run for the front door? What could I use as a weapon? My eyes darted around the room. It was futile. I was running blind. Dammit.

I edged down the steps slowly, listening for sound. A footstep. I crouched down and peered through the railing to the ground floor. All shadows. I tried to distinguish shapes. There . . . Was that a body . . . or the couch? Panic wiped memory of the room's layout from my mind.

Movement. Look for movement, I told myself. My eyes began to adjust slowly. Just below me, near the kitchen counter, something wavered. I riveted on the shape. The room started to lighten, the fog bouncing silvery light into the room. My eyes narrowed to tight slits. Something glinted in the dark. I knew the shape well. Remembered all too well what a gun barrel looked like in a black space, the cool metal catching the smallest fragments of light.

I shook the memory out of my head and looked above me. The second-floor deck was about ten feet off the ground. If I was careful, I could make the jump. But what if I broke a leg, or worse. I'd be completely helpless. I glanced back down. The shadow was moving toward the stairs.

I had no choice. I inched up the stairs on my knees, a sharp pain shooting around my stitches. I held my breath like a diver. One more step. A small squeak, but loud enough to give me away. A blast rang out behind me.

I sprinted to the deck with every ounce of energy. I had just opened the glass door when a spotlight flashed on me.

"Another step and you're dead."

I dropped my hands and turned around. The figure was nothing more than a silhouette behind the blinding light. But with a dull chill I had recognized the voice.

Patty.

"I'm really sorry about this, Robin," she said quietly.

I opened my mouth, but sound wouldn't come.

"Would you mind placing both hands on your head? I want to make sure you don't make any sudden moves. Good . . . that's better."

She stood the flashlight on the table so that the beam bounced off the ceiling. In the dull light I could see she was wearing a navy peacoat and dark jeans. Her hair was piled on top of her head in a loose French bun. She looked strangely radiant. "I'd turn on a light, but I removed all the fuses."

"Why, Patty?" I finally managed, surprised to find my chief emotion was sadness and not fear.

She looked away briefly. "You wouldn't understand."

"Give me that much. Please. I need to know why." My voice cracked. "Dammit, you loved her!"

Her eyes flashed bullets at me in the dark. "You don't know how much."

"But you killed her. For God's sake, why?"

Her smile was wry. "Interesting use of words . . .

Maybe that's why I did it. For God's sake." She moved closer. I could smell cheap whiskey on her. Of course. Patty was drinking again. I remembered her sipping red wine that first night we all had dinner. I should have known then.

"Do you remember anything about my life?" she slurred slightly. Beads of sweat were marking trails along her brow. I nodded, afraid to interrupt her. "A few years ago, I was worth shit. Ninety-nine percent of the time, I was drunk or stoned. Cathy had had her mastectomy and all she could think about was herself . . ."

Her face was wooden, her eyes flat. "She wanted me to prove she was still attractive. As if I could care about anything at that point in my life." She poked the gun barrel in my direction, her features twisting with emotions I couldn't begin to understand. "I was battling to stay alive and she didn't do shit for me. Nothing."

Then she laughed. "Oh yeah. She left me., That's what she did. She left me. But Mary . . . Mary came through. She flew out from New York and dragged me home. I knew it was do or die. She held my hand as long as she could, and then she scampered home to you."

She coughed, a small tight cough. Her grief and anger were choking her. Keep talking, I pleaded silently.

"Then Pete came along. You will never know what that man did for me. He saved my life. And my soul. Stayed by me through every stinking minute of detox. I put him through hell, but he never left me. Never. We got married and moved back here. And I built a life like I never had. A husband, child, community. I had everything . . . or almost everything."

She waved the gun under my nose and then cocked her head. "Do you want to tell me what I didn't have?"

Words stumbled over me. *I dream of being with you in our glorious bed by the sea, the waves rocking the air the way you rock me with your tongue, your moans.*

"Passion."

She smiled sadly. "Two points. Passion. I turned to Mary because I knew she'd understand. After the two of you broke up, Mary had bungled one relationship after the other. Because they weren't you. Didn't make her feel the way you did. One day, we stumbled into bed. It was sheer accident, chance catching us at a weak moment. But the passion . . . God . . . we exploded. I had never felt that way. Not even with Cathy. I couldn't get enough of her."

She narrowed her eyes. "Do you know about the videotape . . . no, don't answer. I can see it in your eyes. Of course you do. When Mary told me about it, I wanted to die. I was terrified Pete would find out."

She sat on the edge of the desk, the gun barrel pointing at my feet, her voice growing tentative. "Carl's deal was a fair one, I thought. No one would get hurt. But Mary wouldn't let it go. She said it made her sick to lie to Pete. And she refused to let Carl get off scot-free." She looked up at me pleadingly. "I had no other way out. She had made plans to have dinner with Pete before going to the police. I guess the letter in her typewriter was for him. Another hour or so . . ."

Her voice was shaking now. My body went on alert, waiting for her to break.

"I couldn't afford to lose him. He's my life. I begged Mary. But she just refused to listen to reason. I had no choice." She wiped her nose with the back of her free hand. "Once I made the decision, the rest was so easy. It was like someone was watching over me. I got the penicillin and then drove down to the house with Miriam on a Thursday. I knew Mary was going to Big Sur that weekend, so it was just a matter of mixing the penicillin into the yogurt. I figured it would be fast and painless —"

"Fast and painless?" My fury broke. "Why the hell didn't you just run her off the damn road?"

She interrupted, her eyes pleading with me to understand. "I couldn't watch her die. This was the best way. I never wanted her to hurt . . ."

Suddenly, she was crying, the gun's muzzle drifting off target. I sprang forward, but she spun away from me and started to take aim. I had one way out and I took it. I ran out to the deck and leapt off. A thick bush broke my fall. I rolled off and dove toward my car. I smashed into the side door and grabbed the handle. Locked. And the keys were in the house.

I looked up. Patty was at the doorway. I bolted into the woods. My lungs were burning, sweat dripping into my eyes. Fog hung above the ground in thick patches. I didn't care that I could barely see. I only knew I had to get as far away as fast as I could.

Behind me, Patty's voice rang out. "I know this property better than you. You can't hide from me!" Her footsteps were closer than I liked.

I could feel the hill sloping down toward my left. I had to stay away from the edge of the bluff. Bear right. I shifted direction, my heel catching on a loose rock. I fell into a pile of pine cones, scraping my chin and left cheek. My stitches burned. I shook myself off and darted toward a shape I remembered. The boulder. I shot through the fence and started running up the hill, toward the road. Another crack echoed through the night. She was gaining on me, so close I could hear her gasping for air.

"Robin, don't make this harder. It'll be worse if I just wound you first."

I spun between trees, the fog growing thicker as I climbed the hillside. Stay away from the edge, I warned myself over and over, my ears straining for the sound of the surf.

My knee was starting to pull, and Patty's footsteps were rumbling right behind me. I gritted my teeth and put on extra speed. The wind had picked up in the last few seconds. It whipped across my face, heavy with salt.

I fumbled over some mossy boulders and tore out to my left, my sense of direction faltering in the dark. The incline grew steeper till I was running at an angle, my chest heaving and my pulse pounding so loud it drowned out all other sound. I barreled ahead blindly. The road had to be up ahead somewhere. All of a sudden, I felt like my lungs were tearing open. I braced myself against a tree to gasp for air. In that moment, I heard Patty sprinting toward me . . . and the distinct sound of a gun being cocked.

I darted out a split second before the impact hit. I veered to my left, but the bullet crashed into my right shoulder, spinning me around like a top. The next thing I knew, I was tumbling toward the edge of the bluff. My fingers smashed around a prickly root sticking out from the side of the cliff, my feet scrambling madly for a foothold.

The roar of the ocean was directly below me, spray shooting up the bluff and falling on my face in a fine mist. I dug my nails into the soil and started pulling myself up. I flopped my chin onto the ground and swung one arm up. I was losing blood and my head started to spin, flashing lights dotting my vision. I dug my chin into the pebbly soil like an anchor and inched upward.

I hefted my upper torso over the edge, and suddenly Patty was standing over me, the smoking gun barrel pointing between my eyes.

"I told you it was harder this way," she said breathlessly.

"Patty, don't make things worse for yourself."

She laughed. "I'm not." Her face hardened. "You have to understand . . . I'm fighting for my life too."

She raised the gun. I stared into the barrel, my breath catching in my throat. Is this what Carol felt before I pulled the trigger? Disbelief, fear, fascination? Maybe this was right, I thought all at once, my eyes drifting down to Patty's muddied sneakers. Then I remembered the spark in the deer's eye, a fierce reminder of life, strength. I raised my head, counting to two and then barreled the side of my head against her legs. My eyes crossed with the impact, but Patty had stumbled backwards.

I hauled myself over the edge and crashed into her mid-section like a linebacker. She fell like a doll, the gun arching out over the bluff. I bent over her and she kicked at my knee. The pain was dazzling. I fell back across a tree stump. Patty spun around and sprang into the woods, toward the house.

I stood up on rubbery legs, shook my head, and took off after her. By the time I got to the house, the back tires of her car were spitting pebbles into the air. I raced into the house, fumbling in the dark till I found my briefcase and car keys, then I dashed outside and leaped into the car.

Blood was pouring down my shoulder as I shot out of the driveway. I squinted at the road and bit down on my lip. *Stay focused.* The car careened around hairpin turns. At times, I could feel it edging up onto the two outer wheels. I took a deep breath and reluctantly let up on the gas.

I was rocking around a tight curve when a flash of light lit up the night like fireworks. I slammed on my brakes and ran the car into a gravel pit at the base of the cliff to my right.

I bolted out of the car and scrambled to the edge of the bluff. The fog clung to the rocks far below, but I could see the flames clearly enough. I glanced back at the road and saw fresh skid marks tearing over the edge.

At the base of the cliff, Patty's car exploded for the second time.

Chapter 21

I drove myself to an emergency room in Monterey and passed out sometime during the triage interview. I didn't wake up till Sunday morning, my shoulder bound in a blood-stained sling and my body feeling like something that had been recently blenderized.

A set of newspapers lay on the otherwise sterile night table next to the hospital bed. I picked them up. The front pages buzzed with Carl Lawrence's arrest. There was even a picture of a triumphant-looking Ryan dragging Lawrence out of his expensive condo by the shirt sleeve. I cut that one out for my scrapbook.

Buried back on page twenty was a small notice about a car plunging off Route 1 early Saturday morning. The victim, one Patty Allen Walker, had left behind a husband and an infant daughter. Still further back, on the gossip page, was a six-line blurb revealing that Laurel Carter, the famous romance writer, had recently been uncovered as an "active lesbian." I hadn't been as active as I would have liked, but I figured that could be easily remedied.

I spent the later part of the day being photographed, prodded, and poked by various antiseptic instruments. It was not my idea of fun, but at least they had taken my stitches out. When they finally wheeled me into my room and dumped me back in my hospital bed, I discovered Pete leaning on the window sill, his face pressed against the glass like a little boy gazing through a pet store display — the last step in a desperate search for his lost puppy.

"Hey Pete," I said as the hospital attendant draped a coarse blanket over my bare knees.

He waited a beat and then turned around. His eyes were sunk in his face, shadows dulling his features. He shoved his hands deep into his jean pockets and hunched his shoulders. "I just wanted to tell you how sorry I am . . ." He blinked twice and then swiveled back to the window.

I watched the muscles in his jawline jump into relief. "Me too, Pete. I didn't mean for any of this to happen."

He nodded, his lips puckered and quivering. "You

know what really stinks . . . none of this had to happen. Christ, did she really think I wouldn't understand?" He turned questioning eyes at me. I tried to sit up straighter.

"When I met her, she was the most confused creature I had ever encountered. But she touched me . . . here." He pounded his chest, his voice shaking. "I would have done anything for her." He circled the bed and slumped into a cracked vinyl visitor's chair, his hands clasped between his knees, his head bowed as if in prayer.

"The funny thing is . . . I knew all about it . . . the affair with Mary, I mean. It would have been hard not to know. A couple of months back . . . I don't know . . . it must have been after New Year's. Anyway, Patty's entire personality changed. It was like someone had turned her motor on. She was whizzing around the house, smiling and singing all the time. At night . . ." He looked up at me with red eyes. "Is this okay?"

I reached out and squeezed his hand in response. He gave me a sad half-smile and nodded.

"She was never very . . . what's the word? Aggressive. In bed, I mean. But all of a sudden, she was grabbing at me, mounting me in the middle of the night like I was a horse. At first, I was delirious. I mean . . . I thought she had broken through some barrier. Then I started noticing things. She joined this adult literary center . . . or so she said. Two or three nights a week, I had to watch Miriam while she went out to redeem the illiterate." He stared at his hands, scratching at a cuticle with narrowed eyes. "That's how she put it . . ."

I poured myself a glass of water and he smacked

his lips. I passed the paper cup to him and poured myself another cup.

"Thanks. I feel like I'm dying of thirst . . . my mouth's so dry." He downed the water and crumpled the cup in his hand. "The nights she was home, she'd be on the phone with Mary for hours. It got to the point where she'd sneak out of bed in the middle of the night and go downstairs to make a phone call. Then she started visiting Mary in Big Sur on the weekends . . . That's when I knew for sure."

He stretched out his legs and shook his head in a daze. "I didn't say anything to her 'cause I figured it would pass in time . . . and even if it didn't . . ." His eyes bored into mine. "I know I sound like a jerk, but I didn't really care. I knew she loved me and Miriam, and she was a good wife, a great mother. If she needed to take care of some special need somewhere else, it was fine with me . . . as long as I knew she was coming home to me. That's all that mattered." His Adam's apple bobbed crazily.

He stood up abruptly and crossed back to the window. "You have to believe me, I didn't know about the murder. I still don't understand it. Not completely. How could she kill someone she loved that much? How could she think that was better than telling me the truth?"

I watched his back rise and fall with the effort to restrain the tears. "You can't blame yourself, Pete."

He threw his head back and laughed — a bitter, cracking sound. "Yeah. Right."

I swung my legs off the side of the bed and walked over to him. We stared at each other a few minutes. Then I wrapped my free arm around him

and held him while he cried against my good
shoulder.

* * * * *

The next day Cathy called just as I was getting
ready to check out. We fumbled for words for a good
fifteen minutes. She found them first. After
apologizing in ten different ways, she invited me to
spend a week with her in northern California. She
had taken a leave of absence from the paper and
wanted to use that time to rediscover our initial
connection. "Let's start from scratch. Make believe
we met through a personal ad, or something
innocuous like that."

I laughed, remembering how glorious it was to
rest in her arms after making love. I reintroduced
myself and asked her if she'd like to catch a movie
with me in the city that night. She agreed readily.

I packed up my briefcase and scanned the
hospital room. There were four pots of flowers, one
each from Pete, Dinah, Cathy and Detective Ryan. I
picked up Ryan's collection of pink and yellow roses
and exited the room.

* * * * *

Before heading north, I drove back to Mary's
house, averting my eyes from the skid marks that
were still etched into the road. I taped plastic over
the glass door leading to the second floor deck,
plugged the fuses back in, packed my overnight bag,
and grabbed an apple and a Yoo-Hoo from the
fridge. Then I locked the place up, making a mental

note to contact a real estate agent before Cathy and I headed up to Mendocino.

On the drive back to San Francisco, I pulled into the gravel pit just in front of the skid marks. It was a gorgeous day, the sun directly overhead, the hillside pulsing with vibrant foliage, the whitecaps below breaking into a powdery turquoise. Patty's car was upside down in the surf, sea foam drifting between the tires.

My eyes filled unexpectedly. I smoothed my hair back from my face, then walked back to the car and dug into my briefcase. I removed the stack of letters tied with a lavender ribbon and plucked out one of Ryan's pink roses.

I stood on the edge of the bluff and tossed the letters into the wind. They arched into the surf like a bird diving for fish. Then I dropped the rose and watched it flutter to the rocky shore.

A few of the publications of
THE NAIAD PRESS, INC.
P.O. Box 10543 • Tallahassee, Florida 32302
Phone (904) 539-5965
Mail orders welcome. Please include 15% postage.

MURDER BY TRADITION by Katherine V. Forrest. 288 pp. A
Kate Delafield Mystery. 4th in a series.   (HC) ISBN 0-941483-89-4 $18.95
                                          (Paperback) ISBN 1-56280-002-7   9.95

A DOORYARD FULL OF FLOWERS by Isabel Miller. 176 pp.
Stories incl. 2 sequels to *Patience and Sarah.*   ISBN 1-56280-029-9   9.95

THE EROTIC NAIAD edited by Katherine V. Forrest & Barbara Grier.
224 pp. Love stories by Naiad Press authors.   ISBN 1-56280-026-4 $12.95

DEAD CERTAIN by Claire McNab. 224 pp. 5th Det. Insp. Carol
Ashton mystery.   ISBN 1-56280-027-2   9.95

CRAZY FOR LOVING by Jaye Maiman. 320 pp. 2nd Robin
Miller mystery.   ISBN 1-56280-025-6   9.95

STONEHURST by Barbara Johnson. 176 pp. Passionate regency
romance.   ISBN 1-56280-024-8   9.95

INTRODUCING AMANDA VALENTINE by Rose Beecham.
256 pp. An Amanda Valentine Mystery — 1st in a series.
                                         ISBN 1-56280-021-3   9.95

UNCERTAIN COMPANIONS by Robbi Sommers. 204 pp.
Steamy, erotic novel.   ISBN 1-56280-017-5   9.95

A TIGER'S HEART by Lauren W. Douglas. 240 pp. Fourth Caitlin
Reece Mystery.   ISBN 1-56280-018-3   9.95

PAPERBACK ROMANCE by Karin Kallmaker. 256 pp. A
delicious romance.   ISBN 1-56280-019-1   9.95

MORTON RIVER VALLEY by Lee Lynch. 304 pp. Lee Lynch at
her best!   ISBN 1-56280-016-7   9.95

LOVE, ZENA BETH by Diane Salvatore. 224 pp. The most talked
about lesbian novel of the nineties!   ISBN 1-56280-015-9   18.95

THE LAVENDER HOUSE MURDER by Nikki Baker. 224 pp. A
Virginia Kelly Mystery. Second in a series.   ISBN 1-56280-012-4   9.95

PASSION BAY by Jennifer Fulton. 224 pp. Passionate romance,
virgin beaches, tropical skies.   ISBN 1-56280-028-0   9.95

STICKS AND STONES by Jackie Calhoun. 208 pp. Contemporary
lesbian lives and loves.   ISBN 1-56280-020-5   9.95

DELIA IRONFOOT by Jeane Harris. 192 pp. Adventure for Delia
and Beth in the Utah mountains.   ISBN 1-56280-014-0   9.95

UNDER THE SOUTHERN CROSS by Claire McNab. 192 pp.
Romantic nights Down Under.   ISBN 1-56280-011-6   9.95

RIVERFINGER WOMEN by Elana Nachman/Dykewomon.
208 pp. Classic Lesbian/feminist novel.   ISBN 1-56280-013-2   8.95

A CERTAIN DISCONTENT by Cleve Boutell. 240 pp. A unique
coterie of women.   ISBN 1-56280-009-4   9.95

GRASSY FLATS by Penny Hayes. 256 pp. Lesbian romance in
the '30s.   ISBN 1-56280-010-8   9.95

A SINGULAR SPY by Amanda K. Williams. 192 pp. 3rd spy novel
featuring Lesbian agent Madison McGuire.   ISBN 1-56280-008-6   8.95

THE END OF APRIL by Penny Sumner. 240 pp. A Victoria Cross
Mystery. First in a series.   ISBN 1-56280-007-8   8.95

A FLIGHT OF ANGELS by Sarah Aldridge. 240 pp. Romance set at
the National Gallery of Art   ISBN 1-56280-001-9   9.95

HOUSTON TOWN by Deborah Powell. 208 pp. A Hollis Carpenter
mystery. Second in a series.   ISBN 1-56280-006-X   8.95

KISS AND TELL by Robbi Sommers. 192 pp. Scorching stories by
the author of *Pleasures*.   ISBN 1-56280-005-1   9.95

STILL WATERS by Pat Welch. 208 pp. Second in the Helen
Black mystery series.   ISBN 0-941483-97-5   9.95

MURDER IS GERMANE by Karen Saum. 224 pp. The 2nd
Brigid Donovan mystery.   ISBN 0-941483-98-3   8.95

TO LOVE AGAIN by Evelyn Kennedy. 208 pp. Wildly
romantic love story.   ISBN 0-941483-85-1   9.95

IN THE GAME by Nikki Baker. 192 pp. A Virginia Kelly
mystery. First in a series.   ISBN 01-56280-004-3   9.95

AVALON by Mary Jane Jones. 256 pp. A Lesbian Arthurian
romance.   ISBN 0-941483-96-7   9.95

STRANDED by Camarin Grae. 320 pp. Entertaining, riveting
adventure.   ISBN 0-941483-99-1   9.95

THE DAUGHTERS OF ARTEMIS by Lauren Wright Douglas.
240 pp. Third Caitlin Reece mystery. ISBN 0-941483-95-9   9.95

CLEARWATER by Catherine Ennis. 176 pp. Romantic secrets
of a small Louisiana town.   ISBN 0-941483-65-7   8.95

THE HALLELUJAH MURDERS by Dorothy Tell. 176 pp.
Second Poppy Dillworth mystery.   ISBN 0-941483-88-6   8.95

ZETA BASE by Judith Alguire. 208 pp. Lesbian triangle
on a future Earth.   ISBN 0-941483-94-0   9.95

SECOND CHANCE by Jackie Calhoun. 256 pp. Contemporary
Lesbian lives and loves.   ISBN 0-941483-93-2   9.95

BENEDICTION by Diane Salvatore. 272 pp. Striking,
contemporary romantic novel.   ISBN 0-941483-90-8   9.95

CALLING RAIN by Karen Marie Christa Minns. 240 pp.
Spellbinding, erotic love story   ISBN 0-941483-87-8   9.95

BLACK IRIS by Jeane Harris. 192 pp. Caroline's hidden past . . .
                                                   ISBN 0-941483-68-1   8.95

TOUCHWOOD by Karin Kallmaker. 240 pp. Loving, May/
December romance.   ISBN 0-941483-76-2   9.95

BAYOU CITY SECRETS by Deborah Powell. 224 pp. A Hollis
Carpenter mystery. First in a series.   ISBN 0-941483-91-6   9.95

COP OUT by Claire McNab. 208 pp. 4th Det. Insp. Carol Ashton
mystery.   ISBN 0-941483-84-3   9.95

LODESTAR by Phyllis Horn. 224 pp. Romantic, fast-moving
adventure.   ISBN 0-941483-83-5   8.95

THE BEVERLY MALIBU by Katherine V. Forrest. 288 pp. A
Kate Delafield Mystery. 3rd in a series. (HC)   ISBN 0-941483-47-9   16.95
                                    Paperback   ISBN 0-941483-48-7   9.95

THAT OLD STUDEBAKER by Lee Lynch. 272 pp. Andy's affair
with Regina and her attachment to her beloved car.
                                                   ISBN 0-941483-82-7   9.95

PASSION'S LEGACY by Lori Paige. 224 pp. Sarah is swept into
the arms of Augusta Pym in this delightful historical romance.
                                                   ISBN 0-941483-81-9   8.95

THE PROVIDENCE FILE by Amanda Kyle Williams. 256 pp.
Second espionage thriller featuring lesbian agent Madison McGuire
                                                   ISBN 0-941483-92-4   8.95

I LEFT MY HEART by Jaye Maiman. 320 pp. A Robin Miller
Mystery. First in a series.   ISBN 0-941483-72-X   9.95

THE PRICE OF SALT by Patricia Highsmith (writing as Claire
Morgan). 288 pp. Classic lesbian novel, first issued in 1952 . . .
acknowledged by its author under her own, very famous, name.
                                                   ISBN 1-56280-003-5   9.95

SIDE BY SIDE by Isabel Miller. 256 pp. From beloved author of
Patience and Sarah.   ISBN 0-941483-77-0   9.95

SOUTHBOUND by Sheila Ortiz Taylor. 240 pp. Hilarious sequel
to *Faultline.*   ISBN 0-941483-78-9   8.95

STAYING POWER: LONG TERM LESBIAN COUPLES
by Susan E. Johnson. 352 pp. Joys of coupledom.
                                                   ISBN 0-941-483-75-4   12.95

SLICK by Camarin Grae. 304 pp. Exotic, erotic adventure.
                                                   ISBN 0-941483-74-6   9.95

NINTH LIFE by Lauren Wright Douglas. 256 pp. A Caitlin
Reece mystery. 2nd in a series.   ISBN 0-941483-50-9   8.95

PLAYERS by Robbi Sommers. 192 pp. Sizzling, erotic novel.
                                                   ISBN 0-941483-73-8   9.95

MURDER AT RED ROOK RANCH by Dorothy Tell. 224 pp.
First Poppy Dillworth adventure. ISBN 0-941483-80-0   8.95

LESBIAN SURVIVAL MANUAL by Rhonda Dicksion.
112 pp. Cartoons! ISBN 0-941483-71-1   8.95

A ROOM FULL OF WOMEN by Elisabeth Nonas. 256 pp.
Contemporary Lesbian lives. ISBN 0-941483-69-X   9.95

MURDER IS RELATIVE by Karen Saum. 256 pp. The first
Brigid Donovan mystery. ISBN 0-941483-70-3   8.95

PRIORITIES by Lynda Lyons 288 pp. Science fiction with
a twist. ISBN 0-941483-66-5   8.95

THEME FOR DIVERSE INSTRUMENTS by Jane Rule. 208
pp. Powerful romantic lesbian stories. ISBN 0-941483-63-0   8.95

LESBIAN QUERIES by Hertz & Ertman. 112 pp. The questions
you were too embarrassed to ask. ISBN 0-941483-67-3   8.95

CLUB 12 by Amanda Kyle Williams. 288 pp. Espionage thriller
featuring a lesbian agent! ISBN 0-941483-64-9   8.95

DEATH DOWN UNDER by Claire McNab. 240 pp. 3rd Det.
Insp. Carol Ashton mystery. ISBN 0-941483-39-8   9.95

MONTANA FEATHERS by Penny Hayes. 256 pp. Vivian and
Elizabeth find love in frontier Montana. ISBN 0-941483-61-4   8.95

CHESAPEAKE PROJECT by Phyllis Horn. 304 pp. Jessie &
Meredith in perilous adventure. ISBN 0-941483-58-4   8.95

LIFESTYLES by Jackie Calhoun. 224 pp. Contemporary Lesbian
lives and loves. ISBN 0-941483-57-6   9.95

VIRAGO by Karen Marie Christa Minns. 208 pp. Darsen has
chosen Ginny. ISBN 0-941483-56-8   8.95

WILDERNESS TREK by Dorothy Tell. 192 pp. Six women on
vacation learning ''new'' skills. ISBN 0-941483-60-6   8.95

MURDER BY THE BOOK by Pat Welch. 256 pp. A Helen
Black Mystery. First in a series. ISBN 0-941483-59-2   9.95

BERRIGAN by Vicki P. McConnell. 176 pp. Youthful Lesbian —
romantic, idealistic Berrigan. ISBN 0-941483-55-X   8.95

LESBIANS IN GERMANY by Lillian Faderman & B. Eriksson.
128 pp. Fiction, poetry, essays. ISBN 0-941483-62-2   8.95

THERE'S SOMETHING I'VE BEEN MEANING TO TELL
YOU Ed. by Loralee MacPike. 288 pp. Gay men and lesbians
coming out to their children. ISBN 0-941483-44-4   9.95
ISBN 0-941483-54-1   16.95

LIFTING BELLY by Gertrude Stein. Ed. by Rebecca Mark. 104
pp. Erotic poetry. ISBN 0-941483-51-7   8.95
ISBN 0-941483-53-3   14.95

ROSE PENSKI by Roz Perry. 192 pp. Adult lovers in a long-term
relationship.   ISBN 0-941483-37-1   8.95

AFTER THE FIRE by Jane Rule. 256 pp. Warm, human novel
by this incomparable author.   ISBN 0-941483-45-2   8.95

SUE SLATE, PRIVATE EYE by Lee Lynch. 176 pp. The gay
folk of Peacock Alley are *all cats*.   ISBN 0-941483-52-5   8.95

CHRIS by Randy Salem. 224 pp. Golden oldie. Handsome Chris
and her adventures.   ISBN 0-941483-42-8   8.95

THREE WOMEN by March Hastings. 232 pp. Golden oldie. A
triangle among wealthy sophisticates.   ISBN 0-941483-43-6   8.95

RICE AND BEANS by Valeria Taylor. 232 pp. Love and
romance on poverty row.   ISBN 0-941483-41-X   8.95

PLEASURES by Robbi Sommers. 204 pp. Unprecedented
eroticism.   ISBN 0-941483-49-5   8.95

EDGEWISE by Camarin Grae. 372 pp. Spellbinding
adventure.   ISBN 0-941483-19-3   9.95

FATAL REUNION by Claire McNab. 224 pp. 2nd Det. Inspec.
Carol Ashton mystery.   ISBN 0-941483-40-1   8.95

KEEP TO ME STRANGER by Sarah Aldridge. 372 pp. Romance
set in a department store dynasty.   ISBN 0-941483-38-X   9.95

HEARTSCAPE by Sue Gambill. 204 pp. American lesbian in
Portugal.   ISBN 0-941483-33-9   8.95

IN THE BLOOD by Lauren Wright Douglas. 252 pp. Lesbian
science fiction adventure fantasy   ISBN 0-941483-22-3   8.95

THE BEE'S KISS by Shirley Verel. 216 pp. Delicate, delicious
romance.   ISBN 0-941483-36-3   8.95

RAGING MOTHER MOUNTAIN by Pat Emmerson. 264 pp.
Furosa Firechild's adventures in Wonderland.   ISBN 0-941483-35-5   8.95

IN EVERY PORT by Karin Kallmaker. 228 pp. Jessica's sexy,
adventuresome travels.   ISBN 0-941483-37-7   9.95

OF LOVE AND GLORY by Evelyn Kennedy. 192 pp. Exciting
WWII romance.   ISBN 0-941483-32-0   8.95

CLICKING STONES by Nancy Tyler Glenn. 288 pp. Love
transcending time.   ISBN 0-941483-31-2   9.95

SURVIVING SISTERS by Gail Pass. 252 pp. Powerful love
story.   ISBN 0-941483-16-9   8.95

SOUTH OF THE LINE by Catherine Ennis. 216 pp. Civil War
adventure.   ISBN 0-941483-29-0   8.95

WOMAN PLUS WOMAN by Dolores Klaich. 300 pp. Supurb
Lesbian overview.   ISBN 0-941483-28-2   9.95

SLOW DANCING AT MISS POLLY'S by Sheila Ortiz Taylor.
96 pp. Lesbian Poetry   ISBN 0-941483-30-4   7.95

DOUBLE DAUGHTER by Vicki P. McConnell. 216 pp. A Nyla
Wade Mystery, third in the series.   ISBN 0-941483-26-6   8.95

HEAVY GILT by Delores Klaich. 192 pp. Lesbian detective/
disappearing homophobes/upper class gay society.
                                       ISBN 0-941483-25-8   8.95

THE FINER GRAIN by Denise Ohio. 216 pp. Brilliant young
college lesbian novel.   ISBN 0-941483-11-8   8.95

THE AMAZON TRAIL by Lee Lynch. 216 pp. Life, travel & lore
of famous lesbian author.   ISBN 0-941483-27-4   8.95

HIGH CONTRAST by Jessie Lattimore. 264 pp. Women of the
Crystal Palace.   ISBN 0-941483-17-7   8.95

OCTOBER OBSESSION by Meredith More. Josie's rich, secret
Lesbian life.   ISBN 0-941483-18-5   8.95

LESBIAN CROSSROADS by Ruth Baetz. 276 pp. Contemporary
Lesbian lives.   ISBN 0-941483-21-5   9.95

BEFORE STONEWALL: THE MAKING OF A GAY AND
LESBIAN COMMUNITY by Andrea Weiss & Greta Schiller.
96 pp., 25 illus.   ISBN 0-941483-20-7   7.95

WE WALK THE BACK OF THE TIGER by Patricia A. Murphy.
192 pp. Romantic Lesbian novel/beginning women's movement.
                                       ISBN 0-941483-13-4   8.95

SUNDAY'S CHILD by Joyce Bright. 216 pp. Lesbian athletics, at
last the novel about sports.   ISBN 0-941483-12-6   8.95

OSTEN'S BAY by Zenobia N. Vole. 204 pp. Sizzling adventure
romance set on Bonaire.   ISBN 0-941483-15-0   8.95

LESSONS IN MURDER by Claire McNab. 216 pp. 1st Det. Inspec.
Carol Ashton mystery — erotic tension!.   ISBN 0-941483-14-2   8.95

YELLOWTHROAT by Penny Hayes. 240 pp. Margarita, bandit,
kidnaps Julia.   ISBN 0-941483-10-X   8.95

SAPPHISTRY: THE BOOK OF LESBIAN SEXUALITY by
Pat Califia. 3d edition, revised. 208 pp.   ISBN 0-941483-24-X   8.95

CHERISHED LOVE by Evelyn Kennedy. 192 pp. Erotic
Lesbian love story.   ISBN 0-941483-08-8   9.95

LAST SEPTEMBER by Helen R. Hull. 208 pp. Six stories & a
glorious novella.   ISBN 0-941483-09-6   8.95

THE SECRET IN THE BIRD by Camarin Grae. 312 pp. Striking,
psychological suspense novel.   ISBN 0-941483-05-3   8.95

TO THE LIGHTNING by Catherine Ennis. 208 pp. Romantic
Lesbian 'Robinson Crusoe' adventure.   ISBN 0-941483-06-1   8.95

THE OTHER SIDE OF VENUS by Shirley Verel. 224 pp.
Luminous, romantic love story.   ISBN 0-941483-07-X   8.95

DREAMS AND SWORDS by Katherine V. Forrest. 192 pp.
Romantic, erotic, imaginative stories.   ISBN 0-941483-03-7   8.95

MEMORY BOARD by Jane Rule. 336 pp. Memorable novel
about an aging Lesbian couple.   ISBN 0-941483-02-9   9.95

THE ALWAYS ANONYMOUS BEAST by Lauren Wright
Douglas. 224 pp. A Caitlin Reece mystery. First in a series.
    ISBN 0-941483-04-5   8.95

SEARCHING FOR SPRING by Patricia A. Murphy. 224 pp.
Novel about the recovery of love.   ISBN 0-941483-00-2   8.95

DUSTY'S QUEEN OF HEARTS DINER by Lee Lynch. 240 pp.
Romantic blue-collar novel.   ISBN 0-941483-01-0   8.95

PARENTS MATTER by Ann Muller. 240 pp. Parents'
relationships with Lesbian daughters and gay sons.
    ISBN 0-930044-91-6   9.95

THE PEARLS by Shelley Smith. 176 pp. Passion and fun in
the Caribbean sun.   ISBN 0-930044-93-2   7.95

MAGDALENA by Sarah Aldridge. 352 pp. Epic Lesbian novel
set on three continents.   ISBN 0-930044-99-1   8.95

THE BLACK AND WHITE OF IT by Ann Allen Shockley.
144 pp. Short stories.   ISBN 0-930044-96-7   7.95

SAY JESUS AND COME TO ME by Ann Allen Shockley. 288
pp. Contemporary romance.   ISBN 0-930044-98-3   8.95

LOVING HER by Ann Allen Shockley. 192 pp. Romantic love
story.   ISBN 0-930044-97-5   7.95

MURDER AT THE NIGHTWOOD BAR by Katherine V.
Forrest. 240 pp. A Kate Delafield mystery. Second in a series.
    ISBN 0-930044-92-4   9.95

ZOE'S BOOK by Gail Pass. 224 pp. Passionate, obsessive love
story.   ISBN 0-930044-95-9   7.95

WINGED DANCER by Camarin Grae. 228 pp. Erotic Lesbian
adventure story.   ISBN 0-930044-88-6   8.95

PAZ by Camarin Grae. 336 pp. Romantic Lesbian adventurer
with the power to change the world.   ISBN 0-930044-89-4   8.95

SOUL SNATCHER by Camarin Grae. 224 pp. A puzzle, an
adventure, a mystery — Lesbian romance.   ISBN 0-930044-90-8   8.95

THE LOVE OF GOOD WOMEN by Isabel Miller. 224 pp.
Long-awaited new novel by the author of the beloved *Patience
and Sarah.*   ISBN 0-930044-81-9   8.95

THE HOUSE AT PELHAM FALLS by Brenda Weathers. 240
pp. Suspenseful Lesbian ghost story.   ISBN 0-930044-79-7   7.95

HOME IN YOUR HANDS by Lee Lynch. 240 pp. More stories
from the author of *Old Dyke Tales.*   ISBN 0-930044-80-0   7.95

THE SOPHIE HOROWITZ STORY by Sarah Schulman. 176
pp. Engaging novel of madcap intrigue.   ISBN 0-930044-54-1   7.95

THE YOUNG IN ONE ANOTHER'S ARMS by Jane Rule. 224 pp. Classic
Jane Rule.   ISBN 0-930044-53-3   9.95

THE BURNTON WIDOWS by Vickie P. McConnell. 272 pp. A
Nyla Wade mystery, second in the series.   ISBN 0-930044-52-5   9.95

OLD DYKE TALES by Lee Lynch. 224 pp. Extraordinary
stories of our diverse Lesbian lives.   ISBN 0-930044-51-7   8.95

DAUGHTERS OF A CORAL DAWN by Katherine V. Forrest.
240 pp. Novel set in a Lesbian new world.   ISBN 0-930044-50-9   8.95

AGAINST THE SEASON by Jane Rule. 224 pp. Luminous,
complex novel of interrelationships.   ISBN 0-930044-48-7   8.95

LOVERS IN THE PRESENT AFTERNOON by Kathleen
Fleming. 288 pp. A novel about recovery and growth.
    ISBN 0-930044-46-0   8.95

TOOTHPICK HOUSE by Lee Lynch. 264 pp. Love between
two Lesbians of different classes.   ISBN 0-930044-45-2   7.95

MADAME AURORA by Sarah Aldridge. 256 pp. Historical
novel featuring a charismatic "seer."   ISBN 0-930044-44-4   7.95

CURIOUS WINE by Katherine V. Forrest. 176 pp. Passionate
Lesbian love story, a best-seller.   ISBN 0-930044-43-6   8.95

BLACK LESBIAN IN WHITE AMERICA by Anita Cornwell.
141 pp. Stories, essays, autobiography.   ISBN 0-930044-41-X   7.95

CONTRACT WITH THE WORLD by Jane Rule. 340 pp.
Powerful, panoramic novel of gay life.   ISBN 0-930044-28-2   9.95

MRS. PORTER'S LETTER by Vicki P. McConnell. 224 pp.
The first Nyla Wade mystery.   ISBN 0-930044-29-0   7.95

TO THE CLEVELAND STATION by Carol Anne Douglas.
192 pp. Interracial Lesbian love story.   ISBN 0-930044-27-4   6.95

THE NESTING PLACE by Sarah Aldridge. 224 pp. A
three-woman triangle — love conquers all!   ISBN 0-930044-26-6   7.95

THIS IS NOT FOR YOU by Jane Rule. 284 pp. A letter to a
beloved is also an intricate novel.   ISBN 0-930044-25-8   8.95

FAULTLINE by Sheila Ortiz Taylor. 140 pp. Warm, funny,
literate story of a startling family.   ISBN 0-930044-24-X   6.95

These are just a few of the many Naiad Press titles — we are the oldest and
largest lesbian/feminist publishing company in the world. Please request a
complete catalog. We offer personal service; we encourage and welcome direct
mail orders from individuals who have limited access to bookstores carrying
our publications.